"_____ r
chir _____ -
pera _____ f
quie _____

Elle closed her eyes. "They had an early lab."

"So it's just the two of us this morning?"

Elle reluctantly pulled away. "Don't start anything you can't finish, my love."

"You're right. I certainly don't like leaving things unfinished." He reached over for the phone and dialed. "Morning, Ki. I need you to push my meeting back this morning by a half hour or forty-five minutes. Make whatever excuses you have to, and I'll see you soon. Thanks, buddy." He hung up.

Elle shook her head. "I know that had to be his voice-mail."

"It was." He unloosened his tie and tossed it on the chair. "He'll get over it." He unbuttoned his shirt. Then he took it and his undershirt off. Elle couldn't help but smile. Douglas still had the same hard body with great pecs. His shoulders were as amazing as ever. He pulled his pants off. "You know, sweetie, you're still the same sexy mocha goddess I saw on the beach all those years ago. It's like time stood still."

"And you're still the same Adonis I saw on the beach."

He climbed in bed with her. "Thanks, baby but you haven't seen anything yet." He tossed aside his boxer briefs and kissed her fervently.

Sorry Ki. I was gonna go to bat for you but . . . oh God, she thought before she succumbed to her husband's passion. Douglas knew just what to do to drive her crazy.

"I love you, so much, Ella." He gently touched her
and began kissing her more deeply, raising the tem-
ture and the stakes. "Where are the boys? It's kind of
her this morning." He continued kissing her neck.

MIXED REALITY

CHAMEIN CANTON

Genesis Press, Inc.

INDIGO LOVE SPECTRUM

An imprint of Genesis Press, Inc.
Publishing Company

Genesis Press, Inc.
P.O. Box 101
Columbus, MS 39703

All characters in this book have no existence outside the imagination of the author and have no relation whatsoever to anyone bearing the same name or names. They are not even distantly inspired by any individual known or unknown to the author and all incidents are pure invention.

Copyright © 2010 Chamein Canton

ISBN: 13 DIGIT : 978-1-58571-423-0
ISBN: 10 DIGIT : 1-58571-423-2
Manufactured in the United States of America

First Edition

Visit us at www.genesis-press.com
or call at 1-888-Indigo-1-4-0

DEDICATION

My mother always said love was a thirteen-lettered word, communication. This novel is to remind all of us to talk to the one we love, openly and honestly. Remember to back up your actions with words, so there is never any doubt about how you feel and what the love of your life means to you. Actions may speak louder, but words filter straight from the ears to the heart.

ACKNOWLEDGMENTS

My journey as an author has been made more special by all the readers who have taken time to reach out to me. I want you to know that I think of you with every word I type. You inspire me to want to improve and to continue to grow as a writer. Thank you. As always I never forget my family, who is always there to support me in all my endeavors. My dad, Leonard F. Canton Jr, who is the absolute best father I could ask for. Then there is my mother, Mary E. Wallace, who keeps me in stitches with her straight talk. I again thank my sister Natalie and my brother-in-law Donell for always being in my corner when it comes to my career and my children. Again there's my brother in spirit, Joel Woodard, who always cheers for the big girls. I again thank Mrs. Frances Watkins, who taught me how to find joy in everyday life even when there is physical pain. I also am grateful to my sons Sean and Scott, who have grown into fine young men. I also thank my uncles, Calvin and Cecil Canton and Charles Salley, for being great uncles.

Thanks also to the man that puts a smile on my face and opened my mind to delve further into NYC politics, Michael Bressler. He is the most wonderful man, and I thank him for loving me unconditionally. As always I also want to thank those I've lost but carry in my heart every day: Grandma Salley and Grandma Canton; my great-grandmother Dorothy Donadelle; my great-uncle, Ernest "Unc" Donadelle; my Auntie Ruth, Uncle Willis, and Aunt Edna. Thanks also to my friends, near and far: James Weil, Eric Smith, Pearl Alston, Sheri Collins, Kim Bettie and Edward Kemnitzer. Thank you all for being in my life. I also want to thank the mayor of New York City, Michael Bloomberg, and the wonderful tour guides at City Hall for helping me fill in the blanks about life at City Hall.

Finally, thanks to the wonderful folks at Genesis Press: Deborah, Valerie, Diane, Brian, and my new editor Mavis Allen. You are a terrific team and I thank you from the bottom of my heart!

CHAPTER 1

The morning sun shone brightly on the sands of Martha's Vineyard. It was a little after six in the morning and the seagulls were the only creatures stirring as Mirielle Abbott casually strolled along the shoreline. Elle, as she was known to her family and friends, had decided to take advantage of the early morning before the beach got too crowded and the hangover twins awoke. Although just nineteen, Elle passed for over twenty-one and could have easily joined her travel companions in yet another alcohol-soaked night in Margaritaville, but, after she'd spent the previous six months convincing her parents to let her fly solo, she wasn't taking any chances. Her parents, Richard Abbott and Lynette Chambers, may not have agreed about much after their divorce, but they were on the same page when it came to their only child. They wanted her to be safe.

If her parents seemed a little overprotective, they had every reason to be. Growing up on Long Island, Elle had a Doogie Howser life. At age four, when most kids were learning their ABC's and basic counting, she read at a high-school level and her math scores were off the charts. By the time she was eleven years old Elle had graduated high school. So when other teenagers were getting ready for the prom and the SAT's, she was in graduate school, all under the watchful eye of chaperones, tutors and her parents. So it was *no surprise Elle intended to enjoy every second of her new-found freedom, even if it was only for a few days.*

Walking slowly, she closed her eyes as the ocean breeze wrapped her gauzy white halter dress around her curvy figure. She smiled as the wind gently combed through her long, wavy auburn locks. Too bad I can't bottle this feeling, she sighed. Just as she opened her eyes she noticed a shirtless runner heading her way. Oh my. Her eyes widened. Who knew you could find Adonis in Martha's Vineyard? Elle's stomach fluttered as she beheld his broad shoulders, incredible pecs and dark, wavy hair. Before she realized it he had stopped in front of her.

"Good morning." He smiled.

"Good morning," she said shyly.

"I see I'm not the only one taking advantage of this beautiful morning."

"Yes. I like how peaceful it is."

"I do, too. It helps me clear my head."

"I know how you feel." Elle looked down at the sand.

"By the way, my name is Douglas Brennan." He put his hand out.

She shook it. "It's nice to meet you, Douglas Brennan. I'm Mirielle Abbott. Everyone calls me Elle."

"May I call you Elle?"

"Sure."

"So, Elle, are you here on a family vacation?"

"No. I'm here with friends. Are you here with family?"

"Yes. We have a place just up the beach." He pointed. "Are you on a break from school?"

"I guess you could say that. I just graduated."

"Congratulations. Have you decided what college you're going to?"

"Princeton," she began.

"That's a terrific choice. I went to Harvard, but Princeton was one of my top choices."

Elle laughed.

"What's so funny?" He looked a little puzzled.

"I just completed my doctorate in sociology at Princeton."

His eyes widened and his jaw just about hit the sand. "You just finished your doctorate? How old are you?"

"I'm nineteen."

Douglas shook his head. "That blows my mind," he said as he laughed. "Here I am thinking you just left high school. You must think I'm a putz."

"No. It's an honest mistake." Elle looked up as a seagull passed overhead.

"I think we should start walking so we're a moving target."

"I think you're right. But don't you want to get back to your run?"

"No. I think I'm done for now. I'd like to slow it down and walk for a while, if that's okay with you." He smiled warmly.

Elle felt the butterflies swarm in her stomach. "Sure." Just as she turned to walk she nearly tripped on a mound of sand. Douglas quickly grabbed her hand and steadied her.

"Are you okay?"

"Yes. Thank you, Douglas."

"You're welcome, and please call me Doug."

In that moment their eyes met and their hands didn't part as they walked down the beach.

"Elle? Are you awake, baby?"

She slowly opened her eyes to see Douglas sitting on the edge of the bed. "Good morning." She yawned. "What time is it?"

He looked at the clock. "It's not quite 7:00 a.m. I'm sorry I woke you up. You looked so happy."

"That's okay, honey." She covered her mouth as she yawned again. "Oh, excuse me." She paused. "I have to get up and get this day started." Elle sat up.

"Did you have that dream again?"

"Yes." She smiled. "I don't know why I keep dreaming about the day we met. "

He leaned in and kissed her. "That was the best day of my life."

"Mine, too."

"And once this term is over we get to go back to that life."

"Hmm."

"What? You don't believe me?"

Elle had been married to Doug long enough to know the name Brennan was synonymous with politics. Doug's grandfather, Hugh Brennan Sr., came from a family who had owned a pub in Boston when Irish had been a dirty word. His grandmother, Kathleen, was the daughter of Boston's first Irish mayor. Hugh's family could afford to send him to Harvard, but once he was there he quickly learned that if he wanted acceptance and respectability, he would have to buy it. It didn't take long for him to amass a fortune working as a bank president and dabbling in the still unregulated stock market. However, certain country clubs and associations wouldn't accept him regardless of his wealth. The realization led him into the world of politics, and he backed Democrat FDR for his first term as president. After FDR rolled into office, he rewarded Hugh Sr. with a position with the then newly formed Securities and Exchange Commission in New York, making it necessary to move the family to Bronxville, a wealthy enclave in Westchester and a mere train ride from all the action in Manhattan. Nevertheless, his real dream was to make a run for the White House himself. Unfortunately Hugh's business practices made it impossible for him to run for office without inquiry. So he did what every stifled politician did, he passed on his political aspirations to his eight children, including Doug's father, former two-term Congressman from New York Hugh Brennan Jr., who in turn passed the family mantle to his eldest son Doug.

"Let's just say I'm not going to hold my breath."

"You know there are term limits for New York City mayors. It's not like I can change that."

"True." Elle still sounded skeptical.

"Well, technically I could challenge it. But why would I want to? Two terms is more than enough."

"That's easy to say now, but running New York City is a tough act to follow and you love a challenge. What would you do next?"

"I don't know, but it will be nice not having to worry about campaigning for re-election or pissing off this or that group. No more press conferences, budget meetings, special appearances or official dinners."

"You could get back to your civil rights law practice . . ."

"Yes." He leaned closer to her. "I'm also looking forward to more than an occasional morning in bed with my beautiful wife." He kissed her.

"Is that right?" She grinned.

"Yes. That's right." They kissed a little longer. "Mmm. Are you heading over to the office this morning?"

As the President of Community and External Affairs at New York Hospital, Elle developed outreach programs for the community the hospital served and beyond. More importantly as a Brennan she didn't have to take a salary, which meant the hospital couldn't afford not to have her. In return she had the flexibility of working from the office or home, which made it easier for her to stay involved with their children.

"No. There's a parents' meeting at the school. I'm working from here later on today."

"Oh, that's right. Should I be there?"

"That's okay, honey. I think today's meeting has to do with the upcoming winter dance. They're probably looking for chaperones, people for the refreshment committee . . . really interesting stuff like that."

"In other words it's just up your alley."

She smiled. "It is in a way. I never went to a high school dance."

"You couldn't go. You were only ten."

"Right. That's why I'm so into this stuff for Kyle and Kevin. I want them to enjoy being teenagers."

"You know there is such a thing as teen angst."

"True, but at least it will happen in high school. Let me tell you it was no fun to go through it in college. There Melissa and I were, the M & M girls, escorted by our chaperone to every class while eighteen-, nineteen- and twenty-year-olds looked at us like the geek freaks we were."

"They didn't think you were freaks. I bet most of them wished they had a tenth of your smarts."

"You always know just what to say." She smiled warmly.

"I guess that's the mark of a politician."

"No. It's the mark of a wonderful man."

"I love you so much, Elle." He gently touched her chin and began kissing her more deeply, raising the temperature and the stakes. "Where are the boys? It's kind of quiet this morning." He continued kissing her neck.

Elle closed her eyes. "They had an early lab."

"So it's just the two of us?"

Elle reluctantly pulled away. "Don't start anything you can't finish, my love."

"You're right. I certainly don't like leaving things unfinished." He reached over for the phone and dialed. "Morning, Ki. I need you to push my meeting back this morning by a half hour or forty-five minutes. Make whatever excuses you have to, and I'll see you soon. Thanks, buddy." He hung up.

Elle shook her head. "I know that had to be his voice-mail."

"It was." He unloosened his tie and tossed it on the chair. "He'll get over it." He unbuttoned his shirt. Then he took it and his undershirt off. Elle couldn't help but smile. Douglas still had the same hard body with great pecs. His shoulders were as amazing as ever. He pulled his pants off. "You know sweetie, you're still the same sexy mocha goddess I saw on the beach all those years ago. It's like time stood still."

"And you're still the same Adonis I saw on the beach."

He climbed in bed with her. "Thanks, baby, but you haven't seen anything yet." He tossed aside his boxer briefs and kissed her fervently.

Sorry, Ki. I was gonna go to bat for you but . . . oh God. She thought before she succumbed to her husband's passion. Douglas knew just what to do to drive her crazy. He kissed and caressed her neck and shoulders and teased her soft breasts. The smell of his cologne and the warmth of his body next to hers drove her wild. Every time felt like the first time for her, although she'd grown more adept at turning the tables on Douglas.

She rolled on top of him and removed her nightgown. Douglas could barely catch his breath before she began kissing and gently sucking her way down his neck to his chest. She softly blew on his skin as she tickled it with her tongue. Doug's body tensed with anticipation when she grew ever closer to his waist. *Oh, baby, she really knows how to get me. One more centimeter, Elle, just one more kiss.* He closed his eyes and Elle went the distance.

"Okay, baby," he said breathlessly. "You're mine." He rolled her onto the bed and soon their bodies were intertwined as they slowly savored every moment of their lovemaking. When they neared the peak they locked eyes.

"I love you, Elle."

"I love you, too, Doug." Elle was breathless and within an instant sheer ecstasy washed over them.

A few minutes later Elle lay on Doug's chest. He gently rubbed her shoulder. "Soon this will be us every morning."

Elle lifted her head. "Did you say every morning?"

"You heard me. We've got a lot of lost time to make up for, you know. Are you up to it?"

"Of course I'm up to it. I'm just not sure you're really done with politics. You thrive on challenges most people would run from screaming."

"I can't help it. I do love politics."

"Be honest, you also love being in the spotlight. I, on the other hand, would rather be in the witness protection program before I have to put on my Stepford wife act and smile pretty for the cameras."

"You are definitely not a Stepford wife. I know you're tired of all the scrutiny that comes with the job."

"If the media only concentrated on you, I'd be fine. But I did marry into this family with my eyes wide open. I mean, once I realized you were the sexiest man alive."

Doug cringed. "It's been twenty-plus years and I haven't been able to shake that title."

"Most men would still be milking it for all it's worth."

"I'm not most men."

"Hallelujah to that!"

"I'll say it again; in a few months you will have me all to yourself. So I'll ask you again. Are you ready for that?"

She kissed him. "Bring it on, Your Honor."

The phone rang.

So much for our quiet time, she thought. "I bet I know who it is."

"That's a sucker bet." He looked at the phone.

"If you don't answer it he'll just keep calling."

"I know." He sat up took a deep breath and picked it up. "Hello, Ki." He stopped to listen. "Really? Okay. I'll see you then." He hung up.

"That didn't sound bad at all."

"It wasn't bad. He said this morning's meeting was cancelled at the last minute."

"Oh, so you have time to take another shower and get ready."

"I wouldn't say that exactly . . ."

"You wouldn't?"

"No. You know I was a boy scout and our motto is 'be prepared'."

"And?"

"I want to make sure I'm ready for civilian life."

"Excuse me?"

"You heard me, Mrs. Brennan. Class is in session." Elle giggled as he took her into his arms.

With an IQ of 185 Elle easily mastered the world of academia, but the world of fashion confounded her. Before she met Doug, fashion wasn't a priority for this 'big girl' turned full-figured woman. Although she wasn't exactly a fashion 'don't', her choices were based on comfort and not New York's Fashion Week. Her style had been fine for pre-politician's wife, but all that changed the moment Doug announced his candidacy for mayor. This meant that unlike the other mothers at the PTA, who could get away with jeans and the occasional yoga suit, Elle had to be camera-ready at all times. And with a husband who frequently appeared on any given 'best dressed man' list, Elle's curvy size 16/18 body suffered from regular fashion anxiety attacks. She had what most society moms and models didn't have: big boobs, a belly and a somewhat generous butt.

What in the world am I going to wear, Elle thought as she stared at the navy blue suit in their walk-in closet. *This is too dressy for a parents' meeting.* She glanced over at her yoga outfit. *That would be too casual.*

"Babe?" Doug looked crisp in his blue-grey Calvin Klein suit. He adjusted his tie. "Elle, are you okay?"

"I'm fine." She turned around. "And so are you."

"This old thing," he joked.

"Honey, with your body you could make a burlap suit look like it belonged on the cover of *Men's Vogue.*" She looked at his side of the closet with its perfect racks of suits, pants, shirts and ties for all occasions. "It's all so effortless for you."

"Oh, please," he said dismissively.

"It's the truth." She put her hands on her hips. "When I open the closet I'm at a total loss. Do I go casual or dressy? Should I wear pants, a skirt or a dress? Will it look like I'm trying too hard? Then there's the ultimate question, just how fat will my ass look in the photographs?"

"Baby, it's not that bad."

"You don't think so? Do you remember the 'baby girl' sweats you bought me?"

"Oh." He winced.

During the height of the emblazoned-butt yoga pants craze, Doug thought it would be cute to get his 'baby' a pair just for fun. The minute Elle wore them to run errands the press had a field day with her 'junk in the trunk'.

"Oh, he says." She shook her head. "I don't think I'd seen so many photos of my rear since my baby pictures." She sighed. "And if the press isn't enough, I have to worry about the fashion auxiliary police."

"Don't you mean the fashion police?"

Elle was referring to a group of mothers who believed magazine subscriptions to *Vogue*, *Harper's Bazaar* and *Town and Country*, coupled with their Black Amex cards, made them fashion authorities. They attended PTA meetings decked out in creations by Roberto Cavalli, Prada, Armani and Luca Luca with Jimmy Choos and Manolo Blahniks on their perfectly pedicured feet.

"No. The fashion police are real media and fashion people who are allowed to hand out fashion violations. The only thing the fashion auxiliary can give you is a dirty look. But you can't tell them that."

Doug laughed as he kissed her forehead. "I'm sorry, honey." He stopped. "Wait a minute. You can't find anything to wear in here? Isn't that why we hired Sheri?"

Sheri Cole was a stylist with an A-list clientele. However, unlike most celebrity stylists, she was full figured and could relate to Elle. Every month she would fill her closet with finished outfits. Elle relied on her implicitly.

"Yes, but I don't think I have any more ensembles," she said worried.

Doug looked around. "You have a ton of stuff here. Put something together. You can do it."

Elle scanned the closet again. "Listen, honey, if you want to know what's on page 131 of *Building a New American State: The Expansion of National Administrative Capacities, 1877–1920* by Stephen Skowronek under the heading of Patching Business Regulation, I can do that in a snap. Putting an outfit together than won't land me in the 'don't' section of *Glamour* with a black bar across my face might be a stretch."

"You're exaggerating. You didn't have this problem when we first got married."

"We were still private citizens then. Besides, my mother shopped with me, which worked for the most part. Until she'd attempt to turn me into walking sorbet in the spring and summer." She shuddered. "God, I hate pastels."

Doug snickered.

She punched him in the arm.

"Ouch," he said as he feigned injury.

"It was a good thing I met Sheri when she was still a Macy's personal shopper, otherwise I'd never get an appointment."

"That's true. When is she coming?"

"She'll be here this week with some new stuff for me. In the meantime I have to hope there's something in here for today." She let out a deep breath and stared at the racks again.

13

Doug sighed. "Well, honey, I'd like to help you but I've got to head in."

"I know." They kissed. "I'll see you later."

"Okay." He picked up his briefcase. "Good luck."

"Good luck with the parents' meeting or finding something to wear?"

"Both." He smiled and left the room.

Come on, Elle, make a decision. She tapped her foot. *If I could write a doctoral thesis about the new middle class, capitalism and the new working poor, surely I can't be defeated by the fashion equivalent of paper or plastic.* She softly chuckled. *This reminds me of another time I tried to dress to impress.*

It was Doug's twenty-eighth birthday and he was anxious to show off his fiancée. However, Elle was less than thrilled with the pink taffeta monstrosity her mother chose for her. From the moment Elle peaked around in the grand ballroom, she was hit with the sight of sleek designer and mostly black gowns. She felt like a piñata.

"Not sure you want to enter into the lion's den?" Her future brother-in-law Rory asked with a smile.

Elle looked down at her dress. "No. Especially since I look like a bottle of Pepto Bismol."

"You look great."

"Have you seen the gowns in there?"

"Elle, there isn't a woman in that room who wouldn't give her eye teeth to be you right now."

"Rory, you certainly know how to make a girl feel better."

"Are you ready to make your grand entrance?"

"I guess so, but I do wish they were playing better music. This top 40 stuff isn't my cup of tea."

"Mine either." Rory grinned. "I'd much rather the Talking Heads."

"I love the Talking Heads. "Burning Down The House" is one of my all time favorites," she said excitedly.

Without skipping a beat Rory and Elle imitated a couple of scenes from the video and then dissolved into laughter.

"It's nice to know that I have at least one weird music comrade." Elle smiled.

Just then Doug walked over. "There you are." He kissed her. "Now I feel like the party can really get started. You look beautiful."

"You really think so?"

"Absolutely. There isn't a woman here who could hold a candle to you." He turned to Rory. "Thanks for finding her for me, brother."

"You're welcome." He paused. "I'll check with the DJ to see if he has any Talking Heads records with him."

"That would great."

Doug took her by the hand. "There are some people I'd really like you to meet."

Later on that evening, Rory had the DJ play the Talking Heads' "Once In A Lifetime". It wasn't "Burning Down the House", but they danced to it. Caught up in the moment, Rory tried to kiss Elle on the lips that night. He was unsuccessful and Elle dismissed the incident as champagne-fueled. They never mentioned it again.

If I could make a shade of Pepto work, there has to be something in here. Finally she spotted a ready-made outfit of black pants with a chain belt, a white shirt and a black knit sweater to go over it. *Thank goodness. This works,* she thought as she laid the outfit on the bed. She then went over to her dresser and turned on her small CD player. Elle embraced her inner music geek. *Now for a little musical accompaniment. I think it's only right that I pay a little tribute to Rory with something from the Talking Heads. I know just the song.* Elle dressed, put a little make up on and bumped her hair to the tune of the Talking Heads' "Burning Down The House". About to leave, Elle stood in front the mirror and checked her final look. *Not bad.* She turned around for a rear view. *If there are any cameras at least I'm wearing black. I may not know much about fashion, but I do know that black is slimming.*

A little while later Elle sat in her chauffeur-driven limo as it made its way through traffic on the way to the St. Regis Preparatory High School where her identical fourteen-year-old twin sons, Kevin and Kyle Brennan, attended school. *If I'm lucky I'll make it to this meeting just in time.* She looked out at the traffic, which was moving. *It figures the one time I depend on gridlock we're actually moving.* She sighed.

Though she wasn't crazy about PTA politics, Elle pushed that aside when it came to the lights of her life, Kevin and Kyle. Born just after Christmas, they were tall and brunette, with baby blue eyes. Basically they were the spitting image of Doug and had been since the nurses mistakenly brought her sons to the new white mother in the room next to hers for feeding time. Even Elle's parents stood in front of the nursery for ten minutes before a nurse convinced them the two little white babies were their grandsons.

Needless to say Elle spent the first few years of her sons' lives being mistaken for the nanny despite the fact that she went through five months of morning sickness, two incidents of false labor and seventy-two hours of real labor; she had the stretchmarks to show for it. Eventually the world saw more of their family, and the misconceptions were put to rest.

Over the years as her sons grew, Elle took great delight in all the childhood normality. She loved all the bake sales, field days, show and tell, spelling bees, concerts, school plays and the like.

Naturally once Kevin and Kyle entered high school, the types of activities changed. The bake sales and spelling bees were replaced by dances, school clubs, varsity sports and the prom. There were also more distractions, which for the moment were mostly electronic in nature. Although honors students they were obsessed with the latest video games, phones and music. Elle knew that eventually their interests would grow to include girls, and that was the one teenage experience she was in no hurry for.

While Elle was lost in thought the car pulled up to the school. "We're here, Mrs. Brennan." Her driver Ed opened the door.

"Thanks, Ed."

"You're welcome." He helped her out of the car. Her security detail, Zach, stood nearby and then escorted her into the building.

The moment Elle entered the room the fashion auxiliary gave her the once-over. *Oh brother, am I going to get
a thumbs up or down? Oh, who cares?* As Elle scanned the
room the next face she saw belonged to Morgan Thames-
Whitmore, who was the president of the parents' board.
A petite brunette with blue eyes, Morgan's family ran in
the same social and political circles as the Brennans. She
and Doug dated briefly in college and many people
thought they'd wind up together, including Morgan,
until Elle came along. But like any good socialite Morgan
bounced back with a good marriage to financier Kiernan
Whitmore. Their son was the same age as the twins. She
gave Elle a halfhearted smile and Elle responded in kind
as she continued to look for a friendly face. Melissa
waved to her. *Oh, there she is.* Relieved, Elle headed over
to her.

Her best friend and fellow wunderkind, Melissa
Nolan was curvy with long, curly brown hair and olive
skin. She was the one person who truly understood the
challenges of being 'gifted'. After graduation Melissa took
her doctorate in Civil Engineering to the government
and worked on the state's many roadways. Somewhere in
the midst of construction drawings and specifications she
met her husband, Myles Nolan, on the job. She gave
birth to Jason two months after Kevin and Kyle were
born and the three boys were best buddies, much to their
mothers' delight. As Elle approached her she saw
Melissa's nose was scrunched up, a move usually reserved
for equations or blueprints.

"Okay, what's wrong?" Elle asked as she sat down.

"You know I can decipher the most convoluted plans, but I'll be damned if I will ever figure out this parents' schedule. They've got more meetings listed than there are students in the school." Melissa adjusted her reading glasses.

Elle laughed. "It's known as too much time on your hands."

"Is that what they call it?"

"Yes." Elle glanced at the paper.

"Speaking of time, you cut it kind of close this morning."

"I know. It couldn't be helped." Elle grinned.

"Oh, it's like that is it?" she said, suggestively raising her eyebrow.

"I don't know what you're talking about," Elle said innocently.

"That's all right, you don't have to say a word." She smiled. "You know he does have a city to run."

"True. But we only have one more year to go."

"I know you're happy about that."

"I don't know . . ." She shrugged.

"What?"

"Politics for the Brennans is like breathing for other people. So I'm not sure Doug's ready to throw in the towel."

"Does he want to make it a third term for mayor?"

"You know there is a two term limit to consider."

"This is New York City. Anything's possible, especially if you have enough money to make it happen, and, let's face it, the Brennans have more than enough money."

"I know. Still it would be nice to go back to life as a semi-private citizen." As Elle looked up members of the fashion auxiliary waved. She waved back. "I'll be damned."

"What?"

"I guess my outfit passed this morning. Look who's waving."

Melissa looked up. "I see." She looked down at her outfit of black slacks and a sweater. "I guess I got a black bar over my outfit." She snickered. "I've been here for twenty minutes and they haven't acknowledged me."

"You don't speak Prada. Consider yourself lucky."

"Oh, so you speak Prada now?"

"Please," she scoffed. "I wouldn't know Prada from Payless."

Melissa covered her mouth as she tried to stifle her laughter.

Elle looked pensive.

Melissa looked at her watch. "We have a few more minutes before Morgan pounds that gavel of hers. Something is bothering you. Let's talk."

"I was just thinking how great it would be to have Doug come to a parents' meeting with me, but . . ."

"You don't think it's going to happen?"

"No. Doug loves politics. There is nothing he loves more than swimming around in this big aquarium with all eyes on him."

"Meanwhile you're the goldfish hiding behind the diver and coral."

"Right." She nodded.

"Did you tell him that's how you felt?"

"Yes."

Melissa looked skeptical. "You told him, but you really didn't tell him, did you?"

"I could have made myself clearer, but I'm as mesmerized with him as the other eight million people in this city are."

Melissa laughed.

"Maybe I'm fretting over nothing."

"Maybe you are. Just relax," Melissa said reassuringly.

Before Elle could answer a gavel pounded from the front. "Okay, everyone, we're coming to order . . ." Morgan began.

"Here we go." Melissa crossed her legs.

As the meeting got underway Elle couldn't help but think about her morning with Doug. *The idea of Doug being through with politics is novel. But who am I kidding? Politics isn't done with him, and he's not done with it.*

Doug walked into his office at City Hall with a bounce in his step. His secretary, Alice, looked puzzled.

"Top of the morning to you, Alice," he said in his best Irish brogue.

The usually reserved fifty-something Alice chuckled. "Good morning, Mayor Brennan. You're in a good mood today." She handed him a stack of messages.

"I am in a good mood." He smiled as he scanned through the messages. "Is Ki in his office?"

"No. He's in your office sir."

"Is he in a good mood?"

"Yes."

"Really?" He was genuinely surprised. His chief of staff Ki didn't smile much, a fact Doug found amusing since Kiano, his name in Kenyan, meant full of joy.

"Yes."

"Thanks, Alice. I guess I'll enter with caution."

She smiled and went back to work.

When Doug entered the room Ki had his back to the door. Ki Odiembo was still just as long and lanky as the day he and Doug met at Phillips Academy in Andover, Massachusetts. His parents were academics from Kenya who had come to America when Ki was a baby. He and Doug became fast friends, and their personalities complimented each other from the start. Doug was Mr. Personality and loved working the room while Ki preferred to be in the background to make the most of Doug's contacts. They were quite a team in college and law school, so when Doug entered politics, naturally Ki was his right-hand man.

"Good morning, Ki."

He turned around. "Good morning, Your Honor." He put his Blackberry back in his pocket.

"You looked intense before. Anything I should know about?"

"In due time."

Doug stood still. "Uh-oh. I don't know if I like the sound of that. Should I sit down?"

"Stop being so paranoid. Have a seat."

Doug sat down.

"So what happened that you needed me to push your day back by forty-five minutes?"

"I had a pressing matter to take care of, okay?"

Ki looked at him skeptically.

"What?"

"You know what, I'm not going to say anything." He shook his head. "Damn, I give it to you, man. You love your wife."

"I believe Proverbs 5:18-19 reads 'Let your fountain be blessed, and rejoice in the wife of your youth, a lovely deer, a graceful doe. Let her breasts fill you at all times with delight; be intoxicated always in her love.' "

"Oh, my God, you're quoting the Bible." Ki laughed.

"Yes. I take that scripture seriously. I'm happy to say when it comes to Elle, I'm a lush." He smiled.

"You're just one happy drunk." He laughed.

"Guilty as charged." Doug laughed. "I've got a lot to feel good about these days, Ki. We have a new president on his way in, our party seems to be on the rise and I'm in the last year of my term as mayor. It won't be long before I go back to life on earth as private citizen Brennan."

"Yes, about that . . ."

The intercom buzzed. "Hold that thought, Ki." He pressed the button. "Yes, Alice?"

"Governor Pearson's office just phoned. He'll be here in less than ten minutes."

Doug looked confused. "Thanks, Alice." He looked at Ki. "What's this about the governor coming here? I know we've got some serious state budget problems, but why is he coming here? I'm having a hell of a time with the city's budget."

"That's what I wanted to talk to you about."

"Okay." His interest was piqued. "I'm all ears."

Just then there was a knock on the door.

"Hold that thought again, Ki. Yes?"

Alice entered. "The governor is here."

"I thought you said he was ten minutes away," Ki said.

"That's what they told me, but he's here now. Should I send him in?"

"Please do." Doug stood up and buttoned his jacket.

Governor James Pearson was New York's first African-American governor. Tall, brown-skinned with salt and pepper hair, the fifty-six-year-old was well liked on both sides of the aisle.

"Governor Pearson. It's good to see you." Doug walked from behind his desk and the two men embraced. "You look good. Have you lost weight?"

"Have you seen the state budget? Weight isn't the only thing I'm losing. I can't tell you the last time I had a good night's sleep."

"It's good to see you, governor." Ki shook his hand.

"Well, gentlemen, let's take a seat." Doug motioned for them to sit.

"Thanks, Doug." The governor unbuttoned his jacket. "So I guess Ki has filled you in as to why I'm here."

"No, sir. I didn't quite get the chance to do it. I was about to tell him when you arrived."

"Oh." He laughed. "Well then, I get to make your day in person."

"Okay, now I'm really intrigued. What's going on, Governor?"

"It's just us, Doug. You can call me Jim."

"Okay, Jim. I'm on pins and needles."

"Well, you know the president-elect is vetting candidates for secretary of state with his transition team."

"Yes."

"This isn't public knowledge, but Rita Clemson is on the short list for the job, and rumor has it she's going to accept."

"Well, that's terrific news, Jim. Rita's a great choice for the job. She's knowledgeable and respected on both the national and international stage. But what does that have to do with me?"

"Once she accepts her position the seat of junior senator from New York will be open, which means I have to appoint someone to serve the rest of her term." He paused. "I think that someone could be you."

Doug sat in stunned silence. "I'm sorry, Jim, did I hear you correctly?"

"If you heard me say that you're the frontrunner for the appointment, then you heard right."

"I don't know what to say."

"You don't have to say anything at the moment, since the president-elect hasn't made it official yet. You have some time to think and talk it over with your wife. But I hope you want to throw your hat in. Naturally there are other candidates, but I really think the state needs someone with your experience and charisma to represent us in Washington."

"I'm honored."

The governor looked at his watch. "Well, I have to get going, I have to tape an appearance for PBS, and if I'm late my chief of staff will kill me. You know how that is, right?" He winked as he stood up.

"I know it intimately." He laughed as they walked to the door.

He shook Doug's hand. "So give it some thought and let me know."

"I will."

"I'll see you, Ki."

"Yes, Governor."

"Let me walk you to the door." Doug escorted the governor to the door and the two men shook hands again. When he returned to his office Ki was sitting in front of his desk.

"It's pretty awesome, isn't it?" Ki practically bubbled over with enthusiasm.

Doug walked over to his desk and sat down. "You could have given me a little more warning."

"I tried to, but he beat me to it. So what do you think? Are you interested?"

"Of course I'm interested. Who wouldn't be? But this isn't exactly what I had in mind for the next stage of my life."

"I know, but this is an amazing opportunity for you. Besides, being in the Senate is a natural stepping stone for . . ."

"Don't say it. Now you sound like my father."

"Your father's right. You could make it to the White House. Look, Doug, you're young, smart and politically adept, some would say you're even good looking. What else do you need to be president?"

"For one thing I would need the support of my wife to be appointed senator, let alone to run for President of the United States."

"You and Elle have been married for twenty years. She knows the drill when it comes to the Brennans and politics. So ask yourself the question, are you really ready to retire from public life?"

Doug was quiet for a moment. "Are you?"

"This isn't about me. Listen, I'm not exactly making a fortune here. You're the one who can afford to take a one dollar salary for this job. I, on the other hand, am paid like a civil servant."

"I know. You have sacrificed."

"Don't get me wrong, Leslie and I are doing okay. She works in the private sector, so that helps keep our girls in Marymount."

"Life in the private sector as a consultant would make it even easier for you."

"I know, but it isn't up to me. It's up to you."

Doug rubbed his forehead. "You know I was having a good day when I got here."

"It's still a good day." Ki got up and patted him on the back. "Your next meeting isn't for another twenty minutes. Doesn't that make you feel better?"

"Oh yes, I feel lots better," Doug said facetiously. "How am I going to tell my wife?"

"Just tell her about the offer and let her know how you feel about it."

"I'm not sure how I feel."

"Unfortunately, I can't help you there." He looked at his watch. "I've got a staff meeting in few minutes. We'll continue this over lunch."

"Okay."

"I'll see you later, Your Honor." Ki left the office.

A minute later Alice came in with a cup of coffee. "Here you go, sir."

"Thanks, Alice."

"You're welcome." She smiled as she closed the door.

Doug slowly sipped his coffee and stared out into nothing. *The governor wants me to be the junior senator from New York. That would mean three more years in politics and a move to Washington.* He sighed heavily. *I just told Elle I was ready to leave the spotlight and concentrate on us. I don't want to break my word. She's sacrificed so much for me already.*

CHAPTER 2

After the parents' meeting Melissa went back to her office and Elle headed home. She'd decided to make Doug's favorite dinner, Irish stew, as a special treat. When she walked into the entryway of their six-thousand-square-foot townhouse she was met by their sixty-some-thing house manager Frieda Boyle. Frieda had been with the Brennan family for years. So when Elle's pregnancy was labeled as high risk, Hugh and Margaret asked her to help them out until the babies were born. It took Elle a little longer to recover from the twins' birth so Frieda stayed, and she'd been there ever since. A plump woman with striking blue eyes, she wore her long gray hair in a tight bun. Frieda ran the day-to-day happenings in the house for Elle, and she relied on her implicitly.

"Hello Mrs. Brennan. How was the school meeting?"

"It was okay. We mostly talked about the winter dance committees and such."

"Sounds like fun."

"Oh yes." Elle took her jacket off. "By the way, do we have the ingredients to make Irish stew? I want to surprise Doug."

Frieda took her coat. "I think we do." She cleared her throat. "I should tell you that Mr. Brennan is in the living room."

She looked at her watch. "Doug is home?"

"No. Mr. Hugh Brennan is here. He's been waiting for you."

"He is?" Elle was genuinely surprised. Her father-in-law wasn't the type to just drop in.

"Yes."

"Okay. Will you tell him I'll be there in a minute?"

"Sure." Frieda walked away.

Elle checked her clothes and makeup to make sure she was pulled together for a visit from her venerable seventy-four-year-old father-in-law, the patriarch of the Brennan family. Although he'd quit politics for himself, his political mojo was reawakened when Doug was tapped to run for mayor. Hugh threw himself and his money into his son's campaign. It was a proud day when his oldest son was sworn in as Mayor Brennan. Ever the gentleman, he stood when Elle entered the room. Though Elle and Mr. Brennan had a great relationship, she could never quite get used to the near Svengali-like control he had over her husband. Doug never thought about being mayor until his father began dropping hints in all the right parties' ears. A skilled politician, Hugh Brennan used subtlety to make his wishes known and he usually got his way. From the moment Elle saw him in the living room she knew something was afoot.

"Mr. Brennan, this is a surprise. How are you?"

Hugh kissed Elle on the cheek. "I'm well. You look lovely, my dear."

"Thank you. Please sit."

Ever the gentleman, he waited until she sat first.

"Can I freshen up your coffee?"

"No thank you, dear. It's fine."

"So what brings you by?"

"Can't a father-in-law stop by to see his favorite daughter-in-law?" He smiled.

"Of course you can, Mr. Brennan." She grinned. "Just don't let Angela hear you say that."

"Oh, she can get over herself. She's some spoiled brat, I tell you." He sipped his coffee.

Elle covered her mouth to keep from laughing.

"How's it going at the hospital? I hear your autism outreach program is really gaining some traction."

Elle found herself thrown again. "How did you know about the autism outreach? It's practically still in its infancy."

"I have my sources. When you get to be my age you hear things and people tend to tell you stuff. I don't know whether it's because they trust you to keep your mouth shut or they figure you're so old you're likely to forget." He laughed.

"It's certainly not the latter in your case."

"Thank you." He put his cup down. "You know what else I heard?"

"What?"

"The president-elect is set to tap Rita Clemson as his secretary of state."

"Wow, that's terrific. I like Rita. I think she's up to the job."

"So do I. Naturally it will be a little while before the official announcement, but that means her seat will be open."

"It's a great opportunity for Governor Pearson to appoint someone worthy, and an even greater opportunity for whomever he chooses." She crossed her legs.

"I'm glad you feel that way, because I heard something else."

"What?"

"Governor Pearson wants Doug to throw his hat into the running."

Elle was stunned. "He does?"

"Yes. He's down from the capital today, so I'm pretty sure he's floated the idea past Doug by now."

"That's funny. He didn't say a word to me this morning."

"He didn't know anything about it."

"Oh."

"Of course there will be other candidates for the appointment, but Doug is Pearson's first choice."

"So you're telling me because you don't think he's going to tell me."

"I know my son loves you more than anything. I also know he promised you this would be his last year in politics, which means he's probably decided not to take Jim up on the offer."

"And you think that's a bad decision."

He leaned forward. "As mayor your husband has balanced the budget, reformed city schools and put more police on the street to make the city even safer. He's governed over more people in this city than some governors have in their entire state. I believe he has what it takes to go to Washington. Imagine if he had the chance to do for everyone in the state what he's done for the city."

"Mr. Brennan, they could use your to help negotiate in the Middle East. Or at least they should appoint you to the UN."

He laughed. "I don't know if I have the stomach to do that every day, but I certainly don't mind a little gentle persuasion with my pretty daughter-in-law." He smiled.

"Mr. Brennan, it's not me you have to worry about. It's up to Doug. I'll support whatever decision he makes."

"That's all I can ask for."

Elle looked at the clock. "The boys will be home soon and I'm sure they'd love to see their grandpa."

"You know I half expected them to be with you when you came in."

"They're teenagers now, so it wouldn't look cool to come home with their mother. They'd rather come home with their friends on the bus."

"Don't feel too bad about it, they will always need their mother. They're just stretching their wings a bit."

"I know you're right." She paused. "You're welcome to stay for dinner tonight, too. I'm making Irish stew."

"Mmm that sounds good to me, but Mary Katherine and I have a charity event tonight and if I don't eat the rubber chicken she'll kill me. Can I get a raincheck?"

"Sure."

"I'd better get going if I want to get my tuxedo from the tailor." He stood up.

"Okay." Elle got up. "I'll walk you to the door."

Once they got to the door Mr. Brennan kissed her cheek. "Thanks for hearing me out, Elle."

"I'm really going to give this some thought before Doug comes home tonight."

"You really are my favorite daughter-in-law." He winked.

"Please give Mrs. Brennan my love."

"I will, dear." He stepped out and down the stairs to a waiting car. Elle watched as the car pulled away. *Senator Douglas Brennan. Wow. His father knows it's not that far of a jump from senator to the White House.*

"Mrs. Brennan? Are you all right?"

"I'm fine, Frieda. I was lost in thought that's all." She closed the door. "I'm going to head upstairs and get changed and come back down to the kitchen. Would you mind setting up for me?"

"Not a problem." Frieda went to the kitchen.

Maybe while I'm cooking I'll figure out how I bring this subject up to Doug, she thought as she went upstairs. *I think I'll give Melissa a call.* Once she in the bedroom she dialed Melissa's cell.

"Hi, Elle. What's going on?" she asked cheerily.

"Don't you sound jovial. Are you still at work?"

"As a matter of fact I am about to wrap up my day. I finally finished the blueprint calculations I'd been working on for the last two days."

"It took you two whole days? Are you sick?"

"No. Our latest temp misplaced them. I told them I didn't want her near the blueprints, but did anyone listen to me?"

"I guess not. She's not the one who messed up the filing in the front office, is she?"

"And she sang the alphabet song while she did it and she still got it wrong."

Elle laughed. "Who is she related to?"

"Some muckity-muck," she scoffed. "But that's enough about me. To what do I owe this call?"

"You remember what we talked about at the parents' meeting earlier?"

"About Doug retiring from politics? Yes."

"It seems politics is calling earlier than expected."

"Is that right? Can you give me details?"

"I can't because Doug hasn't talked to me about it yet."

"Then how do you . . . ?" She paused. "His father told you, right?"

"I just don't know why Doug didn't tell me himself. He could have called."

"It's not like he wanted to know if you want Chinese or Thai for dinner. It's more of a face-to-face conversation."

"You're right about that, but I really don't know how I feel about staying in the spotlight."

"If anyone knows how you feel, it's me. I hated being stared at in college, too, but we got through it."

"That's easy for you to say. When you walk into your office no one is lurking around trying to take your picture or report your latest fashion faux pas."

"But I also don't get seats behind home plate at Yankee games or center court at the US Open or tickets to opening night at The Met. It's not all bad."

"It is pretty cool to go to opening day at Yankee Stadium."

"See? So do yourself a favor and be prepared to hear him out before you shoot him down completely. Make sure you have all the facts."

"That's very sound advice coming from a numbers gal."

"Thank you." She paused. "Well, I'd better get out of here if I'm going to pick dinner up tonight. I may give good advice but I'm not a gourmet like you. Speaking of gourmet, what are you making for dinner?"

"Irish stew."

"I rest my case. I'll talk to you later. Let me know what happens."

"I will."

Elle hung up and headed downstairs to get dinner underway. Melissa was right. She needed to think about what a run for Washington would mean for their family. They'd managed to weather New York City politics relatively unscathed, but Doug's favorite uncle Boston Senator Robert Brennan's longest relationship was with the senate while several marriages fell to the wayside. Elle wondered whether their luck would hold once Washington entered the equation.

Doug was going over his notes for the weekly radio address to the city the next day. It was time to talk about the executive budget, a subject he wasn't looking forward to discussing. *At least the city's budget is $59.1 billion.* He sighed. *But we're keeping city spending down. I mean, who can complain if it grows by 0.1percent? Who am I kidding? I'm sure someone will find something to be unhappy about.*

He stopped. "My thoughts are beginning to sound like a press release," he said and sighed.

Files tucked under his arm, Ki entered the office. "Are you as tired as me?"

"More."

"Are you calling it a day?"

"What do you think?" Doug closed his briefcase.

There was a knock at the door. "Yes?" Doug called.

"It's me, sir," Alice answered.

"Come on in."

Alice walked in with a large bouquet of flowers. "The florist just delivered these." She put them on the desk.

"Thanks, Alice. Why don't you knock off for the day?"

"Thanks, sir. I'll see you tomorrow."

"Okay."

"Goodnight, Alice." Ki smiled.

"Goodnight." She closed the door after her.

Ki looked at the flowers. "What's the occasion?"

Doug put his jacket on. "There's no occasion. I just wanted to give my wife flowers."

"You know you really are making it hard on the rest of us husbands."

"What do you mean? They're just flowers."

"It's not just the flowers. It's the hand-holding everywhere. The way you grin when you swat her bottom.

And do I have to mention the number of times the press has caught you making out with your wife?"

"This is a problem for you?" Doug laughed.

"It's a problem for me when my wife asks me why I'm not more like you. And I'm pretty sure I'm not the only married man to hear that."

"What can I say? I can't help it." He shrugged.

"I'm just teasing." Ki chuckled. "Don't you remember? There you were, the tabloid's newly crowned sexiest man alive, away on vacation and having the time of your life, When you came back to the compound from your morning run that day you had stars in your eyes and a dumb grin on your lips. I knew you were smitten the minute I saw you that fateful morning on Martha's Vineyard," he reminisced.

"What can I say? When you find the one, you know it."

"So I guess that means we're not heading to Washington."

"I'm sorry, Ki," Doug said as he opened the door.

"That's okay. I understand. All I need is a good reference."

"You don't even have to ask."

"Thanks."

"Are you coming?"

"I have a few things to finish in my office and then I'm going to pick up my flowers for no reason and go home."

"Good man." Doug pointed. "See you tomorrow."

Once they devoured their after-school snacks, Kevin and Kyle did their homework at the kitchen table under Elle's watchful eye. Homework time meant no cell phones, iPods, video game systems or television. To say it wasn't Elle's most popular decision was an understatement.

"Mom, why can't we do our homework upstairs? It's noisy down here with all the pots clanging around," Kevin whined.

Elle looked at Frieda. "Can you believe what you're hearing? The pots are too loud. This from the child who listens to his iPod in his ears on full blast."

Kyle snickered.

"Shut up," Kevin growled at him.

"I didn't say anything."

"Now don't you two start up again," Elle warned.

"We're not little kids anymore, Mom. You can trust us to do our homework."

"There are far too many diversions in your rooms."

"It's not fair, Mom."

"I don't have to be fair, Kevin. I'm your mother." *Oh, good Lord, I sound like my mother.* "Dinner will be ready soon."

"Is Dad going to be home for dinner?" Kyle asked.

"I know he'll try. You know how busy he is."

"Anybody home?" Doug called.

"Dad!" Kevin and Kyle chorused.

Doug walked into the kitchen with one hand behind his back. "Here's my family." He grinned. Doug kissed each son on the forehead. "How was school today?"

"It was good, Dad," Kevin answered.

"How about you, Kyle?"

"I had a good day."

"Did you get your lab completed this morning?"

"Yes," Kyle answered.

"Good man." He began walking toward Elle. "How's my best girl?"

"She's wondering what you have behind your back."

He handed her the flowers. She took a whiff. "They're beautiful and they smell so good. What's the occasion?"

"No reason. I just wanted to give you flowers."

"Oh." Elle turned to Frieda. "Would you put these in a vase for me?"

"Sure."

"Thank you. Now I have to thank my wonderful husband." Elle put her arms around him and they kissed.

"Come on, you guys. There are children in the room." Kevin sounded completely disgusted.

Elle pulled away slightly. "We're grossing our children out."

"I guess they don't know how they got here." Doug gave her a quick peck. "I thought we had *the talk*."

"Dad," Kevin groaned.

"Okay." Douglas laughed.

Elle went back to the pot on the stove. "Dinner will be just a few more minutes."

Doug slid his arms around her. "Is that Irish stew I smell?"

"Yes."

"You're the best, babe." He kissed her.

"Thank you." She looked at the boys, who were fooling around. "I take it you two are finished with your homework?"

"Yes, Mom."

"Okay. So go upstairs and get washed up for dinner." They picked up their books and dashed out.

"I'm gonna head upstairs and change for dinner, too." He kissed her cheek.

"All right, honey." As Elle stirred the stew she watched Doug walk out. *He's really not planning to tell me about the senate. It looks like I'm going to have to open the door for this discussion.*

Dinner finished the family sat around the table talking.

"So, Mom, there's this concert we've been invited to," Kevin started.

Elle put her glass down. "Oh? Who's going?"

"Steve Friedman, Dan McCullough, Jordan Hamilton and Ted Springfield are going. Ted's dad got Akon tickets."

"Tickets for what?" Elle asked.

"Akon isn't what, babe, he's who."

"He's the guy that did the background on that Gwen Stefani song, right?"

Kevin and Kyle looked at each other in disbelief. They only knew of their mother's penchant for weird music by people like Kate Bush, Tori Amos, Beck and the Talking Heads.

"That's right, I know who he is. Give your mother some cool points."

"Wow, Mom, I didn't think you listened to our music."

"Given what they're allowed to say in songs these days, I listen. So when's the concert?"

"The Saturday after Thanksgiving."

Elle looked at Doug. "What do you think, honey?"

"Is Sam going to the concert?"

"Mr. and Mrs. Springfield are going," Kyle answered.

"They're braver than I. It's okay with me, babe."

"All right, then you can go."

The boys cheered.

"But I'm going to call Sam and Simone to get the details."

"We're cool with that." Kevin grinned.

"In case you didn't know, Kevin, Gwen Stefani is closer to my age than you think."

"She's that old?" Kevin laughed.

"Hey!" Elle threw her napkin at him.

"You're mother is still a young, hip thing," Doug said as he kissed her hand.

"Thank you, honey."

"Oh, God." Kevin rolled his eyes. "If you guys are going to keep this up, can I be excused?"

"Yes. You're both excused. Don't forget to take your plate into the kitchen and put it in the dishwasher."

They stood up. "Okay, Mom," Kyle said.

"Do we still have those chocolate chip cookie ice cream sandwiches you made Mom?" Kevin asked.

"Yes. Help yourselves but you only get two apiece."

"Okay, Mom."

Kevin and Kyle disappeared into the kitchen.

Doug put his wine glass down. "You know you've spoiled us with that ice cream maker of yours."

"You're the one who bought it for me. You know how I can't resist a kitchen gadget."

He patted his stomach. "But if you keep this up I'm going to have a hard time keeping this boyish figure."

"Don't worry, I'll watch your figure." She kissed him lightly on the lips. "So when were you going to tell me about the governor's visit?"

He was floored. "You know he stopped by City Hall today?"

"Yes. I also know why he was there."

"What?"

"Your father was here this afternoon."

"It figures. He knows things before they happen."

"It's his gift." She rubbed his hand. "What did you say when he asked you?" Deep down she hoped he'd said no in no uncertain terms, but from the look on his face, she knew better.

"I told him I was honored."

"But you didn't tell him no, either."

"They haven't made an official announcement about Rita taking the secretary of state position. So technically the seat isn't available."

"But it will be."

"Listen, baby, I told you this was my last year in office. I'm getting out of the political arena." He took her hand in his. "I want to spend more time with you and the boys." His words were sincere, but they lacked the weight of truth.

"I've been a politician's wife long enough to know that you're saying what I want to hear, but that was before they put this on the table. Are you trying to tell me that the idea of being senator doesn't appeal to you at all? Be honest."

"Of course it appeals to me. I'd be in the halls of power with the movers and shakers in Washington."

"And you'd like to be there where it all happens, and it's just a stone's throw from 1600 Pennsylvania Avenue."

"Now I wouldn't go that far."

"Come on, it's crossed your mind."

"Maybe once or twice." He shrugged.

Elle looked down as Doug took her hand in his. "Baby, this isn't a decision I can make without you, and we'd be going from life in a fishbowl to the ocean. But I really think I can make a difference for the people of our state."

With every word, Elle saw her dream for a quiet private citizen's life evaporate.

"What do you think, baby?"

If I say no, I'll be the shrew who kept him from attaining his dreams. "I'll go wherever you are, honey. It doesn't matter if it's here or in Washington."

"I love you, baby. You won't regret this. I promise I won't let this interfere with our lives."

Elle smiled. *Where have I heard that before?* She picked up both their plates. "I'm going to put some decaf on."

"Great." He leaned back in the chair.

"You have your radio address tomorrow, right?"

"Yes." He sighed. "I need to go over a few more details to make sure I'm prepared."

"Why don't you go in your study and I'll bring you a cup of coffee and a slice of pound cake."

"I didn't think there was any cake left."

"There wasn't much left, but I managed to hide away a slice for you," she said.

"Thanks, baby."

"You're welcome." Elle went to the kitchen.

It wasn't long before Doug had papers sprawled across his desk. Elle walked in and put the coffee and cake on the table. "I see you're already hard at work."

He looked up. "Oh yes." He looked over at the table. "Thanks for the refreshments."

"You're welcome." She started out of the office.

"You're not keeping me company?"

"You've got work to do. We can talk later. Besides, I hear thumping upstairs." She pointed to the ceiling.

"Are the boys playing their music too loud?"

"No. If you can believe it I think they're jumping on the bed."

Doug chuckled.

"All this talk about how they're growing up and they're jumping up and down like they're eight years old again."

"You go get 'em, Mom."

"I will." Elle left the room.

What I wouldn't give for a little play time. Doug tapped the desk. *If I were senator it wouldn't be much better. I'd*

45

have even less time since the Senate has even more personalities than the City Council, and that's says something, but I'd like to mix it up with them. He sighed. *Enough of this Washington dreaming I have to get back to work.*

A couple of hours later Doug flopped on the bed and covered his eyes. "I'll kill myself if I have to read another spreadsheet, report or memo."

"Was it that bad?"

"Worse." He lifted his hand. Elle was in her red silk bathrobe. "Look at you."

She smiled as she went over to her dressing table.

"The kids are in bed. Why are you all the way over there?" He patted the bed.

"I want to continue our talk about the Senate. I'd like to know what's next. You have made up your mind to go for it."

"Yes and no. On the one hand it's an honor to take up Senator Clemson's mantle. However it's one thing to be mayor of New York City. Being senator is a whole other ballgame. Do you know how many residents I'd have to answer to?"

"As of July, 2008 about 19,490,297, give or take a few people, and 42.2 percent of them live in New York City."

"We've been married for twenty years and it still amazes me when you spout statistics just off the top of your head."

"My point is you already answer to nearly half of the state's residents."

"And I already work with the governor and legislature."

"So what's stopping you from throwing your hat in the ring? And don't say it's me."

"I promised you this was our last year of public life. If I were appointed we're talking about three more years in politics. Can you handle that?"

"On one hand, I'm a Brennan. Of course I can handle it," Elle said, spouting the family line. "But it hasn't been a bowl of cherries sharing you with eight million people, and now I'd have to share you with nearly twenty million. It could give a girl a complex. Still, I have to admit there have been more cherries than pits."

"That's because you're my girl and you'll always be number one."

"How many times have I heard that on the phone when you're running late from a budget meeting or fundraiser?"

"Elle, I'd rather not play this passive-aggressive game. If you don't want me to go for senator, then tell me."

"I want you to do what makes you happy, and you'll never forgive yourself if you don't give it a shot." *More truthfully I won't forgive myself, and I don't want Doug to hold it against me.*

"Are you sure that's something you could live with? You know they're going to turn up the scrutiny."

"I've been through it before." She got up and walked over to the bed. "That's the good thing about being 'gifted'. I lived a sheltered, structured life. I don't have much of a past to speak of at all. No illicit relationships or bitter ex-boyfriends lurking about. Heck, I only had one boyfriend, and I married him."

"You're delightfully squeaky clean," he said and winked at her.

"And don't think for one moment I believe you'd only serve three years." She crossed her arms. "I know we'd be looking at a minimum of nine years."

"You don't think I'd leave after three years?"

"No," she said bluntly. "To be honest, I think you'll be there more than nine years, just like your Uncle Rob."

Douglas's favorite uncle, Robert Brennan, had elected to move back to Boston in the sixties. In 1970 he was voted the senator from Massachusetts and had recently won another term.

He kissed her hand. "What about your Martha's Vineyard dream?"

"I'll tell you what. If you promise that we'll make it a family vacation at least twice a year no matter what, I'm cool."

"You've got a deal. In fact, we'll do one week with the kids and one for just the two of us. We can send them to their grandparents."

"That's easy for you to say, your parents are still married. My parents aren't, so that's a fight waiting to happen."

"The boys can do three days with my parents and two days of each with yours. I think that's fair and democratic."

"That's very diplomatic of you, Doug. However, the only ' *d* ' word that applies to my parents is *done*. I don't think *democracy* enters the picture at all."

Elle's parents divorced when she was thirteen years old after eighteen years of marriage. Though their north/south union, her father was from New York and her mother was from South Carolina, had worked for a time, they grew apart and spent the last four years of their marriage reenacting various battles from the Civil War. Once the divorce was final, Elle thought they'd get on with their lives and get along. She was wrong. Suddenly Elle became an air traffic controller of sorts, having to guide her parents' 'landings' to avoid near misses or worse whenever she invited them for special occasions, which included her wedding, holidays, and anything involving her grandsons.

"We'll work it out."

"You're more hopeful than me." She got up. "I'm going to take a bath. Why don't you give Ki a call and give him the news. You know you want to." Elle walked into the master bath.

Doug paused and then picked up the phone.

"Hello?" Ki answered in a low voice.

"Is that you, Ki?"

"Yes."

"What's wrong?"

"Nothing's wrong. I decided to take Proverbs to heart, too."

Doug grinned. "I'll let you go."

"What's happening?"

"Let's just say don't print your consultant cards yet."

"I knew it."

"Whatever. Go back to the lush life. I'll see you tomorrow."

"You bet, Your Honor."

Eyes closed in the large sunken tub, Elle let the hot water and massage jets relax her mind and body. Although a shower was more environmentally correct, it was an indulgence Elle found hard to live without. When she opened her eyes she saw Doug in his robe.

"I know taking a bath isn't the best thing for conservation, but at least I'm using candles instead of the lights."

"Now Elle, you know we have to lead by example."

"Yes."

He took his robe off. "If you insist on taking a bath, at least we can make it an energy efficient activity."

"And how are we doing that?"

"We'll make it a bath for two," he said, stepping into the tub. "The water is nice." He sat down. "The temperature is almost right."

"Almost?"

"Yes. We just need to heat it up a bit." He lifted her leg and slowly began to kiss her foot.

Elle laughed. "Stop you know my feet are ticklish."

He put her foot down and came towards her. "I'll find something else to tickle." As he and Elle kissed he let his hand slip down under the water.

"Oh," Elle moaned softly.

"Come with me." Doug took her by the hand as they both got out the tub. "Wait a minute. I don't want you to catch cold." He reached over and grabbed a towel. "Let me dry you off." Doug toweled and kissed every curve of her body until her skin was dry, though she was quite the opposite elsewhere.

Knowing he had her just where he wanted, Doug led Elle to the bedroom and onto the bed. They were both on fire. Elle stroked Doug's strong back. She could feel every muscle tense in his body. He kissed and nuzzled her breasts in his hands, taking time to explore every inch of them. Soon their bodies came together in a flash of white hot passion.

Later on they lay in each other's arms.

"Honey?"

"Yes, baby?"

"When do you think they're going to make the announcement about Rita?"

"Here I thought you were going to say something about our conservation efforts."

Elle chuckled. "I think you know how I feel about it. I think we should conserve more often."

"Maybe I should consider this as a PSA campaign."

"You want to make an X-rated PSA? Your constituency would love that."

They laughed.

"Seriously, Doug, when do you think the president-elect will make the announcement?"

"I'm pretty sure it won't happen until after Thanksgiving, but we could be jumping the gun. Politics is a fickle business. What you think should happen and what actually happens are two different things."

"Maybe so, but Rita is smart and ambitious. Trust me, she's taking the position. So when are you calling the governor to let him know you're interested?"

"Let's slow it down a little, Elle. It doesn't work that way."

"You are going to let him know you're interested, right?"

"Yes. Then the ball's in his court from there. He might have someone else in mind."

"I doubt it."

"Anyway, I'll worry about it later."

She let out a deep breath. "It's just as well, I've got to focus on Thanksgiving."

Doug squeezed and kissed her shoulder. "Oh, yes, I'm looking forward to this year's menu."

"I am, too, once I finally figure out what's making it to the table this year. You know I think all your cousins are coming."

"Of course everyone's coming this year. They heard about the food last year and decided not to miss it this time."

"Oh boy," she groaned.

"That's what you get for being a great cook."

"I appreciate the compliment, but you have so many cousins for someone with just one brother."

"What can I say? My grandparents had eight children."

"Being that I'm an only child I can't imagine that many kids fighting for attention."

"It's a way of life for the Brennans, believe me."

"I noticed." She paused. "The radio address is at eleven, right?"

"Yes."

"Hopefully my meeting won't run overtime so I can listen to it."

"At least you're looking forward to it. I have to talk about the city budget, and it's not going to be popular."

"I'm sure you're ready."

"I'm as ready as I'll ever be." He sighed. "Is anything else on your agenda tomorrow?"

"Yes. I'm having lunch with Rory tomorrow."

"Oh yeah, what's going on with him?"

"To tell you the truth, I don't know. We haven't gotten together in a little while so we're just gonna catch up."

"Sounds good." He yawned.

Elle curled up next to Doug. "I can't believe how tired I am." She yawned.

"Me, too." He kissed her. "Good night."

"Good night."

He turned the lamp off and they fell asleep in each other's arms.

When Doug's secretary Alice arrived she found him already hard at work at her desk.

"Oh, good morning, sir. You scared me."

"Good morning, Alice. I didn't mean to scare you. I'll get up."

"Oh, no, sir, you don't have to get up on my account. You can use my computer no problem."

"Thanks."

"Is yours moving slowly again?"

"Yes. I called IT but they're not in yet."

"I know Charlie's cell phone number. I'll give him a call." She opened her cell.

"Thanks, Alice."

"Not a problem, sir." She dialed the phone.

Ki walked in. "Good morning." He looked surprised.

"Good morning and do mark the calendar. I beat you here this morning."

"I will." He looked at the computer. "Is your computer on the fritz again?"

"Yes. Alice is calling Charlie for me."

"Good." He looked at his watch. "I'm going to put my briefcase down in my office, and then I'd like to talk to you in your office."

"No problem."

Alice hung the phone up. "Charlie is on his way."

"Thanks, Alice." He got up. "It's all yours. I'll be in my office."

"Yes, sir."

Doug sat down at his desk. "Aw, come on." He hit his monitor.

"You know you won't be able to use that tactic in the Senate."

"I bet I'd get a lot done if I did."

"Yes, we'll spin you as the senator with the smack attack." Ki sat down.

"So do you want to run through the radio address?"

"We can do that in a few minutes. I really want to talk to you about the senate appointment."

Doug saw that familiar look on Ki's face. He wanted to talk turkey. "Okay. You have my attention."

"I'm happy you've decided to consider Jim's offer, but you do know what you're up against, don't you?"

"Naturally there will be a lot of scrutiny," Doug conceded.

"Rita's a popular senator and she'll be a tough act to follow."

"She'd be a tough act for anyone to follow."

"I know, but the fact is Jim is taking a risk picking a man to fill the seat."

"He would have had a tough time anyway because the perfect candidate for the job would be a gay, black, Roman Catholic female with a Latino father and a mother who was born to Christians who converted to Judaism. She would have to come from the suburbs of Long Island or upstate New York, preferably Buffalo, Rochester, or even Albany. She'd also need to be a graduate of the Ivy League."

Ki was impressed. "You really thought about this."

"My father was a two-term Congressman in the late sixties and early seventies. What do you think?"

"You've got me there. Is Elle ready for this?"

"She's the one who told me to go for it. You know if she wasn't on board I wouldn't do it."

"I know. You realize that once Rita's nomination and acceptance is announced, you'll have to start making moves like you want the job."

"Yes, and that means making appearances with all the right people."

"Exactly," Ki said emphatically.

"I got it. Now you know what I need you to do."

"I'll make the call."

"Thanks." He looked at his frozen computer screen. "Now if this thing would work I'd be in business."

There was a knock on the door.

"Yes?"

"It's Charlie, your Honor."

"Come on in, Charlie."

Charlie entered the room. "Good morning, Mayor Brennan, Mr. O. I hear you're having some issues with your computer this morning."

"Yes." Doug got up from behind his desk.

"You got here just in time, Charlie. I think the mayor was about to assault his monitor," Ki said with a chuckle.

"Well, let's see what I can do to revive the patient."

"Thanks, Charlie." Doug picked a folder up. "Ki, why don't we go to your office and finish up."

"Sounds good to me."

"I'll keep you posted on the patient's status." Charlie smiled.

"Good deal."

Doug and Ki worked up until it was time for him to go live on the air.

Elle rushed from the conference room to her office where her assistant Pamela Walters had the radio on.

"Have I missed much?"

"I think he's almost done."

"Damn!" Elle sat down in front of Pam's desk.

Doug's voice continued. *"And even with all the measures I've proposed we still have rough waters to navigate. Unless there is a dramatic turn in the country's economy, we're still expecting a budget gap of $1.3 billion in the next fiscal year. So many New Yorkers are already dealing with the ill effects of this economic downturn, and unfortunately there will likely be more rough times ahead of us. There are no easy solutions or magic formulas to get our city through this. However, we do have the knowledge to make it through for a speedy economic recovery. We will push the dollar forward by guarding services that will bring jobs to grow our communities and by sticking together as New Yorkers. This is Douglas Brennan. Thanks for listening."*

"Well that's it." Pam turned the radio down.

"I'm sorry I missed it. How did he sound?"

"Great for someone talking about spending cuts and three thousand city positions cut."

"He told me it wasn't going to be popular."

"He can't help it. He's responding to the overall economy."

"I know but not everyone is going to be as reasonable as you." Elle got up. "Any messages?"

"Yes. Sheri called. She said she's ready for you when you are."

"Fabulous." Ellé was excited. "Would you call her back and ask her to be at my house tomorrow morning around 10:30 a.m."

"Will do."

"Thanks." Elle went into her office and put her notes down on her desk. "Cuts must be the word of the day."

She sighed as she sat down. *I need to find money for autism services, but it's like trying to figure out which foot to shoot. Whether it's the left or the right one, it's going to hurt. Except the trick is, I have to figure out which one will hurt less.* Elle buried her face in her hands. *At least it's nearly lunch time.* She looked up at the knock on the door. "What's up, Pam?"

"I spoke to Sheri. She said she'll be there tomorrow."

"Great."

The way Pam waited in the doorway reminded Elle of when her sons want to ask her something and they're not sure what's she's going to say. "Is anything on your mind, Pam?"

"The nurse from Jessica's school called and she's got a fever. Woody's in Staten Island and I need to pick her up and take her to my mother's place until I can get her to the pediatrician later. So I wondered if you'd mind if I knock off now for lunch. The school and my mother's place aren't too far from here. I can get back in time."

"Don't be silly, Pam. Take the rest of the day and get Jessica to the pediatrician."

"Dr. Brennan, I couldn't . . ."

"Yes, you can. I won't hear another word. Go and take care of your daughter."

"Thank you so much, Dr. Brennan. I'll make up the time."

"You have plenty of time, don't worry about it." Elle got up from her desk. She and Pam walked back to the reception area. Pam grabbed her jacket and purse.

"Thanks again, Dr. Brennan."

"I hope Jessica feels better."

"Thank you." Pam dashed out.

Elle sat down at Pam's desk. The phone rang. "Dr. Brennan's office."

"Elle, is that you?"

"Hey, Melissa."

"Why are you answering the phone? I know you said the hospital was making cuts, but I didn't think it was this bad."

"It's not. Pam had to leave for a family emergency."

"Oh, I see. Are you taking lunch?"

"Yes."

"Do you want to meet? I have some time this afternoon."

"I wish I could, but I'm having lunch with Rory today."

"Oh, that's nice. You two haven't gotten together for lunch for a while now."

"It's been six months at least."

"So you two are going to play a little catch up?"

"Yes."

"Tell him I said hello."

"Will do."

"So what happened with Doug and this mysterious political opportunity the other night?"

"Well it won't be mysterious for much longer. Governor Pearson wants Doug to fill Senator Clemson's senate seat."

"I didn't realize she was leaving the Senate."

"The word is she's been tapped to be the next secretary of state."

"That's quite an honor. I know Doug's excited about it."

"He is, and I told him that I'd support him." Elle didn't sound too enthused.

"Now that doesn't sound like a ringing endorsement."

"Don't mind me. It's probably because it's getting closer to lunchtime and I'm hungry. Not to mention Rory will be here any minute."

"Okay. I'll let you go for now. We'll catch up later. In the meantime I have to see what I can grab for lunch."

"Don't forget you and I have a rain check for a spa day or chocolate-fest coming up soon," Elle added quickly.

"Are you kidding? I wouldn't miss it for the world."

"Good. See you later." *I hate to lie to Melissa about the real reason I'm meeting with Rory, but I have to play this meeting a little close to the vest,* she thought as she hung up.

"She's smart enough to figure out Einstein's theory of relativity, able to bend hospital boards to her will, and she answers her own phones. Is there anything you can't do, Superwoman?" Rory grinned.

Only two years younger, Doug's brother Rory was just as handsome. Six feet, one inch tall with an athletic, even muscular, build, he had sandy brown hair and the same crystal blue eyes as his brother. Although born into a competitive extended family, Rory, a successful plastic surgeon, was happy to see his older brother fulfill their father's political ambitions, and he relished his brother's success. The only hint of green in his otherwise blue eyes was over Doug's marriage to Elle. Unbeknownst to her he often wondered what would have happened if it had been him running down the beach that fateful morning in Martha's Vineyard.

"Hey there," Elle said as she got up to hug him. "How are you, stranger? It seems like I haven't seen you in ages." Elle leaned on the desk.

"I've been busy tightening up the faces, stomachs and butts of the rich and famous. It seems quite a few of them weren't too happy with what they saw under the summer sun. And don't get me started about Botox."

Elle laughed. "I don't know how you do it."

"The pursuit of physical perfection and the fountain of youth is practically recession proof."

"I bet. " She touched her face. "I'm forty-one. Do I need any help?"

"No, you're perfect." He quickly rebounded. "My patients would kill to have your skin."

"That's good to know." She smiled.

"I have a little present for you."

"You do?"

He took a CD case from his pocket and handed it to her. "It's selections from one of your favorite singers, Kate Bush."

"Thank you." She gleefully opened the case. "Is *Suspended in Gaffa* and *Wuthering Heights* on it?"

"Of course they are."

"Cool."

Rory still shared Elle's love of weird music by out-there artists. He was also one of the few people who didn't want her to show off her IQ on demand. With Rory, she didn't have to perform and she could be her quirky self.

"It would have been easier to upload it on an iPod."

"I don't like IPods. I still have my Sony Walkman."

Rory winced. "A Walkman? You've got to be kidding me."

"No. I'm not."

He shook his head in disbelief. "You know eventually the CD is going to go the way of vinyl. It's practically a horse and buggy."

"Then I'll wait until that day comes. In the meantime I like the feel of putting on a CD and pressing play."

Rory snickered. "You're impossible."

"I know." She smiled.

"Are you hungry?"

"Yes."

"Well then we're going to just the place for lunch."

"Where?"

"Let's get your coat. You'll see."

Instead of lunch at some fancy Manhattan eatery Rory took Elle to The Viand Café, which happened to be one of her and Doug's favorite places to eat. While they enjoyed upscale dining, there was something comfortable about the diner décor and atmosphere. It also didn't hurt that the food was good with large enough portions to satisfy her walking garbage disposals Kevin and Kyle.

The host, Dean, welcomed them. A jolly man with stark white hair, he could have easily doubled for Santa Claus.

"Mrs. Brennan. How nice to see you."

"Hello, Dean."

"And you're the brother-in-law, the doctor."

"Yes." Rory scanned the diner, which was kind of crowded. "It looks like you're busy. Do you think we'll be able to get a table?"

"Absolutely." He waved one of his waitresses over. "Leah, please clear table four in your section for me."

"Yes, sir."

"It won't take a moment."

"Not a problem," Rory said. He took a whiff. "Do you know what you're going to order?"

"Oh, yes. I'm having a cheeseburger deluxe."

"No turkey burger for you?"

"With Thanksgiving for fifty just around the corner? You're kidding me, right?"

"Point taken."

"Your table is ready." Dean smiled.

They followed him to a spot near the window.

"Thanks, Dean." Elle slid in the booth and took her coat off.

"You're welcome. Enjoy." He put two menus down.

Rory took his coat off. "This is nice."

"Yes." Elle folded her arms on the table. "It's good to see you, Rory."

"I'm tickled you even missed me."

"Of course I missed you. It's been what? Six months? Besides, who else can I bellyache with about all the cousins coming to dinner next week?"

"It's your own fault for being a good cook and hostess."

"What hostess skills? I just walk around the room and hope I remember everyone's name."

"Don't be so modest. Anyone who remembered all thirty-one of my second cousins' names the second time you met them is batting a thousand in my book."

"I have two words for you, photographic memory. Doug wrote all the names down for me."

Lea came over to the table. "Sorry for the delay. Can I get you something to drink?"

"Yes. I think we're ready to order. Right, Elle?"

"Oh, definitely. I'll have a cherry Coke and the cheeseburger deluxe with regular fries."

"I'll have the same."

She picked up the menus. "Very good. I'll be right back with your drinks."

"So have you given any more thought to the clinic situation?" Elle asked.

"You don't miss a beat, do you?"

"Not when it comes to something like this. Granted Dr. Campbell's clinic is out of the geographic region for the hospital, but she's doing such great work for the community. Besides I know she could really use your help."

"I have to admit it was hard to look at so many pictures of children with cleft palate."

"And what's keeping them that way is money and a lot of bureaucratic nonsense."

"What does Doug say about this?"

"I haven't talked to Doug about it."

"Why?"

"He's already dealing with a major fiscal crisis. He has to cut city jobs and services, so I figured now isn't the time to tell him I need extra funding for a clinic to help patients, some of whom are illegal aliens, get surgery for their kids. I know it sounds noble, but I'm pretty sure the three thousand city staffers who are getting laid off wouldn't see it that way."

"Point taken."

"Listen, if you're still on the fence why don't you come with me to visit the clinic after Thanksgiving? This way you can meet Dr. Campbell and see what she's dealing with firsthand."

"That's fair enough."

Elle placed her Blackberry on the table and got her pocket calendar from her bag. "How about the Tuesday after Thanksgiving? Do you think you can swing that?"

"I'll make it happen."

"Thanks, Rory." She marked her calendar. "All right, now that we've got our business out of the way, what's happening at home?"

He shrugged. "Nothing. It's still the same silent war zone. She shops and I stay at the office."

Leah returned with the drinks.

"Thanks." Elle put the straw in her glass. "That's no way to live, Rory." She took a sip.

"We've been to the professionals and the priests. Nothing's helped. It's time to stick a fork in it, but Angela won't do it." Rory looked like a little boy lost.

"I'm sorry."

"Thanks." He sipped his drink.

"Let's change the subject, shall we?" Elle smiled.

"I'm all for that."

"I'm trying to figure out what to make for Thanksgiving." She searched her bag for a notebook. "What do you want?"

"What are you looking for now?" He laughed.

"My notebook."

"Why don't you just use your Blackberry?"

"Don't laugh, but I like writing things down. You know, actually putting ink to paper? Doug and the kids are the only reason I even have a Blackberry. I use it for texting and phone calls and that's it."

"You do know it can do a whole lot more than that."

"I know. Doug showed me how to check my email, surf the Internet, get music downloads, and a bunch of other bells and whistles. I don't know why he wasted his time telling me, all I'm interested in is whether it rings or not."

He shook his head. "That is what kills me about you, Elle. You can figure out complex math equations in your head but you're baffled by a phone."

She shrugged. "Figuring out the square root of 345,684 is 587.948977 is easy, but figuring out how to set up Outlook on my phone so I can check email blows my mind." She continued to shuffle through her bag. "Any special requests for Thanksgiving?"

Rory lost his head for a moment. "You."

She turned to him with the notebook and pen. "Excuse me?"

"You. I want you to make your famous cheesecake."

"Cheesecake is a forgone conclusion. It's your brother's favorite. It figures you'd have the same taste as him." She smiled.

Leah returned with two plates. "Careful, the plates are hot," she said as she put them down. "Do you need anything else?"

"No. I think we're good," Rory answered. "This looks delicious."

"Let's dig in." She raised her cheeseburger. "Cheers."

He lifted his. "Cheers."

Elle savored a few bites of her burger. "Mmm, that hits the spot."

Rory swallowed. "I have to agree with you." He paused to wipe his mouth. "You look like you've got something else on your mind. Do you want to talk about it?"

She sipped her soda. "Well you're going to hear about it soon enough. Doug is considering stepping into Rita Clemson's senate seat once the new administration begins in Washington."

"So Governor Pearson wants to appoint him?"

"Yes."

"That's great for Doug, but how do you feel about it?"

"I'm fine with it."

"Somehow I don't believe that."

"Well, believe it. Doug asked me and I told him to go for it."

"You're a good wife."

"Was that some kind of backhanded compliment?" She sounded defensive.

"No. I was just stating a fact, that's all."

"Oh. I'm sorry. I guess my nerves are a little jumpy with all this holiday planning."

"Then I won't mention another word. We'll just enjoy lunch."

"Thank you. Besides, the fries are calling my name."

"They're talking to me, too," Rory smiled as he ate a few fries.

Elle wanted to enjoy the comfortable and relaxed times she spent with Rory without having to endure an impromptu therapy session about her real feelings. Lunch with Rory was a high point on her schedule and she wanted to keep it that way. For Rory time with Elle was the high point of any day. However, with all the attention the senate vacancy would bring, that fact wouldn't be a secret for much longer.

CHAPTER 3

By the end of the day Doug heard from nearly every sector of the city's government. The axe was going to swing, and everyone was concerned about their necks.

Ki walked in as Doug hung the phone up. "I thought we left Me-ism in the eighties."

"Not when it comes to budget cuts we haven't. People are scared."

"Are you as inundated with calls as I've been?" Doug asked.

"Oh yes. Everyone in City Hall paid particular attention to the part about cutting the authorized headcount at the Mayor's Office."

"I bet they did."

"By the way, I made the call."

"Good. Now it's up to them." Doug looked at the clock. "Is that the right time?"

Ki checked his watch. "Yes."

Doug stood up. "It's seven-thirty."

"Time flies when you're having fun. Everyone else left a while ago. I think it's you, me and the cleaning staff."

"I'd better get out of here if I want to see my sons before they go to bed." He grabbed his coat and briefcase. "As a way of reducing my carbon footprint I'm taking the hybrid home. You're on the way home, why don't you join me?"

"I think I will. Give me a minute to get my coat and briefcase."

After he dropped Ki off Doug went home. He walked into a quiet house.

He took his coat off. *Where is everyone? Was there something at school I forgot about,* he wondered as he headed toward the kitchen. Finally he heard voices and turned for the living room.

Elle and Frieda were on the sofa, notebooks in hand.

"I wondered where everyone was," Doug announced.

"Hi, baby. You had a long day." Elle smiled.

"Indeed I did." He bent down and kissed her.

"It was a tough day, too." She ran her hand through his hair.

"That's an understatement." He looked at Frieda. "Hi, Frieda."

"Good evening, Mr. Brennan."

"What are you two putting your heads together for?"

"We're working on next week's Thanksgiving menu," Elle answered.

"Nice."

Frieda stood up. "If we're done, Mrs. Brennan, I'll go put Mr. Brennan's dinner in the oven."

"Thank you, Frieda."

Once she left, Doug stretched out on the sofa and laid his head on Elle's lap. "Ah, that's better."

"My meeting ran over, but I did get to hear the end of your radio address."

"Then you know how the rest of my day went."

"I do. The hospital meeting had the same theme. If I want to keep all my programs I'm going to have to do more than rob Peter to pay Paul. I have to hold up all twelve apostles."

Doug laughed. "I know you don't want to hear this but I have one word for you *fundraiser*."

Elle groaned. "It's one thing to attend a fundraiser, but it's a whole other thing to plan one."

"That's why you hire an event planner. He or she will take care of everything from the music to the food." He patted his stomach. "Speaking of food, what did Frieda make tonight? I'm starving."

"Frieda didn't cook. I did. I made chicken pot pie."

"Mmm, that sounds good." He paused. "Wait, you went in today. When did you have time to cook?"

"Rory and I had lunch at The Viand Café, and since it's so close to home I called it a day."

"Must be nice."

"I don't get paid the big bucks like you," she teased.

"Oh yeah, I make more money than you."

"One dollar beats zero."

"True." He chuckled. "So how's my little brother?"

"Good. He's working overtime on the nip and tuck crowd, but we'll see him next week." She stroked his hair.

"Mom! Is Dad home yet?" Kevin yelled.

"I'm home!" Doug yelled back.

Elle gave him a dirty look. "Doug, don't encourage him. You know I hate when he yells inside the house. We're his parents, not his buddies on the street."

"Sorry, babe."

The boys thundered down the stairs and rushed in.

Elle shook her head. "How in the world do two of the skinniest people in the world make so much noise on the stairs?"

"Sorry, Mom," they chorused.

"Hey, guys, what's going on?" Doug sat up.

"I got a 99 on my English test. It was the highest grade in my class," Kevin said.

"And I got a 99 on my math test," Kyle added.

"Wow! I'm proud of you two. It looks like we're on our way to another trip to the honor roll.

"Thanks, Dad," they chorused.

"Mom, can we have another piece of cake please?"

"You just had a big slice after dinner. You're still hungry?"

"Yes."

Elle looked at the clock. "Go ahead, it's still early enough."

"Thanks, Mom," they chorused and then made a beeline for the kitchen.

"I don't know where it goes." Elle shook her head.

"They're fourteen with a lot of energy and they need to refuel to keep the engines running. I'm going to join them so I can refuel, too." He leaned closer to her. "So I can expend some energy upstairs a little later." He kissed her and then stood up.

Elle blushed.

"I love that after twenty years I can still make you blush."

Later on that night and the next morning, Doug made good use of his newfound energy.

Elle watched Doug get dressed the next morning.

"You're wearing your Brooks Brothers suit. You must have a photo op."

He adjusted his tie in the mirror. "I have the Broadway Goes Green launch."

"That sounds like fun."

"I'm sure it will be." He walked over to the bed. "But it's still only the second high point of my day." Elle couldn't help but blush. "You are too much."

"I love when you blush. It's so cute." He kissed her. "So Sheri's coming this morning right?"

"Yes, and not a moment too soon. The holiday season is nearly upon us, which means more functions and clothes."

"I'm looking forward to it. I think it's fun to get decked out."

"Of course you love it. All you need is a few good suits, shirts and ties and you're good to go. I've got to worry about dresses and pants and skirts, oh my!"

"That's why you have Sheri. She does all the worrying for you."

There was a knock at the door. "Mom?"

"Come in, Kevin."

Kevin and Kyle burst through the door in their school uniforms.

"How did you know it was me and not Kyle, Mom?"

"I'm your mother, that's how," Elle said.

Doug grinned. "I see you two are ready to bounce."

"Did you say bounce, Dad?" Kevin asked.

"Yes. Your old dad is pretty hip, don't you think?"

"Okay Dad. You're the man," Kevin said.

"Don't you take that smart-aleck tone with your father."

"Yes, Mom. I'm sorry, Dad."

"That's okay."

"Now how about a good morning Mom and Dad."

"Good morning, Mom and Dad," they chorused.

"You did that under duress, but we'll take it." Doug smiled.

"Good morning, boys. What's on your minds?" Elle asked.

"We came in to remind you that we need money for the winter dance tickets," Kevin said.

"You did say we could go," Kyle added.

Doug reached into his pocket and produced the money. "Here you go."

"Thanks, Dad." Kyle grinned.

"Yeah, thanks, Dad," Kevin added.

Elle looked at the clock. "Have you two had breakfast yet? The bus will be here soon."

"We're going down now."

They ran over and kissed Elle.

"See you later, Mom." Kyle waved as he closed the door.

"Okay." She yawned. "Oh, excuse me. Theo and Jake should be here by now, right?"

"They're probably downstairs in the kitchen with Frieda."

"You know we should give them a raise before the holidays."

"The accountants will go nuts. I just gave them a raise. What should I tell the accountant the raise is for now?"

"Combat. They do ride the school bus with five teenagers every day."

Doug laughed. "I think I'll try that." He looked at his watch. "Speaking of security, I'd better get downstairs for my ride. I'll see you later."

They kissed. "Have a good day, sweetheart."

"You, too."

Ki was already in the car when Doug got in.

"Good morning, Your Honor."

"Good morning, Ki. This is different for you," Doug said as he settled into his seat.

"I wanted to talk to you before we get to City Hall."

"What's up?"

"The buzz has already started about you being the one Jim is set to appoint to the senate seat."

"In other words my detractors are ready to pounce."

"That's right. The good news is Congressman Richards likes you and would probably back your appointment."

"That's good news. It doesn't hurt to have the Chairman of the Committee on Ways and Means, Chairman of the Board of the Democratic Congressional

Campaign Committee, and Dean of the New York State Congressional Delegation on my side."

"I know, but we're going to have to be extra careful. We don't want to give them anything to run with."

"I'm not new to this game, Ki. I'm ready. My life is an open book."

Dressed and ready for her appointment with Sheri, Elle quietly enjoyed a cup of coffee in the kitchen. She put her hospital business on the back burner so she could concentrate on fashion, not in a department store dressing room but in the comfort of her own home.

The phone rang. She picked up. "Hello?"

"Elle?"

Elle's mother, sixty-four-year-old Lynette Abbott-Williams, was known as the 'mouth from the South'. An attractive, trim woman with silver hair, she managed to remain wrinkle free in spite of her thirty-plus years in teaching. Her retirement was filled with travel, gardening, *HGTV* and Home Depot. Elle knew she and her husband Abe were in the midst of one of her many household projects. So she was genuinely surprised to hear from her.

"Hi, Mom. Is anything up?"

"Does something have to be up for me to call?"

"No. I just know you've been busy working on your kitchen."

"We're still working. Abe just ran to Home Depot to get another wrench."

"They haven't given you a personalized parking space yet?" Elle joked.

"Very funny, young lady. No, they have not. We're not there that much."

"Mom, you're at Home Depot at least three times a week. I know contractors who spend less time there."

"That's what happens when you have an old house. It requires a lot of work and upkeep."

"I know, Mom, but you wouldn't have to work so hard if you scaled down a little with a condo."

"A condo?" she scoffed. "You mean one of those New York City condos on the fifteenth floor and up? No thank you. I don't care if it has a doorman and gold elevators, it's still a birdhouse in the sky."

"Okay, Mom, point taken." Elle laughed in spite of herself. "They do have two-story condos on Long Island with manicured grounds and a maintenance crew to shovel snow, mow the grass and fix the plumbing."

"That last one is tempting, but I didn't call to talk about my plumbing issues. I wanted to let you know that we'll be there for Thanksgiving."

"Great." *Wait for it,* Elle thought as she held her breath.

"Is your father coming?"

And there's the other shoe. "Yes. Are you going to be nice, Mom?"

"I'm always polite."

"So you're going to speak to Dad first if he's here before you."

"What do you mean? I always speak."

"No, you don't. Dad always has to speak to you first."

"That's only proper etiquette," she insisted.

"Not when you walk into a room and he's already there."

"Where did you read that? *Emily Post?*"

"No. You told me."

"Fine, I'll be on my best behavior. Is he bringing anyone?"

Divorced or not, Elle knew that was a loaded question. Unlike her mother, who remarried a few years after the divorce, her father, Victor, preferred the life of a reconfirmed bachelor.

"I told him he could bring someone. Whether or not he's going to, I don't know."

"I just want to make sure we're not seated together."

Elle shook her head. "Don't worry, Mom. There will be plenty of tables."

"Good. By the way, why aren't you at work?"

"I'm working from home today. I have someone coming this morning. In fact, she should be here shortly."

"All right, I'll let you go. If I don't speak to you I will definitely see you soon."

"Okay, Mom. Love you."

"Love you, too." She hung up.

I should really consider becoming an air traffic controller. Goodness knows I've got experience. Elle sighed as she picked up her mug. A moment later the doorbell rang.

Elle looked at the clock. *It's not ten o'clock yet.*

She heard Frieda go to the door. A minute later Rory walked in.

"Hey there, gorgeous. I was in the neighborhood."

"Are you playing hooky, Dr. Brennan?" Elle asked jokingly.

"Maybe I am. Are *you* playing hooky, Dr. Brennan?"

"Now you sound like my mother."

"Sorry. Was that a loaded question?"

"No. My stylist is coming so I'm working from home today. Have a seat," Elle said, pointing to a chair.

"Thanks," Rory said and sat down.

Elle got up and poured him a cup of coffee. "Here you go."

"Thanks." He sipped it. "So what time will your style guru be here?"

"She and her band of elves will be here in about thirty minutes."

"I can be gone by then if you'd like. I know how you are about trying on clothes."

"Oh, don't be silly, you don't have to leave. Besides I'm only weird about trying on clothes because the designer boutiques don't carry my size and I end up feeling like a hippo in a sea of gazelles."

"How is that possible? You own every room you walk into. You have style and grace most size twos wish they did."

"I seem that confident to you?"

"Yes."

She chuckled. Despite being raised by a weight-conscious mother, Elle never thought about her size growing up until Doug got into politics. She was okay with being a big girl. The numbers geek in her had done the math.

At five feet, nine inches she wasn't supposed to weigh 115 pounds; it just didn't compute.

"What's so funny?"

"Nothing." She smiled. "Thanks for the compliment."

"You're welcome."

Elle studied him more closely. "Rory, aren't those the clothes you wore yesterday?"

He looked down and closed his jacket. "It appears so."

"You didn't go home last night?"

"No. I went to a friend's place for a few drinks. To make a long story short I wasn't in any condition to travel so I stayed over."

"Oh. Am I a part of your alibi?"

"I don't need an alibi. I can assure you Angela wasn't worried. I spend more nights sleeping in my office than I do at home."

Elle stared at him for a minute.

"What's wrong?" he asked self-consciously.

"Did you use your friend's razor or something?"

"Why?"

"It looks like you nicked yourself just above your collar." She pointed.

"Oh." He rubbed his neck.

"Doug has something for that in the bathroom. You should put some on."

"Thanks, but I'm sure I have something for it at my office. I am a doctor. "

"That's true." She sipped her coffee.

Just then Sheri entered the kitchen.

Elle was a little startled. "Hey, Sheri. I didn't hear the doorbell."

"That's because Frieda opened the door before I could press the bell."

"Well it's good to see you," Elle said as she turned to Rory. "Sheri Cole, this is my brother-in law, Dr. Rory Brennan."

"Nice to meet you, Dr. Brennan." They shook hands.

"Same here."

"So what goodies do you have for me?"

"You'll see. Is it okay if I wave my assistants in?"

"Please do," Elle said gleefully.

She and Rory followed Sheri to the front door and watched as three assistants brought armfuls of clothes in.

"You know the drill, guys. Head upstairs and to the left," Sheri directed. Once the last assistant made it upstairs they went up to the master bedroom's walk-in closet.

"The clothes have been divided into four sections; casual, work, semiformal and formal. Naturally I included a cross-section of plus-size designers," Sheri explained.

"Wow, Elle, this is something," Rory said.

"Sheri's the best."

"Now you told me you needed options for Thanksgiving." She removed two dresses from the racks.

Elle looked them over. "They're pretty."

"I know you're not crazy about trying things on, but I'd really like to see how they look on you." Sheri waved the dresses in front of her.

"Oh, I don't know." Elle hesitated.

"Go ahead, Elle, try them on for her. You're the only gazelle here." Rory smiled.

"Okay, which one do you want me to try on first?"

"Try on the plum dress first." She handed her both hangers.

"Okay." Elle went into the bathroom with them.

"Thank you, Dr. Brennan. She usually never wants to try anything on for me."

"You're welcome." Rory smiled.

"I don't think she realizes she's got a great shape."

"Yes, she does." Rory caught himself. "Elle doesn't know how pretty she is."

"You're right." She paused. "Would you excuse me for a minute?"

"Certainly."

Sheri knocked on the door. "Elle?"

"Yes?" she answered.

"Did you have a chance to go through the casual look book I put together for you?"

"Yes."

"What did you think? Did anything catch your attention?"

"Everything looked great." She paused. "There was one look that got my attention."

"Oh, which one?" Sheri seemed excited.

"It was the picture of the spice woman who's married to the soccer player."

Sheri giggled. "You're talking about Posh Spice. She's married to David Beckham."

"Right. Is she trying to look like a praying mantis in high heels, big sunglasses and a little skirt?"

Rory let out a guffaw.

"I'm sure that wasn't the look she was going for, Elle."

"Don't get me wrong, I wasn't trying to be snide. I just know that designers and fashionistas are inspired by a lot of different things. So I thought perhaps she was inspired by a praying mantis. They are long and elegant in a weird bug-like way."

"Well, fashion people find inspiration in a lot of different things. But the question is did you like the skirt?"

"The skirt was cute. It was just a little too short, and I am a woman of a certain age. Besides, I've learned it's in my best interests not to bring too much attention to my butt."

Sheri had worked with Elle long enough to know that was code for she didn't like it or any of the other looks. "I got you," Sheri answered. "I'll bring you another look book."

"Thank you." She paused. "Here I come." Elle walked out and over to the mirror. "I love the color."

Sheri walked up behind her. "I do, too. It's the Camilla wrap dress by IGIGI," Sheri said as she gazed at Elle's reflection in the mirror.

"What do you think, Rory? Is this too much for the church's soup kitchen?"

"No. You look great." He downplayed just how good she looked to him.

"Good. Now for the other dress and I'm done." She went back to the bathroom.

Rory turned to Sheri. "You've got a great eye. I see why you do this for a living."

"Thank you."

A few moments later Elle emerged from the bathroom in a body-conscious black dress that hugged all of her in just the right places. Rory struggled to keep his jaw off the floor.

"I may not know much about fashion, but this feels very Audrey Hepburn in *Breakfast at Tiffany's* to me," Elle said with a grin.

"Audrey Hepburn wished she could have filled out a dress like you," Sheri said. "Go look in the mirror."

Elle looked at her reflection. "What do you think about this one, Rory?"

He gulped. "You look good. You look very good."

Elle grinned. "It's a done deal. Thanks, Rory." She went back to change again while Sheri finished removing the plastic from the rest of the garments in the closet.

"Sheri, you've done it again." Elle hung the dresses up. "Now I don't have to worry about my clothes for a while."

"It was my pleasure."

"Now all I have to worry about is my makeup. Do you think Rochelle will do it? I know it's a holiday, but I'll pay her double."

"I'm sure she will. I'll give her a call. What time do you want her to come over?"

"I'll be back from the soup kitchen around one and I'll probably be in the kitchen for at least an hour. Shall we say around three o'clock?"

"Done." She clapped her hands. "By the way, Fashion Week will be here again before we know it. Would you like to go again?"

What the heck? Elle thought. "Sure. I'd like to see next summer fashions before the end of winter."

"I know it sounds crazy, but there's a method to the madness." Sheri smiled.

"There is?" Rory asked, surprised.

"Yes. Do you really want to know why?" Sheri asked.

"No." Rory nodded. "I'll leave that to the fashion gods."

"What I don't get is why Fashion Week is in September instead of October. I mean if they're going to have so many skeletons walk the runway, it should be closer to Halloween. That's a theme, isn't it?"

Rory and Sheri laughed.

"Elle, what I'd give to be in your head for just a few minutes." Rory chuckled then looked at his watch. "Well, ladies, this has been terrific, but I have to get going."

"Okay," Elle said.

Sheri looked at her watch. "Where did the time go? I have to get going, too."

"I'll walk you both out," Elle said as she led them out of the room and downstairs to the foyer.

Sheri stopped to search her bag. "I think I dropped my keys. Do you mind if I go back up?"

"No. Go ahead."

Sheri dashed upstairs.

Elle opened the door. "I suppose I'll see you next week."

"I wouldn't miss it for the world." Rory kissed her on the cheek. "See you then."

"Bye." She waved.

Sheri returned waving her keys. "I've got them."

"Good. Thanks again for coming today. I really appreciate it."

"You're welcome." She looked around. "Your brother-in law left?"

She nodded. "He has to take care of that cut on his neck before he heads back to his office."

"That was a cut?" Sheri looked confused. "I must need glasses. It looked like a hickey to me."

Elle laughed. "A hickey? That's funny."

Sheri shrugged. "Anyway, you enjoy your holiday and we'll get together for your winter stuff soon."

"Okay."

She closed the door behind Sheri. *Rory has a hickey? That's crazy. He's forty-six years old. Then again, he's unhappily married and he did have the same clothes on.* "Oh, this is too much for me," Elle said aloud.

"Mrs. Brennan? Did you say something?" Frieda asked.

"I'm just mumbling to myself, Frieda." She sighed. "I'll be in the office for a while if anyone needs me."

CHAPTER 4

Before anyone realized it, Thanksgiving Day was upon them. That meant Doug, Elle and the boys were working in St Stephen's of Hungary's soup kitchen. Despite the city's financial troubles Doug increased the resources for soup kitchens and pantries around the city. Moreover the Brennan family made a point to donate to most of these facilities year-round to help New Yorkers through tough times. With hair nets, gloves and serving spoons Doug, Elle, Kevin and Kyle helped prepare and serve food. Though the press usually covered the event with a few city desk reporters, this year there were an unusual number of local and national newspaper and television reporters in the mix as well.

Elle leaned over to Doug. "Did these reporters lose a bet or something? I don't think I've ever seen so many of them here before."

"I can't say for sure."

Ki walked up to them. "Happy Thanksgiving, Elle." He kissed her cheek.

"Thanks, Ki. Same to you."

"We're looking forward to dinner."

"That's great, because there will be plenty of food."

Doug checked the clock. "It's nearly two o'clock. Elle has to get home."

"That's not a problem. I'll take her place." Ki donned a hair net, apron and gloves.

Doug snickered. "That's a lot of look for you, Ki."

Kevin and Kyle chuckled.

"Very funny." Ki wasn't amused.

"Play nice, you two." Elle said as she took her hair net and apron off. "I'll take the boys home with me."

"Okay," Doug said, and turned to Kevin and Kyle. "I'll see you two in a little while."

"Okay, Dad," they chorused.

Doug kissed Elle. "See you later, baby."

Elle waved. "Come on, guys." The press took some pictures as she and the boys left.

Ki waited until the reporters were out of earshot. "Word is the president-elect is making the announcement about Rita on Monday."

"Really?"

"Yes. A friend of mine from *The New York Times* told me they're running a story on Sunday about possible potential replacements, and your name was mentioned favorably."

"Good."

"As for how receptive members of the Senate are about it, I don't know."

"I'm sure Uncle Rob knows. He'll be at the house tonight," Doug said.

"Between him and your dad we'll get the whole picture."

"Speaking of pictures, smile."

A photographer snapped their photo. Doug spent the next couple of hours serving people on the line, taking photos and talking with parishioners, while Ki worked the reporters. It was time to put Doug's best foot forward because it was likely he would meet with just as much disapproval as approval to be the next junior senator from New York.

Elle had spent the better part of two days getting reading ready for the big dinner. Although she had plenty of staff on hand to help, she enjoyed leaving her own culinary mark on the meal. However, on the day of the party she left supervising kitchen duties to Frieda.

After making sure the dining area was set up, Elle went upstairs and changed into her dress for the evening. She was in the midst of putting her makeup on when there was a knock at the door.

"Come in," she called.

"Happy Thanksgiving," Melissa answered.

"Happy Thanksgiving to you, too." Elle turned around and they hugged. "I'm so glad you came early."

"So am I. The dining room looks great."

"Thanks. Do the boys know . . ."

Before she could finish her sentence, Elle heard a stampede of feet descend the staircase.

"Yes. They know Jason's here."

"Where's Myles?"

"He's in the den watching a special on TLC." She shook her head. "You know how those science geeks are."

Elle laughed.

"Looks like you're going to have a full house tonight."

"I know."

"Is Cousin Margaret coming?"

Margaret Brennan-Sanford was Doug's Aunt Evelyn's daughter. Margaret was as flashy as her mother, the former lieutenant governor of Maryland. A born tease, she enjoyed showing off her figure in short skirts and plunging necklines, which explained her 0-6 marriage record even though she was only a year older than Doug.

"I think so."

"She's a character."

"No kidding." Elle put her mascara on. "It kills me when she pulls that innocent act when men come on to her. I mean the woman walks around like an ice cream cone and then acts surprised when someone wants to take a lick. I don't get it."

"Neither do I." Melissa paused. "I thought you had someone to do your makeup for tonight."

"I decided against it. I'm not in the mood for full war paint. Besides it's just family and friends tonight, no flashbulbs."

"Good. Where's Doug?"

Elle checked the clock. "Doug should be back any . . ."

"Hey, babe," Doug said as he entered. "Happy Thanksgiving, Melissa."

"Same to you, Doug." She kissed his cheek.

"Where's your husband?"

"He's in your den. In fact, I'm going to get him so he doesn't get hooked on another TLC show and forget why we're here. I'll see you two downstairs."

"Okay."

She closed the door as she left.

Elle stood up. "How did it go at the church?"

Doug was staring at her.

"Doug?"

"You look exquisite."

"Thank you." Elle turned around to give him the 360 view. "Sheri did a great job."

"Sheri may have picked it, but you're the one making that dress work." He winked as he took her into his arms for a long kiss.

"Oh, you've got lipstick on your mouth. What will people think?"

"Who cares? I think red's my color. Besides, it wouldn't be the first time a mayor of New York wore lipstick."

Elle laughed.

"You think anyone would notice if we're a little late?" He patted her butt.

"They most certainly would notice, Doug. We're the hosts of this shindig."

"You're such a party pooper."

"Sorry." She glanced at the clock. "We'd better get downstairs. I'm pretty sure my parents are here by now."

Holding hands, Elle and Doug left their bedroom. As soon as they neared the staircase they heard Elle's mother.

"It sounds like your mother is already at it."

"Of course she is. I bet she's got an earful for you."

As they descended the stairs the topic of conversation was revealed.

"Well I just don't understand it at all. Just this week alone, Abe and I had to pay several bridge tolls. So I want to know why the MTA claims it doesn't have any money and they have to get fare and toll hikes. It's ridiculous.

I'm telling you there must be two sets of books." Lynette handed her coat to Frieda. Standing next to her was her husband, seventy-three-year-old Abe Williams, who was as tactful as Lynette was blunt. A retiree and contract negotiator from the heyday of Motor City, he learned when to speak after years with the automobile workers' union.

"If they're saying they don't have money Lynette, there isn't much to do." Elle's father, sixty-five-year-old financial analyst Victor Abbott, answered. At six feet tall with a smooth, dark complexion, the only thing that gave his age away was the hint grey in his hair and well-trimmed beard.

"Happy Thanksgiving, Mom and Dad," Elle said as she walked over and hugged both of them.

"How's my girl doing?"

"I'm good, Dad."

"Happy Thanksgiving, Mr. Abbott." Doug shook his hand.

"Thanks, Doug."

Doug then turned to Mr. Williams. "Happy Thanksgiving, Mr. Williams."

Doug faced his mother-in-law. "And how are you, Mrs. Williams?" He hugged her.

"I'm fine except for those tolls. What are you planning to do about that?"

"Well . . ."

Mr. Williams interrupted. "Lynette, it's the holiday. Leave the man alone about the MTA. Besides, he's the mayor. He doesn't have anything to do with that." He shook Doug's hand. "Happy Thanksgiving, Doug."

"Thanks, Mr. Williams."

"So where are those grandsons of mine?" Elle's mother looked around.

"They're probably in the family room with their Wii."

"Their what?"

"It's a game system, Mom."

"That's what's wrong with these youngsters. They spend too much time in front of those video games."

"I'm going to say hello," Elle's dad said.

"So am I. Come on Abe," her mother said.

As the three of them went down the hall, the doorbell rang.

"Okay, honey, you do the meet and greet. I'll be right back. I'm going to check on things in the kitchen," Elle said and went to the kitchen.

A minute later Doug welcomed his father, mother, Rory and Angela when they arrived together.

"Mom, you look wonderful." Doug said as he hugged her.

A tall, striking woman, seventy-two-year-old Mary Katherine Brennan was the epitome of style and elegance. Educated in the best schools, she spoke several languages and was an accomplished photojournalist from a small, quiet family, she'd reluctantly become a part of the large and boisterous Brennan clan. Her greatest joy came from her children, whom she managed to protect from the slings and arrows of public life during Hugh's two terms in Congress. Overall, Mary Katherine wasn't crazy about the business of politics, but she supported

Doug's decision to enter the political arena as she had his father. She knew when to toe the family line and when not to.

"Thank you, dear." She looked around as a maid took her coat. "The house looks and smells wonderful."

"I'd love to take credit, but it's all Elle."

"Where is my favorite hostess?" Mr. Brennan asked, smiling.

"She'll be out in a minute. She's checking on things in the kitchen." He turned to Angela. "Hello, Angela. You look terrific," Doug said as he hugged her.

Angela Smithson-Brennan was forty-six years old, and, like many of the society set, she was rail thin, blonde (courtesy of *Clairol*) and concerned with status. Like Elle, she came from a modest, middle-class family, and for a time they got along. However, unlike Elle, she let society life go to her head. Their relationship deteriorated after Angela realized her husband had more than just a little crush on his sister-in-law.

"Thank you, Doug," Angela said.

"Happy Thanksgiving, everyone," Elle said as she walked over to greet them.

Mrs. Brennan hugged her tightly. "Thank you."

"Where's my hug?" Mr. Brennan asked.

Elle obliged. "I'm glad you're here."

"You're a brave woman to host this bunch." Mr. Brennan winked.

Rory kissed her on the cheek. "Hey there, Elle."

"Hey, Rory." She turned to Angela. "Hello Angela. Happy Thanksgiving."

"Thanks."

Doug clapped his hands. "How about we move this into the living room. We have cocktails and hors d'oeuvres."

"Elle, did you make the hors d'oeuvres?"

"I made a few, Mr. Brennan, but not all of them."

"Now, dear, you mustn't load up on the finger food. I'm sure Elle has a feast prepared," Mrs. Brennan said.

"Oh, you take the fun out of everything, Mary."

Within an hour the rest of the guests arrived and the party was in full swing with everyone mingling, drinking and laughing before dinner. Elle ducked out to inspect the dining room. Drink in hand, Melissa watched as Elle put the finishing touches on the tables.

"That should do it." Elle stepped back to admire the tables.

"You've done it again."

"Thanks. Now all I have to do is get everyone in here for dinner."

When Elle and Melissa went back the living room and den were nearly empty.

"Where is everyone?" Melissa asked.

Elle and Melissa heard a burst of laughter from the family room and went to investigate. Their faces fell when they saw Elle's mother playing the Wii tennis game with Kyle.

Melissa laughed.

"Oh, my God. Who is that woman and what has she done with my mother?"

Rory walked over. "You think this is something? You should have seen my mother."

Elle laughed. "Well, I hate to break this up but dinner is ready. Can you rally the troops for me?"

"Sure thing."

After dinner, Hugh and his younger brother, Senator Robert Brennan, held court in the den like two silver-haired lions. Though he resembled his older brother, Robert's waistline was a bit more generous than his slender brother. The senator enjoyed the trappings of good food, good wine and good women.

"All right, now that we've had a great meal, we can talk a little business." Senator Brennan sipped his brandy. "Have you made any decision about taking the governor up on his appointment offer, Doug?"

"He didn't say he was going to appoint me. He said I was a frontrunner and there will be other candidates. Besides, he could change his mind."

"Why would he change his mind?" Hugh asked.

"He might want to appoint himself to the position. It was something he talked to me about when he was lieutenant governor."

"It's not likely he'll do that now," Ki piped in. "With all the trouble happening with the state's financial situation, he'd look like he was abandoning New York during a fiscal crisis."

"He's got a point," Hugh agreed.

"Besides, any appointee would have to run again in 2012. I don't think he's interested in two campaigns.

He'd rather run for governor on his own steam later on," Ki added.

"You're really on your game, Ki." Senator Brennan was impressed.

"Thank you, Senator." He paused. "So, Senator, have you heard any rumblings about Doug?"

"To tell you the truth most of the Senate would welcome you. I know Chuck Schuler likes you."

"That's nice to hear, Uncle Rob."

"What do you think about your son-in-law joining the Senate, Victor?"

"Well Hugh, I think Doug would make a great addition to the Senate. But if you think your mother-in-law has a lot to say now, you just wait."

The men laughed.

Doug noticed Rory staring out of the window. He walked over to him and put his hand on his shoulder. "Hey, are you all right?"

"I'm fine," Rory said as he sipped his drink. "Senator. That's a pretty big move."

"I know," Doug said. "I'm sorry I didn't call and tell you about it personally."

"That's okay. How does Elle feel about it?"

"You know Elle, she's so supportive. In fact, she was the first one to say go for it."

"That sounds like Elle."

"What's that supposed to mean?" Doug's jovial demeanor suddenly became serious.

"I'm just saying, it's just like her to get behind whatever you want."

"She's not a worker drone, Rory. If she had a problem she would have told me."

"Relax, Doug, I'm not implying anything. It's just that this will be a big change for her and the kids. You'll have to spend a lot of time in Washington."

"We'll make it work," Doug said.

"I'm sure you will." Rory walked back over to the sofa.

Doug looked out the window. *I know we'll make this work. It has too.*

"Hey, are you okay?" Ki asked.

"Yeah, I'm fine," Doug said.

"Then come join us. Your uncle's talking about what's ahead for the Senate with the new president. You should hear this."

Elle was sitting on the sofa with Leslie, Ki's beautiful brunette wife, having coffee.

"So Elle, are you ready for the holidays?"

"No. Are you?"

"No." She laughed. "Every year I tell myself that I'm going to do better, but I still manage to put the bulk of my preparations off to the last minute."

"I know what you mean." Elle nodded.

"Mommy! Ashley's bothering me!"

"No, Mommy. Hannah bothered me first!"

Leslie put her cup down on the table. "Excuse me. I don't know what I'm going to do with these girls."

"No problem."

Melissa chuckled as she walked in. "Your mother and mother-in-law are having a Wii tennis match."

"I hope someone took a picture."

"I think Mr. Williams got a couple of shots."

"For blackmail, I'm sure." Elle laughed.

Melissa looked over at Angela, who was doing her best to ignore the hostess. "What's her problem?"

"Who knows?"

"She could be a little more sociable. She is a guest in your home."

"Leave her be. I gave up trying to figure it out years ago." Elle picked up the coffee pot. It was empty. She got up. "I'm going to refill the pot. You want to come with me?"

"No. I'm going to see how the tennis aces are doing. I have a video feature on my phone. I have to get this for posterity."

"Are you looking for a little blackmail material, too?"

"Forget blackmail. I need it for evidence. Otherwise no one will believe me."

"That's true." Elle laughed. "Go get your close-up, Ms. De Mille."

Elle made her way past her guests to the kitchen. She checked the coffee pot. She poured more decaf into the coffee urn.

"Oh, Mrs. Brennan, I can do that."

"It's not a problem, Frieda. But you can take this back out once I get . . ."

"Your Princeton mug." She smiled.

"Yes. Those little china cups are pretty, but they only hold about two sips of coffee." Elle went to the cabinet and retrieved her mug.

Frieda poured for her.

"Thanks, Frieda. Now this is a cup of coffee."

Frieda chuckled as she left the kitchen.

Elle fixed her coffee and took a long sip. "Ahh."

"Does it taste better in a Princeton mug?" Rory asked.

"You caught me. I didn't want to clash with the Wedgewood."

Rory smiled. "So I just heard about the senate."

"I figured as much."

"I know what Doug said, but how do you really feel about it?"

"I'm happy. I know it's something Doug wants."

"I know he wants it, but do you?"

"I want whatever makes him happy. I also know if the shoe were on the other foot, he'd support me," Elle said earnestly.

"I just thought I'd ask since I know a little something about living life around Washington politics. It's a whole other universe."

"Thanks for your concern, but I lost a quiet civilian life when Doug became mayor of the largest city in the world. As far as I'm concerned, we've been on the national stage for nearly eight years."

"I just thought I'd offer a listening ear if you needed it. You really didn't seem to want to get into it when we had lunch the other day."

"I appreciate it, Rory, but I know my own mind and I know what I'm getting into."

"Okay. Can I get a 'no hard feelings' hug?"

"Sure." Elle put her coffee down and they hugged.

"So this is where you're hiding," Doug said as he walked into the kitchen.

Rory backed away from Elle, who went over to Doug. "Elle and I were having a little chat," Rory said.

"I see. Well, Angela's looking for you. I think she's ready to leave."

"Thanks. I'll see what's happening with her," Rory said and left the kitchen.

"What were you two talking about?"

"Stuff. It's not important."

Doug looked at her mug. "Now I see why you were in here."

"Guilty."

"Can I have a sip?"

"Sure."

"How did you make it?"

"Dark and sweet."

"Good. That's just how I like it, and my woman." He playfully kissed her neck.

Elle giggled.

Rory watched longingly from the doorway before turning away.

Later on that evening after the Wii tennis tournament was declared a draw, Doug lay in the bed waiting for Elle, who was in the midst of her nightly beauty routine.

"I think the party went pretty well, don't you?" she asked as she dabbed moisturizer on her face.

"You hit out of the park again, baby."

"Thanks, sweetie." She brushed her hair. "You know what I'm really happy about?"

"What?"

"I now know what to get your mother and mine for Christmas. A couple of Wii game systems."

"Who knew it would be as easy as following what we get for the boys?"

"They're the last two people I would have ever thought would be the least interested in video games."

"Yes, they are." He leaned on his elbow. "The president-elect is making the announcement about Rita on Monday."

"Oh really? I guess that means Governor Pearson will have to pull the trigger soon, too."

"It looks that way."

Elle got up, took her robe off and climbed into bed. Doug put his arm around her. "Are you sure you're okay with everything?'

"Yes. Have you been talking to Rory?"

"We talked," Doug said.

"Doug, this is the last time I'm going to say this, so listen carefully. I know this is going to be a big change for us and I'm okay with that. I know this is important to you."

"What would I do without you?"

"I don't know, but I don't plan on giving you the chance to find out."

CHAPTER 5

The Thanksgiving weekend offered something Doug rarely had, time to spend with his family unimpeded by city business. Naturally Elle took full advantage of it to get the family ready for the Christmas season. Doug, Kevin and Kyle shopped for electronics on Black Friday. That Friday evening they put up the Christmas tree, followed by a family night movie marathon. The kids helped decorate the tree before they went to the Akon concert on Saturday, which gave Elle and Doug some alone time. However, by the time Sunday afternoon rolled around Kevin and Kyle were itching to make another break for it.

They were putting their coats on when Elle came downstairs.

"Where do you two think you're going?"

"Over to Noah Bradley's house to play *Guitar Hero*," Kevin answered.

"Dad said we could," Kyle added.

"He didn't say anything to me."

"I'm sorry, babe, they asked me after breakfast. I meant to tell you," Doug called from the top of the stairs.

"Are you driving them?"

Just then Theo emerged from the kitchen. "I'll be driving them there and bringing them home, Mrs. Brennan."

"Oh, okay. You can't be out too late, it's a school night."

"We know, Mom." Kevin kissed her cheek. Kyle did likewise.

"I'll see you later. Thanks Theo."

"You're welcome, Mrs. Brennan." He held the door open for Kevin and Kyle.

"Catch you later, Dad," Kevin called.

"Okay, boys, have a good time."

"We will, Dad," Kyle answered as he walked out.

Theo closed the door.

Elle was about to head to the kitchen.

"Elle?"

"Yes?"

"Can you come up here for a minute, please?"

She went back upstairs. "Where are you?"

"I'm in the bedroom."

As soon as she walked in Doug pulled her into a passionate embrace. "Now that the boys are out I figured we could have a play date of our own." He lifted her up and carried her over to the bed.

Like two randy college students, Elle and Doug undressed in a flash. Doug explored the peaks and valleys of Elle's curves with a slow hand and a gentle touch. He savored the sweetness of her skin with every kiss. Elle could barely contain herself as she ran her hands through her thick wavy hair and down his back. Soon the sensation of her soft lips on his hard muscles drove him wild.

"I want you now," he whispered as her legs parted. In an instant their bodies came together. With every move the fire of their love grew hotter until they were consumed by total pleasure.

After another surprising round, Doug and Elle lay in each other's arms.

"Mr. Brennan, I don't know what got into you, but wow."

He smiled. "Thank you, baby, you were pretty outstanding, too." He kissed her. "I'm a little thirsty. I'm gonna get something to drink. You want something?"

"Mineral water would be nice. Thanks."

"Your wish is my command." He got up and put on a pair of pants and a shirt.

Elle started to get out of bed.

"Wait. Where are you going?"

"Nowhere, I was just going to put something on," Elle said.

"No, don't do that."

She looked at the clock. "The boys will be home in a little while. They get grossed out over us kissing. They'd be mortified to know their parents had sex, and in the afternoon at that."

"The kids won't be home for a least a couple of hours. So stay naked. I'll be right back to join you."

"Okay." Elle lay back in bed.

Doug went downstairs to the kitchen and searched the fridge. He grabbed a bottle of water and eyed a bottle of beer. *I'd love a cold beer.* He reached for it, but then stopped. *Elle can't stand the taste of beer and even if I don't get lucky one more time, I at least want to make out.* He grabbed another bottle of water.

The phone rang.

Doug put the water on the counter. *Maybe I'll take some grapes and strawberries.* He took the platter out and put it on the counter.

"Pardon me, Mayor Brennan." Their second maid, Elsa, interrupted him. Frieda was off visiting her relatives until Monday.

"Yes, Elsa?"

"Your son Kevin is on the phone for you."

"Thanks." He picked up the phone. "Hello, Kevin."

"Hi, Dad."

"What's up?"

"We know it's a school night, but . . ."

"You want to stay out a little later."

"Can we Dad, please?"

"Your mother is going to kill me, but you can stay until nine and not a second later," Doug said.

"Thanks, Dad. You rock."

"I'm glad you think so. Please put Theo on the phone. I'll see you later."

"Okay, Dad."

"Yes, Your Honor."

"They've got one more hour and that's it. They have to leave by nine."

"Yes, sir."

"Thanks." He hung up.

Doug looked at the refreshments. *It might not be champagne but that doesn't mean I can't make mineral water more romantic.* He took two wine glasses out of the cabinet.

"Excuse me, Mayor Brennan. Your brother, Dr. Brennan, is here."

Doug was genuinely surprised. "Oh. Send him in."

"Very good, sir."

Rory entered the kitchen. "Hi, Doug."

"Hey Rory, this is a surprise. What brings you by?"

"I had some business in the area and I thought I'd stop in."

"You had business in the area on a Sunday? You're a plastic surgeon, Rory. I didn't think you made house calls."

"Listen Doug, Botox, Collagen and Restlyn injections might be common and accepted, but there are still some that prefer a don't ask, don't tell policy."

"So you bring the fountain of youth to them."

"Right."

"Talk about service with a smile."

Rory laughed. "The house is quiet. Are Elle and the kids out shopping?"

"No. The boys are over a friend's house and Elle's upstairs."

Rory focused on the two wine glasses and fruit on the kitchen counter. "Forgive me for being so dense. I should leave and let you and Elle get back to . . . whatever you were doing. I'm sorry I barged in on you."

"You're my brother. You can stop in whenever you'd like," Doug said reassuringly.

"Thanks. I'll take you up on that some other time. As for right now, I'm going to head back home." He turned to walk out.

Doug patted him on the back. "How are things going with you and Angela?"

"I'm making house calls to Botox bitches on a Sunday. What do you think?"

"Enough said. Things will get better, little brother."

"I hope so."

Doug walked him to the foyer.

"I'll see myself out. Tell Elle and the boys I said hello."

"I will. Take it easy, Rory."

Once his brother left, Doug quickly went to the kitchen, got the tray and headed upstairs. When he opened the door, Elle's eyes were closed.

"Room service."

She opened her eyes. "Oh sweetie, you're the cutest bellman I've ever seen."

"I aim to please." He put the tray down on the night table.

"I wondered what was taking you so long."

"I would have been up sooner, but Rory came by. He had some business in the area."

"He did? On a Sunday?"

"He was visiting the Botox-and-brunch set."

"Blinis and Botox, that's some menu combo."

Doug laughed. "By the way, the boys called. They're staying out until nine."

"Oh they are, are they?"

"Yes." He slipped back into bed and put his arms around her. "So we can continue with our play time."

"You're incorrigible," she laughed.

"I know, but you love me anyway," he said just before he kissed her.

Elle tingled from head to toe . . . she forgot about the water.

CHAPTER 6

After a great four-day holiday that was capped off by an afternoon in bed with her sexy husband, Elle had a hard time concentrating on work Monday morning as she poured over budget reports.

These budget figures lay out like a game of three card Monty. She sighed. *Calculus on manifolds and functional analysis was easier than this.*

Pam knocked on the door.

"Yes Pam?"

"The president-elect is on. He's announcing his appointment of Senator Clemson as secretary of state."

"Thanks. I didn't realize it was on." She turned on the television and put it on mute.

Pam hung around in the office.

"Is there something else, Pam?"

"Did you see the *Times* today?

"No. I've been trying to get through this stuff."

She put the paper down on her desk. Elle looked at the headline.

Pearson's picks for Clemson's seat.

Pam excitedly pointed to Doug's photo. "Dr. Brennan, your husband's in the article. Is he thinking about being senator? I think New York couldn't do better."

Elle had been a politician's wife long enough not to show her hand. "Thanks, Pam."

"You'd be the senator's wife."

"Yes I would." Elle chuckled. She loved Pam's enthusiasm.

Pam looked up at the television. "I guess this proves the saying if you can't beat them, join them."

"I think you might be right."

"This is so exciting." She sighed. "Well, I'd better finish off the donation letter so you can sign it before your committee luncheon."

"Oh, that's right. I nearly forgot. Thanks for reminding me."

"You're welcome."

Elle took her pocketbook out of the desk drawer and rummaged through it to get her calendar out.

"I still can't believe you don't use the calendar on the Blackberry. It's so much easier."

"For who?" Elle asked as she put the calendar back in her bag. "There are far too many buttons to bother with to get to the calendar feature."

"It would give you more room in your bag." She stared for a moment. "Is that Dooney & Bourke's tear drop hobo handbag?"

"Who?"

"Dooney & Bourke, they make high end designer handbags and accessories."

Elle looked at the tag. "Yes, it's by Dooney & Bourke, but as for it being the tear drop hobo bag, I have no idea.

I have three shelves of handbags Doug bought for me as presents. They're nice, but I just grab whatever is handy."

Bemused, Pat shook her head. "Three shelves of designer bags?"

"Oh." She covered her mouth. "Do I sound pretentious? I'm sorry."

"No, Dr. Brennan. I know you're not like that."

"Good," she sighed. "I thought those committee ladies' ways were beginning to rub off on me."

"No. I think you're good." Pam smiled as she left the office.

Thank God, Elle thought.

In keeping with the family's philanthropic endeavors Elle served on the planning committee for Mrs. Mary Katherine Brennan's Education and Arts New York City School Initiative. Her mother-in-law had created the foundation in the 70s to provide public schools with more educational materials for classrooms and to keep the arts programs. As the times changed, the initiative's mission evolved to include computers, better after-school mentoring programs and a partnership with the NYC Council of Arts. While Elle loved the implementation part of the organization, she was less than thrilled with the planning luncheons. The committee spent more time dishing the latest dirt and precious little time on the matters at hand. Gossip wasn't Elle's cup of tea, but her sister-in-law Angela, who also served on the committee, lapped it up.

Two hours with these ladies. I'm going to need an antidote. Elle picked up the phone.

"Hello?"

"Melissa?"

"Elle? You must have read my mind. I was going to call you."

"Then I saved you a phone call." She smiled. "Listen, what are you doing around three-thirty?"

"That's the end of my work day, and since Jason has basketball practice until six, I'm free."

"Good, that makes two of us with children at basketball practice. So how about we split a hot fudge sundae at *Serendipity 3*?"

"Don't you have a luncheon this afternoon?"

"It's the education and arts committee luncheon. Those women don't eat. They graze like rabbits for two hours. Whenever I leave I have to fight the urge to say 'What's up doc?' "

Melissa laughed. "I'll meet you there."

"Cool. I'll see you then."

She hung up and glanced at the newspapers on her desk. Her eyes fixated on a *Post* headline.

Mayor Brennan, qualified senatorial candidate or heir apparent?

"Oh, good grief," she groaned. *It hasn't been a day and already the Brennan butchers are hacking away.*

The Brennan butchers was the nom de plume the family had given to the circle of reporters, politicians and constituents who were anti-Brennan at all costs, no matter what.

It's been twenty-two years and I haven't gotten used to this yet. She put the paper down. *At least Doug's the Teflon mayor.*

Ensconced in his office at City Hall, Doug was in the midst of working his way through a stack of papers when there was a knock on the door.

"Yes?" he answered without looking up.

"It's me, Mayor Brennan," Ki answered.

"Come in."

Ki walked in carrying newspapers. "Where's Alice? She's not at her desk."

"She's taking lunch."

"Oh, okay." He put the newspapers on the desk. "The speculation has officially begun."

Doug glanced at the pile. "We knew that was going to happen."

"I've been taking calls all morning, and the general consensus is positive."

"That's good to hear." Doug shuffled through the papers until he came to *The Post.* "I see Mort is at it again."

Mort Barnes had been a Republican stalwart since Nixon. He was also a vocal critic of Doug's father when he served in Congress and continued to be critical of his uncle at every turn.

"You can't teach an old dog new tricks. He's been after my family for years."

"True. You know we're going to have to schedule some appearances with key people to get their support."

"In other words I have to traipse upstate to visit key cities like Buffalo and Syracuse."

"Yep."

"Okay, who called? My father or my uncle?"

"Both. They think it might be a good idea to get out so people can meet and get to know you."

"I see. I assume some calls have been made."

"Naturally. They'd like you to meet with the mayor of Buffalo."

"When is this supposed to happen? I still have a day job."

"We still have to figure out the logistics."

"Then we have time. Besides, Jim said he's not making any announcement until after Rita's confirmed. So I think we should keep it somewhat local for the time being. I don't want the good people of New York City to think I'm abandoning them in the midst of a fiscal crisis."

"Duly noted. I'll make some calls to see what we can do in our backyard."

"Thanks."

Ki left the office.

The merry-go-round has begun. Doug sighed and went back to work.

As expected without the senior Mrs. Brennan present, the committee luncheon devoted an hour to gossip, fashion and accessory talk. Just as Elle was about to nod off into her salad the talk finally turned to committee business. Vivienne Porter, the committee chair, tapped her wineglass. "Okay ladies, I think Kelly and Helen have to leave us soon, so we should get down to committee business. But I'd love to get the number for your Bee bag before you go, Kelly."

"Sure, Vivienne." She smiled.

Elle rubbed her eyes so no one would see her roll them.

"Delia has secured all the donations for the silent auction. Thank you, Delia." Vivienne grinned.

"I got a little help from my friends." Delia grinned.

Between the light and the porcelain veneers, I'm bound to go blind, Elle thought as she sipped her water.

"Now all we have left is the ticket pricing and signage so we make our goal of $100,000 for new instruments and computer upgrades," Vivienne said as she looked down at her notes. "I think we have eight sponsors for the signage at $5,000 each, so we're halfway there."

Elle raised her hand. "No, we're not. That's only 40 percent. We need two more sponsors to equal half."

"Thanks for the clarification, Elle," Vivienne said through her clenched teeth.

Elle looked down at the committee's information packet. "Also according to this you're talking about two hundred attendees at $150, that would only raise $30,000. If you want to raise $100,000 you'll either have to price the tickets at $250 or up the count to 334 people, which would raise $50,100." When Elle looked up she was met with a sea of blank looks. It reminded her of the blank looks she'd gotten in college whenever she answered a question other students couldn't. *Great, my inner calcu-*

*lator strikes again. I might as well be thirteen again. Then
again, I never did play well with others,* she thought.

"Thank you, Elle." Vivienne shook her head. "The
venue we chose only holds two hundred people, so I
guess we should raise the ticket price." She looked at her
watch. "Okay, unless there's any new business, I'd like to
adjourn the meeting."

All the ladies rose and began giving each other air
kisses and toodles.

Elle stood up and turned her cell phone back on.
*That's an hour of my life I'll never get back. At least we
ended a little early.*

"Elle?"

She turned around. "Yes, Angela?"

"Can I speak with you for a minute?"

"Sure." *This can't be good,* Elle thought to herself.

They walked over to a window in the restaurant.

"I want you to know that I know what you're up to."

"What?" Elle was completely confused.

"I know what you're up to with my husband."

"I'm not up to anything with Rory. He's my brother-
in-law."

"You have it all, don't you? The kids, a great husband,
and now you're probably going to be the wife of the next
senator."

Elle took a deep breath to control her voice. "Angela,
I realize you're unhappy and I'm sorry. But the fact is I
don't have anything to do with your unhappiness."

"You have everything to do with it. I just wanted to
put you on notice."

"I don't have time for this. You have a good day, Angela." Elle walked away. *What the hell had the restaurant put in Angela's salad? It figures she waited until Mrs. Brennan wasn't here to flip on me. Hmm, I think Melissa and I will order a double hot fudge sundae. I could use an extra dose of chocolate.*

Half an hour later Elle filled Melissa in about Angela's antics over a giant sundae at Serendipity 3.

"What's her problem?"

"She and Rory are unhappy and somehow she thinks I'm to blame."

"The idea of you being involved with Rory is preposterous."

"I know. Rory is more like a brother to me than a brother-in-law. We've been getting together for lunch since Doug and I were dating."

"I remember. I used to hang out with you two sometimes."

"That's right." She went for a spoonful of fudge. "Rory is a great guy but Doug's my first, last and only love."

"Anyone with eyes can see that, Elle."

"Anyone but Angela." Elle began to reflect. "I can remember all my firsts with Doug like they were yesterday. The first time we met on the beach, our first date and our first kiss." Elle sighed dreamily. "I knew I was going to be with him forever," she said and took another spoonful of ice cream.

"Even though you didn't have a clue to who he was."

"Neither did you."

"Touché. We didn't read *People*. Let alone their sexiest man alive issue."

"I think he kind of liked that I didn't know, it made things more romantic."

"I was always a little jealous of how romantic you and Doug were. Myles on the other hand . . ."

"Don't say that."

"Oh yeah? Doug set up a romantic proposal on the same spot of the beach where you met. What did Myles do? He sent me an equation to figure out," Melissa said with a sulky expression.

"Don't even try it, Melissa. You're a math geek. You loved it."

Melissa smiled in spite of herself. "Okay, I'll admit it was pretty clever. Still it wasn't a catered proposal on the beach complete with a string quartet playing in the background."

"It was nice." She grinned. "We even set the date that night. Wait if memory serves you and Myles set the date the night you got engaged, too."

"Poor guy, he needed to see the finish line." She winked.

Elle laughed. "I know what you mean. There Doug was, the sexiest man alive and he was dating one of the last two American virgins." Elle ate some more ice cream. "Goodness knows we've made up for lost time and then some. Kevin and Kyle always talk about our kissing and stuff," Elle said. "It completely grosses them out." Elle chuckled. "But then again we're their parents, we're supposed to gross them out."

"Don't worry, Jason talks, too. He's equally grossed out," Melissa said.

"So behind the glasses and protractor beats the heart of a sexy beast."

"Oh yes!"

They laughed.

"Not that I don't love talking about this stuff, but what's the deal with the Senate seat and Doug? Is it official? Is he really going for it?"

"It looks that way."

"That's great for him, Elle. I also realize that I'm the one who told you to keep an open mind, but you seem like you still have reservations."

"It's just the same awkwardness issues I always have." Elle sighed. "For God's sake, Melissa, I have a stylist that literally dresses me every day. She might not be there in person to zip me up but she's responsible for every outfit I wear. What's going to happen when we go to Washington?"

"Doug pays pretty well, so I'm sure Sheri would be more than happy to travel." Melissa smiled.

Elle was not amused.

"It was just a joke, Elle, lighten up." Melissa grinned.

"I'm sorry. I guess I'm a little sensitive."

"That's okay," Melissa said reassuringly. "Think of it this way, how much attention does the press really pay to senatorial spouses?"

Elle thought for a moment. "You might have a point."

"Besides, it's not like here in the city. There you'd be one of many spouses."

"True but then there's the kids to consider. We'd have to uproot them."

"No, you wouldn't. Doug can be a commuter senator."

"You seem to have all the answers, don't you?"

"I think it's the hot fudge. I think it makes me think more clearly." Melissa grinned.

"I guess I could stand it."

"I know you can. However it's Doug that will have to weather most of the storms. The papers and pundits are already at it."

"It's nothing he hasn't heard before. Doug can handle it."

"But can you handle finishing this big sundae?" Melissa teased.

"Bring it on." She chuckled as they dug in.

CHAPTER 7

Exhausted, Doug dropped his coat and briefcase at the door. The sound of his family at the table beckoned him to the dining room.

"Hello, family."

"Hi, Dad." Kevin looked up.

"Hey, Dad," Kyle echoed.

He mussed their hair after he walked over to them. "How are my boys tonight?"

"Good," Kyle answered.

"How was practice?"

"It was pretty good today. Coach Best says my outside shot has improved."

"That's great, Kyle." Doug bent down to kiss Elle. "How's my best girl?"

"I'm good, sweetie. You look tired, though."

"I am tired." He plopped down in a chair.

"Are you hungry? Frieda made red snapper."

"That sounds really good to me."

"Frieda?" Elle called.

"Yes, Mrs. Brennan?"

"Would you please bring Mr. Brennan a plate?"

"Certainly." She disappeared back into the kitchen.

"So, Kevin, how's your jump shot?"

"Coach says I'm making improvements."

"Good."

"He was much better today because his shorty Karen was there," Kyle said.

Kevin shot his brother a dirty look.

"Who's Karen?" Elle asked.

"She's a cheerleader Kevin likes," Kyle said with a smirk.

"Shut up, Kyle," Kevin growled.

"What exactly is a shorty?" Elle asked with a serious expression on her face.

"A shorty is a girl that you like," Kyle explained.

"But why call her a shorty? Is she petite?" Elle asked, genuinely puzzled by the terminology.

Kevin and Kyle laughed. Doug covered his mouth to stifle his laughter.

"It sounds like it could be misogynistic. Is it?"

"No, Mom, it's just a phrase. You hear it a lot in hip hop," Kevin said.

"Kevin wouldn't do that to his shorty," Kyle teased.

"Shut up, Kyle!"

"All right, that's enough you two," Doug said, quickly stepping in.

"He started it, Dad," Kevin protested.

"Keep it up and you two can forget about dessert," Elle warned.

"Mom!"

"You heard me."

Order was quickly restored while Frieda served Doug.

"Thank you, Frieda."

"You're welcome, sir."

"Frieda, we still have brownies, right?"

"I believe so."

She turned to Kevin and Kyle. "Since it appears you're both done, you can take your plates into the kitchen, put them in the dishwasher and then you can have a couple of brownies."

"Thanks, Mom," they chorused as they stood up with their plates.

"You're welcome. Listen, you two, I better not hear anymore quarreling," she warned.

They quietly went into the kitchen.

"You realize they didn't answer you."

"I know. There's going to be another scuffle any minute now, but for the moment let's enjoy the peace."

Elle still looked mystified while Doug continued to eat.

"What's on your mind, babe?"

"If shorty isn't about height, is about the clitoris?" Elle asked matter-of-factly.

"What?" Doug laughed so hard he had to cover his mouth with a napkin to keep from spraying the table.

"Well some consider the clitoris and penis equivalent in all respects except for their arrangement on the human body. And judging from the number of penis size references in some of the hip hop lyrics I've heard, I can only assume that shorty is a sexual reference." Elle sounded like a documentary narrator.

"I can't say that I've ever thought about it." Doug laughed as he got up and kissed Elle on the forehead. "Thanks, sweetie. I needed that." He sat back down.

"I really don't know what I did, but you're welcome." She smiled. "I guess it was that kind of day."

"Do I have to say it?"

"No."

Doug sipped his water. "So, how was your day? You had the organizer's luncheon, right?"

"Oh, yes, that."

"That doesn't sound good. Don't tell me they spent the entire two hours gossiping."

"No. It wasn't that."

Doug put his fork down. "Now I'm intrigued."

"Angela sort of flipped out on me."

"What?"

"She babbled on about being onto to me and that I'm the reason for her trouble with Rory."

"Was she drinking?"

"No more than usual."

"What did you do?"

"What could I do? I told her I was sorry she and Rory had trouble, but any problems they had weren't my doing. Then I left. I didn't want to deal with it."

"Do you want me to talk to her?"

"No thank you. I'm sure it will blow over." Elle sipped her water. "Oh yes, before I forget, Joan Sanders called for you."

"Joan called here?"

"She said she tried your cell but your voicemail was full."

"That's because I haven't cleared any of my messages. Did she say what it was about?"

"No. She just wanted me to give you the message and ask you to give her a ring back."

"You're hogging all the ice cream!" Kyle shouted.

"You took the biggest brownie!" Kevin shouted back.

Elle got up. "I really need a referee's whistle."

"Go get 'em, Mom," Doug said and laughed as Elle rushed away.

Elle went into the kitchen. "I told you I didn't want any noise."

Doug took his cell out and dialed Joan.

One of his oldest friends, Doug met Joan in college. A striking, petite blonde, Joan was a real looker on campus. Doug served as her beard until she came out in their senior year. After graduation she began a career in journalism and worked her way up to managing editor at *The Times*. Given their schedules, she and Doug usually kept in touch via email or by texting, so the fact she'd called piqued his interest.

"Joan Sanders."

"Hi, Joan, how are you?"

"Hey, Doug."

"Elle gave me your message. What's up?"

"I know you're busy, but I wondered if you had a few minutes to spare for me tomorrow?"

"If you don't mind meeting early you can come around eight."

"That works for me."

"What's going on?"

"I'll catch you up tomorrow. Okay?"

"Okay." He put his phone on the table.

"Did you get her?"

"Yes. We're going to talk tomorrow." He paused to listen. "I don't hear anything."

"The great brownie war has been averted." She put a dessert plate with a large brownie on the table. "I managed to save one for you."

"Thanks, baby."

"You're welcome. You look like you could use a big dose of chocolate." She kissed his cheek. "Oh, by the way, I'm going to be in the Bronx tomorrow."

"You're going to the Bronx?"

"I'm meeting with Dr. Campbell about the clinic."

"What time?" Doug asked.

"It's a morning appointment. Why?"

"I'll be in the Bronx making an announcement at the Work Center in Hunts Point, but it's not until the afternoon. I thought you could stop by."

"That would have been nice. Maybe next time."

"Yes, definitely."

"Would you like a cup of decaf or a cold glass of milk to go with that?"

"What do you think?"

"A cold glass of milk it is." She left the dining room.

I wonder what's going on with Joan? It's unlike her to be so secretive. He looked at his watch. *Why does tomorrow suddenly seem so far away? It's going to be a long night.*

Early the next morning, Doug was trying his best not to wake Elle when he stubbed his toe on the settee. "Oww." He grimaced.

"Now I know you must be in a hurry." Elle sat up. "That settee hasn't moved in years, but whenever you're in a rush you run smack into it every time."

Doug sat down on the offending settee to nurse his toe. "Sorry if I woke you. This thing smarts like the dickens." He rubbed his toe.

"Oh, my poor baby."

"I'll live."

"What time is it?"

"It's almost five-fifteen."

"My goodness, I guess you've got a big day in store."

"Every day is a big day when it comes to being mayor of this city."

"That's true." Elle lay back on the bed.

Just as he was about to say something he noticed how sexy Elle looked with her tousled hair and silky red chemise. "Now there's a picture."

"What?"

"You look so sexy."

Elle fussed with her hair. "I must look a fright."

"Not at all." He got up and went over to the bed. "In fact, I'd say quite the opposite." He leaned in to kiss her.

She put her hand up. "I haven't brushed my teeth, Doug."

"Does it look like I care?"

He softly pressed his lips to hers. His soft kissed gradually increased in intensity and passion with each moment, soon he was on top of her.

"Doug." She whispered as he kissed her neck.

"Yes, baby?"

"I thought you had to get to City Hall early."

"So?"

"I don't think we should start something we can't finish."

"Who says we can't finish? Haven't you heard of a quickie?"

"Yes. Have you?"

He stopped kissing her neck. "What's that supposed to mean?"

"Mind you I'm not complaining, but you're not exactly a minuteman."

"Now that sounds like a challenge," he said as he unbuttoned his shirt.

"Oh, how could I forget the Brennan competition gene?"

He stood up and took off his pants. "That's right, honey, we believe in rising to challenges."

She looked down. "I can see that."

He slid under the covers and off came Elle's night chemise. Fast or slow, Doug wanted to savor every inch of Elle's body. He loved that when he held her he could feel her softness while her curves led him to even softer and sweeter spots, none of which he missed. Elle melted under his touch. In the blink of an eye, their bodies wrapped around one another until they became one. It didn't quite qualify as a quickie, but it was a defeat both Elle and Doug were more than happy to live with.

Doug still managed to get to City Hall early enough to arrive with his secretary, Alice. He was eager to see Joan and got an early start on some work to keep his mind busy until she got there.

The intercom buzzed. "Yes?"

"Mayor Brennan, there's a Joan Sanders here to see you but she's not on your calendar . . ."

"It's okay. I'm expecting her. Send her in."

"Yes, sir."

A moment later Joan walked in. "Good morning, Mr. Mayor."

Doug got up. "Hey, Joan." He hugged her. "Have a seat."

"Thanks." She sat down.

He followed suit. "How's Rachael?"

Rachael Madsen was Joan's life partner of ten years. A brunette with medium-length hair and soft features, she was also the host of a very popular news program on one of NBC's affiliates. Doug and Elle had attended their wedding in Vermont a few years back.

"She's doing well, thanks. She's still hunting down the big political stories."

"I know. I'm usually too tired to stay up for the show but Elle TIVO's them for me."

"Good woman." She smiled. "Well, I know you're dying to find out what I'm here about."

"It drove me crazy all night."

"Then let me put you out of your misery. Rachael was approached by someone who is shopping photos of Elle around, and given the fact that you're the mayor of New York and a possible Senate appointee, if they approached her, they went to everyone."

Doug looked confused. "Someone has some photos of Elle? This is crazy. Can you tell me if *The Post* is on that list?"

"I don't have anything that specific, but you can be sure that if it's a chance to lob a missile at your family, they'll take it."

"I don't understand this." Doug scratched his head. "What kind of photos are we talking about? It's not like Elle nude sunbathes on the beach or even hangs around the party scene. She's a card-carrying member of the NAACP, MENSA and the PTA, for goodness sake."

"They're pictures of her with Rory." Joan pulled a folder out of her bag and placed it on the desk.

"Where did you . . ."

"Don't ask."

He opened the folder. There were pictures of Elle having lunch with Rory and a couple of shots of her kissing him on the cheek outside of the townhouse. "There's nothing here."

"I agree, but even the most innocent photos can be taken out of context."

"To be honest they look like surveillance photos."

"You're right. They have P.I. written all over them."

"Who would hire a private investigator to follow Elle?"

She shrugged her shoulders. "I don't know, but if I were you I'd look into this as soon as possible. It won't be long before these photos are published somewhere."

"I will. Thanks for bringing this to my attention, and thank Rachael for me."

"Thank us for what?" She winked.

Doug laughed.

"I'd better get over to my office. Newspapers may be dying, but I'm hanging on to the printed word with both hands." She stood up.

Doug got up and walked her to the door. "Thanks again, Joan." He kissed her cheek.

"Anytime," she said as she walked out.

Doug went back to his desk and looked at the photos. *Who in the world is following Elle and why? This doesn't make any sense.*

From his grandfather's rumored affairs and supposed mob connections to his Uncle Rob's three ill- advised marriages, media attention was par for the course when it came to being a Brennan. It was no different for Doug. He'd spent his twenties as a much sought-after bachelor who dated a bevy of beautiful A-list actresses and models, much to his mother's chagrin. The gossip columns loved him, and when Doug was single his love life sold newspapers. He could have cared less; it came with the territory. However, this time it was personal. Someone was feeding the tabloids a "Cain and Abel" scenario by making it seem like Elle and Rory were having an illicit affair. This was just the kind of thing that spelled disaster and could easily derail his appointment before it got on the rails.

Ki poked his head in. "Was that Joan Sanders I saw leaving?"

"Yes. Come on in." He beckoned him.

"What's up?"

"Take a look." He opened the folder.

Ki look through the photos. "What in the world? Where did she . . ."

"Does it matter? Suffice it to say if Joan had them, someone else has them, too, and it's only a matter of time."

"I'll get on it." Ki quickly left the office.

Doug dialed Elle's cell phone. "Damn! Voicemail." He hung up and dialed again.

"Dr. Brennan's office."

"Hi, Pam."

"Mayor Brennan, how are you?"

"I'm fine. You?"

"I'm well. Thank you."

"That's good to hear. Is my wife available?"

"She's not in the office today. Did you try her cell?"

"Yes. It went straight to voicemail."

"She's in the Bronx at the Children's Clinic."

"That's right. She did tell me she'd be there today." Doug said.

"I can give you the number there if you'd like to call the switchboard."

"No, that's all right."

"She did say that she's going to work from home afterwards, so you might just want to call her at home later."

"That's a good idea. Do you know what time she's supposed to wrap up?"

"I imagine she'll be done around lunchtime."

"Thanks Pam. Have a good one." He hung up.

Ki poked his head in. "You have a public meeting with council members Wagner and Romero about the Belmont Business District in the Bronx. You remembered that, right?"

"Yes. It's on my calendar." As he searched his desk for the paperwork, Ki walked over and handed it to him. "Thanks."

"You're welcome. Listen, don't worry about the other stuff. We'll handle it," Ki said and patted him on the back.

"I know." *If I'm lucky I'll get to Elle before this news breaks.*

They walked out and down to the meeting room.

With the tour of the clinic over, Elle waited in Dr. Campbell's office while Rory met with a few patients to discuss their cases. Like Doug, Rory was fluent in three languages, including Spanish. Elle spoke eight languages and usually would have joined in but she felt a little light-headed. Rosario let her lay down on the sofa in her office.

"Hey, Elle, I see you've made yourself comfortable." Rosario smiled as she entered her office.

Dr. Rosario Campbell was born and raised in the Bronx. A gorgeous brunette with a sharp mind, she went to college on an academic scholarship. She completed her medical studies at Johns Hopkins. Although she had her choice to practice anywhere in the country, she decided to give back to her community in her beloved borough. The Children's Clinic was her baby and she took great care of it and its many small patients.

"Yes. Thanks for giving me the chance to get off my feet."

"No problem. Are you still feeling lightheaded?"

"No. It passed."

"Did you eat this morning?"

"Yes, Doctor." Elle could see the wheels turning in Rosario's mind. "It's nothing. It's happened before and it always passes."

"When you say before, do you mean in the past or more recently?"

"Maybe two or three weeks ago, I guess. Why?"

"Have you noticed anything else?"

"Like what?"

"Well, have you felt a little more tired than usual, or have you had any changes in your appetites?"

"In my appetites? Plural?"

"Yes. Have you craved more food or maybe sex lately?"

Elle was a little taken aback. "What?"

"I'm a doctor, Elle. You can tell me."

"Well, I have to say I have been a little more randy recently, but I think that's pretty good considering I'm forty-one years old."

"Do you think you could be pregnant?"

Elle sat up straight. "Pregnant? No." She shook her head. "The last time I was pregnant I had morning sickness the minute the rabbit died."

"No two pregnancies are alike."

"I can't be."

"When was your last period?"

Elle dug through her bag, got her calendar and leafed through the pages. "I think it was before Thanksgiving."

She studied November. It had no tell-tale X's. She then leafed through to October, which also had no X's. Her mouth was agape.

Rosario reached for a plastic bag with a specimen cup. "You know the drill. You can use my bathroom." She held the bag.

Too discombobulated to argue, Elle took the specimen cup and went into the bathroom. A few minutes later she walked out and handed it to a waiting Rosario.

"Thank you. I'll be right back," the doctor said and then left the room.

Elle plopped back onto the sofa. *I can't be pregnant. Maybe I forgot to mark the calendar. It wouldn't be the first time.* She sighed. *Oh, my God, if I am pregnant the timing is awful.*

Rosario walked back in and handed her a test with a big plus sign. "You're pregnant."

"I'm pregnant?" Her jaw dropped. "How?"

"When a man and a woman love each other . . ."

"Very funny, I know how. I just can't believe it didn't even occur to me," Elle said in a bewildered whisper.

"I'm pretty sure you would have noticed eventually."

"I guess." She rubbed her forehead. "I'm forty-one, for goodness sake."

"These days age doesn't matter. One of my colleagues has a forty-eight-year-old first-time mother who's due in December."

"Wow, forty-eight," she said in disbelief.

"So you're definitely not alone in the pregnant over forty category." She paused. "Are you okay?"

"Yes. Sure. I'm just stunned."

"I can imagine. Listen, even though urine pregnancy tests are a little better than 98 percent accurate, you should make an appointment with your gynecologist for a blood test, just to be sure."

"In the interest of time can you draw blood and have the results sent over to Dr. Aranow? I'd like to know exactly where I stand sooner rather than later."

"I can do that. I'll be right back."

Elle rolled up her sleeve. *Oh, my God, Doug and I are going to have another baby.*

Rosario came back, drew blood and labeled the tubes.

"Thanks again, Rosario," Elle said as she put her coat on. "You can bill me for the lab. I don't want to take away from any of the clinic's resources."

"Don't worry about it."

"No. I insist."

Just then Rory walked in. "Wow, this is some place you have here, Rosario."

"Thank you." She quickly slipped the tubes in her pocket.

"Are you done?" Elle asked.

"Yes. Are you ready to go?"

"Yes."

"I'll walk you both out."

As they headed for the parking lot, Elle was on autopilot while Rory excitedly chirped away. "Elle?"

"Yes?"

"Where were you? I've been babbling away and you haven't heard a word I've said."

"I'm sorry, Rory. My mind was someplace else. You were saying?"

"I was saying that I'm excited to work with Rosario. I'm sure I can get a few other doctors to sign on to work pro bono with the clinic."

"I was hoping you'd say that, Rory." Rosario grinned as she walked up behind them.

"It's hard to look at all those little faces and walk away."

"It's especially hard when the only thing keeping them from living a normal life is money," Elle added.

"You're right about that, Elle," Rory agreed.

"Ooh, it's a little cold out here." Rosario shivered.

"You should get back inside. I'll call you and we'll go over some details."

Rory and Rosario hugged.

"Thanks again, Elle," Rosario said as she hugged her.

"You're welcome."

"Don't worry, I'll put a rush on the lab work," she whispered in Elle's ear.

"Thanks."

Rosario went back inside as Rory and Elle walked towards the car. Elle's mind wandered again.

"Are you sure you're okay, Elle?"

"I'm fine."

"If you say so."

"I do." She stopped by the car and Ed opened the door. "Need a lift?"

"That's okay, I have a ride."

"Oh, all right. Thanks for coming. I'm so glad you're going to work with the clinic."

"I'm glad you thought of me. It will be nice to know all those tummy tucks, boob jobs and Botox injections are going to help pay for people who really need my help."

"Just don't tell them. I know some of your clients. I'm pretty sure they'll try to get it written off as a charitable donation."

Rory laughed. "I'll see you later."

They hugged and Elle got in the car. "See ya." She waved.

As the car pulled away a black sedan pulled up with an attractive black woman behind the wheel. Rory got in. He and the driver embraced passionately before pulling off.

Meanwhile Elle called and made the earliest appointment she could get with Dr. Aranow. Afterwards she stared out the car window with her hand on her stomach.

"Mrs. Brennan?"

"Sorry, Ed. Yes?"

"Would you like me to take you back to your office or home?"

"I'd like to go home, please."

"Home it is."

Elle stared out the window as if she would find answers to her questions in the clouds. *When am I going to tell Doug? Heck, how am I going to tell him?* She sighed. *I don't even want to think of the conversation I'll have to have with Kevin and Kyle. If they're grossed out over kissing, the thought that their mom and dad actually had sex to make a baby might tip them over.* Her thoughts continued to race until she snapped out of it. *Wait a minute. I have to slow this down. I'm getting ahead of myself. I should wait until I've seen the doctor and I know where I stand. After all I'm not twenty-seven anymore, and pregnancy at this age is a lot different.* She took a deep breath. *That's it, I will wait until it's official . . . and then I'll freak out.*

After making his announcement at the Work Center, Doug took a few questions and posed for a few photos before heading to a waiting car.

He looked at his watch. *It's after three o'clock. Elle should be home by now.* As he walked out he was surprised to see Ki waiting by the car. "Fancy seeing you here." He smiled. "I thought you had a staff meeting."

"I canceled it."

Doug was suddenly filled with a sense of dread. "What's going on?"

"I'll tell you in the car."

Doug got in followed by Ki.

"There's something you should see in today's late edition of *The Post.*" He handed Doug the paper, which was opened to a page with the pictures of Elle with Rory. The caption read *Mayor's Wife Cited in Brennan divorce.*

The article went on to read:

Angela Brennan, wife of Dr. Rory Brennan, filed for divorce today. In addition to citing extramarital affairs she also cites her husband's relationship with Mirielle Abbott Brennan as a contributing factor to the breakdown of the marriage. Her lawyer Jasper Lyons told The Post *Rory's relationship with his sister-in-law had been a bone of contention within the marriage, saying that Mrs. Brennan felt emotionally abandoned by her husband.*

In the divorce papers, Angela asked for financial support to maintain her lifestyle, including sole ownership of their Fifth Avenue townhouse and equitable assets. The couple married in 2000.

Doug angrily tossed the paper on the car floor. "Damn!"

"I agree."

Doug rubbed his forehead.

"I know you said Rory and Angela were having trouble, but I had no idea it was this bad. Why didn't you tell me they were getting divorced?"

"I didn't know anything about it. Rory hasn't said a word to me."

"Hell, it's possible he didn't know either. The whole thing smacks of a tactical matrimonial move."

"Of course it's tactical. She hired Jasper Lyons," Doug said matter-of-factly.

A dairy farmer's son from the Midwest, most people said Jasper put the 'con' in Wisconsin. Clean-cut, tall, red haired and as white as the milk from one of his father's dairy cows, Jasper looked like Richie Cunningham from *Happy Days*. However, that's where the similarities ended. Unlike good guy Richie, he knew his way around a courtroom. Jasper's special talent was his ability to court the media to get his client what he or she wanted, and sometimes more.

"You know the New York press and gossip rags are going to be all over this."

"You think?" Doug said sarcastically.

CHAPTER 8

Later that afternoon Elle's powers of concentration for work were nowhere to be found, so she did the only thing she could do; she took a nap.

"Mom?"

She answered with her eyes closed. "Yes, Kevin?"

"How did you know it was me, Mom? You didn't even open your eyes."

She opened her eyes and sat up. "I've told you this a thousand times. I'm your mother. When no one else could figure out who was who, I could tell you and Kyle apart, no problem."

"You could tell us apart when we were babies?"

"Sure. You might be identical twins, but you've always had your own distinct personalities."

"Wow, that's kind of wild, Mom."

"I know." Elle rubbed her eyes.

"Are you okay, Mom?"

"I was a little tired so I took a nap. That's all." She paused. "So, how was school today?"

"It was good." He produced a piece of paper. "I'm thinking of running for president of the student council since Stephanie Hawkins moved away."

Oh Lord, he's been bitten. It really is genetic. Elle looked at the paper. "Great. What do you have to do next?"

"I just have to put my name in and get a campaign going. I'm going to talk to Dad about it."

"He's the person who would know."

Kyle walked in. "Hi, Mom."

"Hey, Kyle, how was your day at school?"

"Good, Mom. I need you to check my answer for math homework."

"Sure. Hit me."

"If functions f and g have domains Df and Dg respectively, then the domain of f / g is given by the intersection of Df and Dg without the zeros of function g. Am I correct?"

"Yes. You know why, don't you?"

"Sort of," Kyle mumbled.

"Division by zero is not allowed in mathematics. Don't forget that."

"I won't, Mom. I have another question."

"Is it about math?"

"No. I just wanted to know why a bunch of reporters is outside?"

"What?"

"You didn't know? There are a bunch of news vans and reporters outside. Kevin and I came in the back way."

Elle immediately got up and went over to the window. *This can't be good.* Then she noticed Doug's car pull up. *Doug's home? Now I know this isn't good.* "I guess we can ask your dad, he's home."

"Dad's home?" Kevin echoed.

"I'm sure he'll be up in a minute." Elle went back and sat on the bed.

Doug looked out the window and the reporters pressed up against the car. "Would you look at this circus? It's crazy."

"I didn't think they'd get here so quickly," Ki said.

"You're kidding me, right? This is New York City. Politics and gossip are blood sports here. The media gather like piranha looking for the slightest bit of flesh to feed on."

"It's going to be a long night," Doug said, disgusted.

"What time is Wendy getting here?"

"She said she'd be here around six, but she's going to try to get here sooner."

"Okay. I'm ready to get out, guys."

"Yes, sir," Theo answered as he and William got out and went around to his door. The minute they opened it, Doug was hit with flashbulbs and a barrage of questions coming at lightning speed.

"What's your wife's relationship with Rory?"

"Any comment on your wife being cited in your brother's divorce?"

Doug smiled and calmly walked through the crowd flanked by Theo and William.

"The mayor isn't making any statement. Thank you," Ki said as they went up the stairs. Frieda opened the door to let them slip in.

"Thank you, Frieda," Doug said, slightly out of breath.

"You're welcome, sir." She took his and Ki's coats.

"Is Elle down here or upstairs?"

"She and the children are upstairs, sir."

"Thanks." He turned to Ki. "I'm going upstairs."

"I'll be in the living room. I have to call Leslie and let her know I'm going to be late."

Doug went upstairs and entered the bedroom.

"Dad," both boys chorused.

"Hey, guys. How are my boys?" He hugged them.

"Good, Dad." Kyle grinned.

"I'm good, Dad. I think I'm going to run for president of the student council," Kevin said excitedly.

"Oh, that's great. We have to talk about that, but first I need to talk to your mom."

"Okay."

"Is your homework done?" Elle asked.

"Almost," Kevin answered sheepishly.

"You know almost doesn't count. Finish your homework. That goes for both of you," Elle said sternly.

"Yes, Mom," they said in unison.

"I'll be downstairs in a little while and you can tell me all about the student council. Okay?"

"Okay, Dad."

Kyle and Kevin left the room.

"Do I want to know?" Elle asked tentatively.

"Elle . . ."

"Please don't spin it for me, Doug. I'm your wife and I want the straight skinny."

Doug knew the best way to explain it was to let her see it for herself. He handed her the paper. "Here, you can read it," he said.

Elle's eyes widened. "What the hell?" She read the rest of the story. "This is total bull. Where did they get these pictures? I can't believe this!"

Doug sat down and put his arm around her. "I know."

"You know this is ridiculous." She pointed to the photos. "This was when Rory and I had lunch before Thanksgiving, and this was taken the morning Sheri was here. You can even see her van in the photo." She pointed it out.

Doug took a closer look. "That is her van."

"I should have known Angela was up to something after that show she put on the other day. She's playing the part of the wronged woman." Elle reached for the phone. "I'm going to give her a piece of my mind."

Doug stopped her. "Elle, you can't do that."

"Why?"

"You'd be playing right into her and her lawyer's hands."

"Are you telling me I have to sit here and take these lies she's heaving my way?"

"Yes and no. All I'm saying is that I still have to talk to Rory, and then we can assess the situation and make our move."

"What do you mean assess the situation? Make our move? The divorce is between Rory and Angela, period. We don't enter into the equation. I think we should make that clear to the media. Doug, we have children, and they have to go to school every day. This stuff affects them just as much as it does us."

"I know, and we're going to handle it as quickly as possible."

"Handle it? This isn't something you handle. If I take a baked potato out of the oven and toss it your way, that's something you have to handle. When your sister-in-law accuses your wife of having something to do with their divorce, this is something to be addressed head-on."

"I know, but this is a very delicate situation."

"Why? Because of the appointment? Are you saying that's a deciding factor?"

"Of course not." Doug was a little offended. "The important thing is to make sure this doesn't get any bigger than it should."

"Doug . . ." Elle wasn't convinced.

"Do you trust me?"

"Of course I trust you," she conceded.

"Then let me handle this. I'll talk to the kids and explain what's going on."

"Fine." She folded her arms. "Then once you're done telling them, you can explain it to me again."

Doug kissed her forehead. "Baby, it will be all right. I promise." He kissed her and then stood up. "Why don't you lie down? You look a little tired. Are you coming down with something?"

"I have the sniffles," she lied. *Maybe I should just tell him that I'm not getting a cold I'm pregnant. Then we can get this whole thing nipped in the bud now and the press won't have anything to feed off of.*

"Doug?"

"Yes?" His cell phone rang. He checked the number. "Hold that thought. It's Rory." He answered it on speaker phone. "Hey, Rory. Are you on your way over now?"

"Yes."

"What's your ETA?"

What's his ETA? I don't think Eisenhower said that when he was planning D-Day, Elle thought.

"I'll be there in five minutes or so," Rory answered.

"Great. I'll see you then." He hung up. "Sorry, sweetheart, what were you going to say?"

"Can you ask Frieda to put the clover honey in the tea, please?"

"Sure. I'll send her right up. You just rest."

"Thank you." Elle stretched out on the bed.

"No problem, baby." He left the room.

Elle rubbed her stomach. *This morning I discovered that I'm pregnant and by evening time I'm a home-wrecking adulteress. This has been some day. I really hope this thing blows over soon. Hope? I know hope floats but when it comes to scandals, hope sinks faster than a boulder. Not to mention the fact this is a social registry divorce, which means that like old soldiers they never die, they just fade away. Please let it fade before I start showing.*

Doug sat down at the table while Kevin and Kyle did their homework. "What are you working on?"

"I have math homework," Kyle answered.

"I have a short essay on why the battle of Trenton was a key turning point during the American Revolution," Kevin said.

"I would ask if you need any help, but you're probably better off asking your mom."

The boys laughed.

"I know you're probably wondering why the media is outside of the house."

"Yeah, they're all over the place," Kyle said.

Doug sighed.

"Dad, we're not babies. Just tell us."

"You're right, Kevin. You aren't babies anymore." He paused. "Your Uncle Rory and Aunt Angela are getting divorced."

"I don't want to sound funny, Dad, but that's not news. They didn't look happy together," Kyle said matter-of-factly.

"Wait, Kyle, I think there's more to it," Kevin said.

"There is more to it. Your Aunt Angela's lawyer went to the newspapers and said that your mother had something to do with the divorce." He put the paper down on the table.

The kids looked at the story.

"This is crap, Dad," Kevin said angrily.

"Are you going to stop her, Dad? She can't do this to Mom," Kyle argued.

"I'm working on it. I have some people coming here tonight and we're going to figure out what to do."

"What about Uncle Rory? What's he doing about this?"

"I'm going to make sure this goes away," Rory replied.

Doug was startled. "When did you get here?"

Rory walked in. "A few minutes ago. I came in the back way." He turned to his nephews. "I'm really sorry about all of this."

"We know it isn't your fault, Uncle Rory," Kyle said.

"That's right," Doug interjected.

"Thanks, guys."

Frieda walked up with a cup of tea in her hand. "May I take your coat?"

"Thank you, Frieda." He handed it to her.

Doug stood up. "Can I speak to you in the den?"

"Sure. I'll see you two in a little while," Rory said to the boys.

"Finish your homework. It smells like dinner is almost ready," Doug said.

"Okay, Dad," they said and turned back to the work.

Doug closed the door behind them once they were in the den.

Rory sat down on the sofa. "I don't know why I didn't see this coming."

"Are you telling me that you didn't know she was going to file for divorce?"

"That's right. I found out when I went home and tried to get into my house."

"What do you mean? You tried to get in?"

"The locks were changed," Rory said bitterly.

"She can't do that, and her lawyer knows it. We'll have the police escort you home. You have rights as a co-owner."

"That's just what I need, a police escort in front of a sea of cameras."

"Sorry, but it has to be done," Doug said.

Rory seemed resigned. "How's Elle?"

"She's upstairs resting."

"Is she okay?"

"It's nothing for you to worry about," Doug said coldly.

"What is that supposed to mean?"

"Nothing. She's coming down with a cold, that's all."

"Oh." He rubbed his head. "Of all the rotten things Angela's done, this one takes the cake. Has Elle seen the paper?"

"I showed it to her."

"She doesn't deserve this. She has had absolutely nothing to do with this."

"I know." Doug sat down. "I contacted Wendy Kulick for you."

"You did? You didn't think I could hire my own divorce attorney?"

"Angela hired Jasper Lyons. You need a big gun, and Wendy fits the bill." Doug's business-as-usual demeanor unsettled his brother.

"Why do I feel like this is more of a political strategy session than my brother trying to help me through this divorce?"

"You know, Rory, I didn't ask for any of this. I'd rather this be a private matter between you and Angela, but she brought Elle into it. And now that it's an open secret that I'm in the running for the senate seat appointment, we have to handle it quickly, which is why we need Wendy."

"Is this about helping me and clearing your wife's name? Or is it just another obstacle on your path to power?"

"I resent the implication that I'd put my political ambitions before the people I love." Doug said angrily.

"Well, it sort of seems that way. You haven't asked me one question about how my marriage got to this point."

Before Doug could answer Ki popped in. "Wendy's here."

"Thanks, Ki." Doug got up. "We'll talk about this later," he said to his brother.

Elle sat on the bed sipping tea. She couldn't watch the news without seeing the sensationalized story running at the bottom of the screen. *This is pathetic.* She groaned.

The phone rang.

"Hello?"

"Elle, are you okay?"

"I'm fine, Melissa. I take it you've seen the news."

"It's all over the place. Are you sure you're okay?"

"I'm as well as any accused home-wrecking sister-in-law can be expected to be."

"You know Angela is full of crap."

"I couldn't have said it better myself."

"What are you going to do?"

"Doug wants to handle it. My first inclination was to call her and curse her out, but Doug stopped me."

"What was your second inclination?"

"To go over there and punch her lights out."

"I would have paid money to see you do either one." Elle laughed.

"By the way, what does *handling it* mean?"

"Calling in a bunch of lawyers and strategists to come up with a game plan." Elle sighed. "It's probably just as well. I have enough to deal with."

"What do you mean? Is there something going on at work?"

Elle knew she had to tell someone her secret, and considering the amount of press around her, she needed someone to take her to see Dr. Aranow. "No. All is quiet on that front."

"Then what is it?"

"I'm pregnant."

"Oh, my God!" Melissa sounded overjoyed. "Elle, that's wonderful," she said. Elle could almost hear the smile on her best friend's lips.

"Thanks."

"You sly thing, you didn't tell me you and Doug were trying to have another baby," Melissa said.

"That's because we weren't trying. And before you ask, yes I experienced a little lightheadedness a few times over the last month but it always passed when I ate."

"I assume you haven't had your period. Usually that's a tell-tale sign."

"I know, but I'm forty-one. I thought I was going through early menopause. I have had my period for over thirty years. The way I figured it, my uterus had quit active duty."

"Well it showed you, didn't it?" Melissa chuckled.

"That's an understatement. I took a pregnancy test at the clinic today and voila, I find out I'm expecting with all this ménage-a-trois stuff going on in the media. How's that for irony?"

"Wait a minute. Did you say the clinic?"

"Yes. I was there for a meeting."

"Good thing you were there." She paused. "Speaking of Doug, have you told him?"

"Not yet. Rosario drew blood to confirm and she's sending the results to Dr. Aranow. I have an appointment with him on Thursday, which is why I'm so happy you called. Would you mind taking me? It's going to be a covert operation."

"Of course I wouldn't mind, but what's the big deal about going to the doctor?"

"Are you kidding me? I'm going to the obstetrician in the middle of this Upper East Side *East of Eden* scenario. What do you suppose the media will report?"

"Oh, you're right," she groaned.

"My thoughts exactly," Elle said.

"What time is your appointment?"

"Nine-thirty. Can you swing it?"

"It's not a problem. I'll go in late."

"Thanks, Melissa, you're a real lifesaver."

"Don't mention it. You should really get some rest. Try not to get too stressed out over this garbage."

"I'll try. I don't know how successful I'll be."

"Hopefully Doug will get a handle on this and the whole thing will blow over."

"From your lips to God's ears."

CHAPTER 9

If Jasper Lyons represented the 'aw shucks' school of law, Wendy Kulick was the polar opposite. Born in Brooklyn, Wendy was a petite brunette dynamo. A no-nonsense attorney, she wielded her strong hand in a velvet glove. She was also just as adept at handling the press as Jasper.

Wendy stood up as Doug and Rory walked into the living room. "Doug."

He hugged her. "Wendy, how are you?"

"I'm fine, thanks." She looked at Rory. "Hey, little brother, how are you?"

"I was okay," Rory said and shrugged.

"Don't worry. I'm here to get you back to being more than just okay."

"Why don't we sit down?" Doug motioned towards the sofa.

Before he could sit down Ki interjected. "Doug, why don't we give them some attorney/client time?"

"What?" Doug seemed taken off-balance.

"Wendy needs to talk to Rory about the divorce, alone."

"Thanks, Ki." Wendy smiled.

"It's no problem. Right, Doug?"

"Right," he reluctantly agreed.

Ki and an agitated Doug stepped out into the hallway. "Why did you do that? Don't we need to know what's happening?"

"No, *we* don't. They're talking about Rory's divorce, and that has nothing to do with us. Relax. We'll figure it out."

"Doug?" Elle was coming downstairs.

He looked up. "Sweetheart, I thought you were resting."

"I was. I came down to see what the kids were doing."

He kissed her on the cheek. "I think they're in the kitchen having dinner."

"Hi, Elle. How are you feeling?" Ki asked.

"Overall I'm okay for a home-wrecker," she said facetiously.

"Don't say that. You're no home-wrecker." Ki shook his head.

"Thanks." She paused to listen. "Is someone here?"

"Wendy's in the living room."

"Wendy's here?"

"Yes. She's meeting with Rory," Doug said.

"When did Rory get here? Let me rephrase that. How did he get past all the media?"

"He came in the back way," Doug answered.

"That was smart." She sighed. "Doug, did Kevin talk to you?"

"About what?"

"He had something he really wanted to share with you. He didn't mention anything?"

"No. Why don't you tell me?"

"I'd rather he tell you. Go in the kitchen and ask him."

"I will."

Just as Doug was about to go, Wendy walked out. "Elle, it's good to see you."

"Hello, Wendy. It's nice to see you, too."

"If you don't mind, I need to steal your husband for a few minutes."

"Sure. Doug, don't forget to ask Kevin."

"I won't."

Elle continued to the kitchen while they went back into the living room and sat down.

"All right, Rory and I have talked things over and we have a plan."

"Good," Doug said as he sat and crossed his legs.

"We're going to get him back into the house tonight. I've already called the police to meet us there, so that's taken care of. As for the situation with Elle, I've advised him to stay away from her until this blows over. Even though we know the whole accusation is bogus, I think it's the best course of action."

"You agreed, Rory?" Doug asked.

"Yes."

"Doug, I know this is something both you and Elle didn't ask to be involved in, but if I were you I wouldn't answer any questions. This is Rory's divorce battle, not yours."

"Right."

"We can issue a statement saying that both you and Elle are saddened by the breakup of the marriage but that it's a private matter, or something like that," Ki offered.

"That sounds good." Wendy looked at her watch. "We'd better get going. The police are going to be there soon." She got up.

Doug, Ki and Rory stood up, too, and Rory helped Wendy put her coat on. "Thank you, Rory," she said.

"You're welcome."

"I'm going to get home, too. I'll see you tomorrow morning. I'll have a statement ready by then," Ki said to Doug.

"Thanks, Ki." He patted him on the back.

"I'll talk to you soon, big brother."

"Hang tough," Doug said and hugged Rory.

"Will you say goodnight to Elle and the boys for me?"

"Sure."

They walked to the foyer. Rory got his coat from the closet and so did Ki.

"Are you ready to walk the plank?" Wendy asked Rory.

"As ready as I'll ever be."

"Remember, don't say anything. I'll do the talking."

"Okay."

"I don't have to say anything to you, Ki. I'm sure you know the drill."

"Intimately," Ki confirmed.

Doug stood out of camera range to open the door. Flashbulbs popped furiously as Doug closed the door. *I hope they don't go blind.* He headed for the kitchen. Elle and the boys were still sitting at the table.

She looked up. "All done?"

"Yes." He kissed her and sat down.

"Did Uncle Rory leave?" Kyle asked.

"Yes. Don't worry, he's going to be all right."

"Okay, Dad," Kyle said.

"Kevin, isn't there something you wanted to tell your dad?" Elle said.

"Yes. Tell me," Doug said to his son.

Kevin produced a piece of paper from his pocket. "I want to run for president of the student council. A freshman has never run before, but I think I have a chance."

Elle watched as Doug's chest filled with pride. "I think you'd make a great student council president. You have my vote."

"You can't vote, Dad."

"I know. But if I could I'd definitely vote for you."

"Thanks."

"Have you thought about your campaign platform?"

"Yes. I'm for personal responsibility and the right to make our own choices."

"You're talking about the vending machines, right?" Elle asked.

"Yes. I think we're old enough to decide whether or not we want a soda or juice with our lunch. The only thing getting rid of the machines succeeded in doing was increasing the number of kids who cut class to go out and get what they want. I think they should put them back and let us make up our own minds."

"It sounds like you really thought this out." Doug was impressed.

"I have."

"Terrific. What about you, Kyle? Are you going to run for anything?"

"No."

"You can be your brother's campaign manager. You can help him design flyers and buttons . . ."

"Don't get carried away, Doug, the school has placed limits on that stuff. Remember most of these kids come from money and flyers could easily become billboards," Elle added.

"That's true." He chuckled.

"I would love for you to help me, Dad."

Elle got up. "I'm going to let you talk strategy and opponents."

"Are you feeling okay, honey?"

"I'm still a little tired. I'm going to lie down."

"I'll be up in a little while."

"Okay."

As Elle walked out she listened to Doug talk excitedly with the boys. *Another Brennan enters the political arena, even if it's just school politics,* she thought as she went up the stairs.

Once Elle was upstairs she slipped into a hot bath. *Doug is tickled pink to have a son follow in his footsteps. I know he'd like to have both of them involved. But Kyle is more like Rory; he has no problem ceding the spotlight to his big brother.* She sighed. *Rory. I hope he's going to be okay. At least he has Wendy in his corner. Hopefully this will go away sooner rather than later. God knows I need it to go away sooner.*

When Doug got to the bedroom he noticed Elle had dozed off while reading. He quietly went over and gently pried the book from her hands.

"Oh," she said and yawned. "What time is it?"

"It's a little after eleven." He put the book on the table.

"Are the boys in bed?"

"Yes." He smiled.

"Did you work on Kevin's campaign?"

"Yes. He's really got a good head for politics."

"Gee, I wonder where he gets that from." She grinned.

"I guess he takes after his old man. And Kyle is going to be his campaign manager and pollster."

"I know he especially loves the idea of crunching numbers."

"I wonder who he gets that from."

Elle laughed.

"Rory was my campaign manager when I ran in high school."

"I know. And now he's going through a rough time with Angela," she said.

"Don't worry about that stuff, baby. It's just a bunch of posturing by her lawyer. Wendy will have everything under control soon. I'm sure of it."

"I hope so." Elle ran her fingers through his thick hair.

He gently kissed her hand. "I love you." He climbed in bed and snuggled with her.

With Doug's arms around her, Elle felt safe and cherished and drifted off to sleep.

CHAPTER 10

Doug was looking forward to a relatively light day at City Hall. Instead of using the Blue Room to make dire pronouncements about the city's budget he was traveling to the Harlem Armory to make an announcement with Tony Evans, the Deputy Mayor of Health and Human Services, about a gain in the life expectancy for New Yorkers. Relishing the chance to slow his morning routine down, Doug took a leisurely hot shower.

Elle poked her head in. "Doug?"

"Yes, baby?"

"Your sons are eager for you to see the campaign flyer they worked on this morning."

"Already?"

"You got them fired up."

"Okay. Honey, can you hand me a towel please?"

"Sure." She walked in to the bathroom and grabbed one. "Here you go."

"Thanks." He pulled the towel and Elle into the shower.

"Hey!" Both Elle and the towel became drenched.

"Aww, honey, we have to get you out of those wet things. It's not good for you."

"Is that right?" she said skeptically.

"Yes." He pulled her nightgown off and tossed it on the floor.

"You know that was one of my favorite nightgowns."

"I'll buy you another one." He pulled her closer. "Besides, I'm kind of partial to your birthday suit."

"Are you?"

"Yes."

They kissed passionately as the hot water streamed down their bodies. Elle's body quivered as Doug kissed her shoulders then softly kissed and caressed her breasts. She then let the water lead her lips down his chest to his waist, hips and just beyond.

Doug moaned. The warmth of the water and her lips drove him wild as she lingered.

"Baby," he said breathlessly.

She continued to explore and tease him until his body was about to explode. He had to have her right there and then. When he lifted her up against the wall, Elle could barely catch her breath as their bodies came together. They held onto to one another tightly as they rode wave after wave of ecstasy.

A little while later Doug joined Kevin and Kyle in the kitchen.

"Good morning, boys."

"Good morning, Dad."

Doug got a cup of coffee. "Your mom said you worked on a flyer this morning."

"Here it is." Kevin handed it to him.

Doug studied it. "It looks good. I like it."

"You aren't just saying that because you're our dad, are you?"

"No, Kevin. I really think it's good."

Kevin and Kyle's faces lit up.

Elle walked in with her head wrapped in a towel.

"You're not dressed yet, Mom?" Kyle asked.

"I've got time. I'm working from home today."

"Dad liked our flyer," Kevin said, beaming.

"I told you it was good." She smiled. *He's still home, I should tell him now.* "Doug?"

"Yes, babe?"

"Can I talk to you for a minute?"

"Sure."

Just then Theo walked in. "Good morning, Mr. and Mrs. Brennan."

"Good morning, Theo. How are you?"

"I'm good, Mrs. Brennan. The bus is here, guys."

Kevin and Kyle jumped to their feet and put their coats, scarves and hats on.

"Do you have everything?"

"Yes, Mom," Kevin groaned.

She picked up a pair of gloves. "Who do these belong to?"

"Mine," Kevin said sheepishly as he took them. "Thanks, Mom." He kissed her on the cheek.

"I'll see you later. Have a good day."

"See ya later, Mom." Kyle kissed her as well.

"You have a good day, too. Let me know about the math homework."

"I will."

"Check you later, Dad. I'm going to submit the flyer."

"Let me know how it goes, Kevin," Doug said.

"I will. I'm out." Kevin made the 'peace out' gesture.

"See ya later, Dad."

They ran out of the kitchen.

Doug looked confused. "What was that Kevin did with the victory sign on his chest?"

Elle chuckled. "That means 'peace out'."

"Oh, I must be getting old or something."

"You're still young, baby." She kissed him lightly on the lips.

"Before I forget, you wanted to talk to me."

"Yes." She took a deep breath. "I have some news . . ."

Suddenly his cell phone rang. It was Ki's distinct ringtone. "Sorry, honey. I have to take this."

"That's okay."

"Hold that thought." He answered the phone. "Yes, Ki." He paused. "You need me to come in now? The announcement at the armory isn't until later. Is there something going on?" He paused. "Okay. I'm leaving now." He shut his phone.

"You have to go."

"I'm sorry. He's got some poll numbers we need to go over." He paused. "But what did you want to tell me?"

"That's okay. It will keep until later."

"Thanks, babe." He kissed her. "We'll pick this up later." He quickly walked out the kitchen.

Elle sat down at the table. Frieda came in. "Would you like anything for breakfast, Mrs. Brennan?"

She rubbed her stomach. "Wheat toast and tea is fine with me."

"No problem."

It figures that Ki would call him about work. But I can't blame him. I had more than enough time to tell him this morning. Elle smiled to herself. *Then again I was distracted by the same thing that got me pregnant in the first place.*

To avoid the media blitz outside the house, Doug went through the back. However when he arrived at City Hall he was met with even more reporters and news vans.

He looked out the window. "Did every outlet send two sets of reporters out? It must be a slow news day." He sighed as the car drove through the gates. As soon as he stepped out of the car, a few reporters called out.

"Mayor Brennan, how do you feel about your brother's love nest?" a reporter shouted.

"How do you think this latest revelation will affect your chance to be senator?" another shouted.

Don't tell me there's something new. What love nest? Doug thought as he smiled, waved and continued walking to the security booth.

"Good morning Mayor Brennan," the police officer said cheerfully.

"Good Morning, Chip." Doug smiled as he put his briefcase on the conveyor.

"Looks like you've got quite a following this morning."

Doug stepped through the metal detector. "Don't I know it." He picked his briefcase up. "You have a good day, Chip."

"You, too, Mayor Brennan," he said and smiled.

Doug knew NYPD would keep the reporters at bay while he made his way up the stairs and into the building, but eventually they'd be in City Hall's press room busily working on their laptops and waiting for another opportunity to ask their burning questions.

Ki was waiting for him when he walked into the lobby.

"If it's possible the press is even crazier today." Doug took a deep breath. "Before you say a word, there's been a new development, right?" They continued walking through the hallway.

"I'm afraid so." Ki handed Doug a copy of *The Post* just as they reached his outer office.

"Good morning, Mayor Brennan." Alice sounded somewhat subdued.

"Good morning, Alice." He opened the paper as he went inside. It was a photo of Rory with an African-American woman. The caption read: *Rory Brennan canoodling with woman at love nest. Estranged wife believes it's his sister-in-law, New York City's first lady, Elle Brennan.*

"Damn!" He dropped his briefcase and tossed the paper on the desk.

"It's been reported in every paper. There are also a bunch of negative articles about your possible senate appointment led by . . ."

"Don't tell me. My old friend Mort," he said sarcastically.

"Yes."

Doug sat at down. "Have we heard anything from Wendy yet?"

"I called her this morning. She says she'll get back to us after she speaks with Rory."

Doug looked at the photo and shook his head. "Just when I thought I could get a handle on the situation, this happens."

"You know it's going to come up during the press conference at the Armory."

"Was there any doubt?"

"I put the statement I prepared last night on your desk. I'm thinking that maybe I should revise it."

"Why?" He leafed through some papers until he found the statement. "Here it is." Doug read it. "This looks good to me. We'll go with this."

"Well, it seems a little too clinical. I think I should flesh it out to give it a little more depth and make it more personal."

"What would you have me say? My sister-in-law is a bitch who is just out to get more money out of the divorce and she doesn't care if she drags me through the mud to get it?"

"No, of course I wouldn't. Even if it is the truth. And by the way she's not just dragging you through the mud; it's about Elle and your family."

"Don't you think I know that?" Doug was offended.

"Sorry," Ki said and backed off quickly.

"No. I'm sorry. I guess I'm a little sensitive."

"I understand."

"Thanks." He checked his watch. "I should give Elle a call before she gets her day started."

"Yeah, you don't want her to get sucker-punched with this."

"Yeah." Just as Doug reached for the phone there was a knock.

"Mayor Brennan?"

"Come in, Alice," Doug called.

Alice opened the door. "Sorry to bother you, sir, but the police commissioner is here."

"Oh, God, I almost forgot. Give me a minute and send him in please."

"Yes, sir."

He dialed the phone. "I have to make this quick." He looked at Ki.

"Good morning, Brennan residence," Frieda answered.

"Hello, Frieda. Is my wife still there?"

"I believe she is but she's in the bathroom. Should I get her for you?"

"No." He looked at his watch. "Will you ask her to call me as soon as she gets out, please?"

"Certainly, Mr. Brennan," she answered.

"Thanks." He hung up. "So what's the story with the polling data?"

"What?" Ki seemed confused.

"Don't you remember? You called me about the polls."

"Oh, that's right. To be honest it slipped my mind once I saw the paper."

"Okay. So how do the numbers look?" Doug asked without missing a beat.

"Sixty-four percent of the people polled think you're doing a good job as mayor."

"That's nice to hear. What about the senate question?"

"Nearly sixty percent think you're a qualified to be in the Senate."

"Not bad."

"Yeah." Ki headed for the door. "I'll have the commissioner come in, and I'll see you before the press conference."

"Thanks." Doug glanced at the newspaper again. *I know it's not Elle in the picture, but if she didn't spend so much time with Rory this wouldn't be an issue. I know I'm wrong to think that, but God help me, I do.*

The commissioner entered. "Good morning, Doug." He put his hand out.

"Hey, Ray, it's good to see you. Have a seat." Doug at least sounded like he didn't have a care in the world.

Elle finally finished blow-drying her hair. As she parted it, she looked at her work in the mirror. *You would think that after twenty years Doug would realize that I'm a black woman. I don't have wash-and-go hair. It's a production just to make it look easy.* She ran a brush through her hair. While Elle wasn't much for clothes she did know how to work a curling iron. Her philosophy for her shoulder-length hair was simple: wash, blow and curl. However she didn't take any chances for special occasions and always called in a professional. *All I have to do is give it a little bump and I'm good to go.* She thought as she turned on the curling iron. Ten minutes later she emerged from the bathroom, coiffed and ready.

She sat down on the edge of the bed and reached for the phone. "Let me see what's happening at the office," she said aloud as she dialed.

"Good morning, Dr. Brennan's office. How can I help you?"

"Hi, Pam."

"Oh, thank God, Dr. Brennan, it's you."

Elle was a little taken aback. "My goodness, what's going on?"

"The phones haven't stopped ringing since I got in, and there are reporters hanging around outside."

"I wonder why? Most of these things have a one day shelf life before they move on to the next thing. I thought the story would be birdcage liner by now," Elle said.

"You haven't seen today's papers?"

"No. Why?"

"I hate to be the bearer of bad news, but they're running another story complete with photo in almost all the New York papers."

"What?" she lamented. "Thanks for the heads-up. I'll check in with you later." She hung up.

Elle retrieved her laptop and quickly booted up. Once she was online she went to *The Post's* website, where she saw the photo and story on the homepage. *What the hell?* She continued to read. *Angela thinks it's me in the picture? She's a real piece of work.* She studied the photo. *Who in the world is this woman?*

"Mrs. Brennan?" Frieda said as she knocked.

"Come in."

"Mr. Brennan called while you were in the bathroom. He'd like you to call him back."

"Okay. Thank you."

"No problem." She stepped out.

The phone rang.

Maybe that's Doug. She picked up. "Hello?"

"Elle?"

"Rory?"

"I wanted to come over to see how you were doing, but under the circumstances I've been advised to keep my distance for the time being. So how are you?"

"I've been better."

"So you've seen the latest pictures."

"At this point, Rory, who hasn't?"

"I'm sure you have questions for me."

"At least now I know why you've been so scarce for the last six months. Also it explains why you had the same clothes on when you stopped by the house the other morning with that hickey," she added.

"You knew it was a hickey?" Rory seemed surprised.

"Well, to be truthful, no. I really did think you cut yourself shaving. Sheri was the one who told me it was a hickey."

"I can only imagine what you must think of me," he said, embarrassed.

"I'm not going to pass judgment, Rory."

"You'd be the only one who isn't."

"Naturally, I don't condone having an affair, even if I don't like your wife. But you said yourself that your marriage has been in name only for a while. All you had to do was get a separation and then it wouldn't matter how many pictures Angela had. She'd be out of ammunition before she could load the gun."

"I know you're right. I really made a mess of things," he said with disgust.

Elle felt badly. "Don't beat yourself up about it. The milk is already on the floor. You can't get it back into the glass now. You just have to clean it up and move on."

"Like it says in one of your favorite U2 songs?"

"That's right. You can't afford to get stuck in the moment." She paused. "Now what did Wendy say about this latest picture fiasco?"

"She said Angela's lawyer isn't stupid. Angela said she *believed* it was you, which is different from saying it was you in the photo."

"Oh, great," she said sarcastically. "So now we're splitting hairs when it comes to my integrity. It figures she'd find a little loophole to escape through." Elle rubbed her stomach as it began to cramp. "I can't talk about this anymore. I suddenly don't feel so good."

As a teenager Elle developed a stomach condition which tended to flare up whenever she felt pressured or stressed. She managed to get it under control as an adult, but with everything going on around her it was the perfect recipe for a recurrence.

"I'm sorry. We can change the subject," Rory said.

"Is it good news?" She quietly let out a deep breath to try to control the pain. "I could use some."

"I managed to get two other doctors and a dentist to agree to work with Rosario. We're going to go over and meet with her next week to discuss logistics. Hopefully we'll be able to begin scheduling surgeries for early January."

"That's wonderful news."

"I thought you'd be pleased. Anyway, I've got to get to my office."

"How's that been going? I can't even go to my office because of the press. I have to work at home."

"Wendy hired a couple of security guys who look like former linebackers to help me through the media maze camped outside."

"You're back in the townhouse, right?"

"Yes. I'm thinking of hiring a painter to put a red line down the middle of it, so we can have our separate corners defined."

Her stomach cramps subsided enough for Elle to laugh.

"Ahh, she laughs. I've done my good deed for the day."

"Thanks, Rory. I guess we'll talk again whenever."

"Okay."

She hung up. *I'd better lay down for a few minutes until this completely passes.* Elle closed her eyes and curled up on the bed. *Okay, I'm pregnant, so I can't take anything, which means I'd better take deep breaths.* Ten minutes passed before she dialed Doug. She got his voicemail and waited for the tone. "Hi, baby, it's me. Frieda told me you called. I know you're busy. We can talk later. I love you."

Now I know why Doug called, Elle thought as she walked towards the window and peered out the curtains.

Look at all those people, just clamoring for a little tidbit. It's a shame that there are fewer reporters covering the wars in the Middle East. But the real shame is they're giving people want they want. More people want to read about inane stuff like this than real news.

Coat in hand, Ki knocked on the open door. "Was that Ray?"

"Yes," Doug answered as he put his coat on.

"I take it he had some much-needed good news."

"Crime is down in the city for the seventh straight year."

"That's great news."

"Too bad I can't lead with it at the press conference."

"Sorry, buddy."

"Is the deputy mayor at the armory?"

"I believe so." Ki put his coat on.

Doug looked at his watch. "I guess we'd better leave now if we're going to get there in time."

"Okay."

They walked into the outer office.

"Alice, we're heading over to the Harlem Armory."

"Yes, sir."

Flanked by security, Doug and Ki made their way through the building to the waiting car. Once they were in, security hopped in the front seats and they were off.

Doug looked out the car window.

Ki looked at his watch. "He's taking the FDR Drive. It shouldn't be too bad this time of day."

"Let's hope not."

A little more than twenty minutes later they arrived at the Harlem Armory, where Doug was quickly ushered inside to the auditorium. When he and Ki walked in there was an unprecedented number of press in attendance.

"You think they're expecting something?" he whispered to Ki.

"No. They're here about the four month increase in life expectancy for New Yorkers." He smirked.

Doug shook Health Commissioner Dr. Tony Evans's hand before going to the podium.

"Good afternoon. It's nice to see that so many of you turned out to hear the exciting news about the life expectancy increase for New Yorkers. I guess you don't mind adding four more months onto your retirement dates."

The gallery of press laughed.

Doug conducted the press conference as planned. Twenty minutes later reporters got less than they bargained for, but they did get an education on what has been done to improve life expectancy in New York.

After taking a few photos, Doug was about to leave.

"Mayor Brennan? Do you have a minute?" Kent Barlow, a reporter for *The Bronx Times,* called after him.

Doug stopped since Kent was always an affable guy. "Hello, Kent. How are you?"

"I'm not bad, sir. How are you?"

"I could complain, but who'd listen?"

"I just wondered if I could ask you about the Bronx Children's Clinic."

"Sure. What did you need to know?"

"Well your wife and brother were seen there with Dr. Campbell just after Thanksgiving and the buzz is the Brennans are going to give some kind of financial aid or something to the clinic. Is that true?"

"The Bronx Children's Clinic is essential to the community, and as there are a number of cuts coming down the pike, we're looking into ways to help fund the clinics privately to keep them running."

"That's good to hear, Mayor Brennan. Thanks."

"No problem, Kent." Doug walked away.

Ki caught up with him. "What did Kent want? I know he didn't ask you about Rory."

"No. He did tell me that Elle and Rory were at the Bronx Children's Clinic together this week."

"You didn't tell me they were going there."

"I only knew that Elle was going. This is the first that I'm hearing about Rory being there." Doug put his coat on.

"You're not thinking . . ."

"I'm not thinking anything. I'm wondering why she didn't tell me Rory was there."

"He is a doctor," Ki said.

"He's a plastic surgeon. He gives Botox injections and does butt lifts. What can a plastic surgeon do at a children's clinic?"

"It almost sounds like you believe the gossip papers."

"I wouldn't call *The Bronx Times* a gossip rag, and I'm not jumping to conclusions. I'm going to ask Elle."

"I think that's a great idea," Ki chimed in.

Why didn't she tell me? How come I had to find out from a reporter? He silently steamed.

After she'd worked through the morning, Elle flipped the television on. *What's on worth watching?* She surfed the channels until she stopped at Noggin. *What's this?* She hit the information button on the remote. *It's a preschool channel. Oh, it's so cute. It's* Blue's Clues. *I remember when Kevin and Kyle watched this show. I think I secretly enjoyed this show more than they did.*

Frieda knocked. "Mrs. Brennan?"

"Yes?"

"Your parents are here."

Elle sat up straight. "My parents? You mean my mother and father? Not my mother and her husband, right?"

"Yes."

Who died? Elle leaped up and raced past Frieda down the stairs. She tore into the living room. "Dad, Mom, who died?" Elle blurted out.

"No one died, honey," her father answered calmly.

"Why would you think someone died?" her mother asked.

She's kidding me, right. "It's not a holiday or the kids' birthday or another special occasion, and you're here together."

"So?" her mother asked.

"So I've spent the last twenty-eight years fine-tuning my divorce diplomacy skills. Are you telling me I didn't have to bother?"

Her parents looked at one another.

"We declared detente when we saw this." Her father showed her *The Post*.

"Oh, that," she sighed.

"Yes, that. What is this nonsense they're reporting in all the papers?" her mother asked vehemently.

"Angela's divorce tactics."

"It's total garbage." Her father threw the paper on the floor. "What are you doing about it?"

"I'm not doing anything. I have to let the lawyers handle it."

"So you're supposed to sit here and wait while she slings mud?"

"That seems to be the plan for the moment, Dad."

"That's ridiculous. Someone needs to take this little hussy out to the shed," her mother snapped.

"I'd love to, Mom, but I can't risk it."

"Who said you had to risk anything? I still remember how to use a switch."

Elle laughed.

"She's serious."

"I know."

"What does Doug say about all of this?"

"He got a top-notch lawyer for Rory, and according to him she's going to work through all of this."

"If this is her idea of working on it, she needs to visit the shed, too."

"Maybe so, Mom, but technically she works for Rory, not us."

"Well, I certainly hope you've learned your lesson about him."

"What?"

"Lynette, she hasn't done anything wrong."

"I didn't say she did. But she is a married woman."

"I'm still in the room, Mom. You can talk to me," Elle said.

"All I'm saying is . . ."

"I shouldn't have gone out to lunch with Rory."

"Mirielle, you're very smart, but when it comes to this stuff you just don't see the whole picture."

"Rory is my brother-in-law. There is nothing going on between us. We went to lunch to talk about him doing some pro bono work to assist Dr. Campbell with all the cleft palate cases she has at the clinic."

"So you had lunch together to talk about the clinic?" her mother asked, surprised.

"Yes." Elle sounded a bit exasperated. "There are a lot of cutbacks in the city's budget. So I thought that if I could get Rory and some of his colleagues to perform these surgeries pro bono, it would really help this clinic, and then maybe we could extend it to other clinics around the city. Other than that day, Rory and I hadn't had lunch together in while."

"Did you tell Doug about this?"

"No, Dad. I wanted to see if I could get if off the ground myself." She sighed. "Clare Booth Luce was right when she said 'no good deed goes unpunished.' "

Her father got up and sat next to her. "I'm sure everything will work out."

Elle didn't say anything, but she hoped her father was right.

CHAPTER 11

It was three o'clock and Doug finally returned to his office after spending the better part of the day reviewing the latest crime stats. Needless to say he was still bothered by Ken's comment. *Why hadn't Elle mentioned meeting Rory to me?* His mind wandered as he sat tapping a hand on his desk.

"Excuse me, Mayor Brennan?" Alice buzzed on the intercom.

"Yes, Alice?"

"Governor Pearson is on line one for you."

"Thank you."

I wonder what's up. He picked up the phone. "Hello, Governor. How are you?"

"I'm good, how are you?"

"I can't complain. I mean, I could complain, but who would listen?" He laughed.

"I hear you."

"So what can I do for you?"

"If you have a wand available you can turn Wall Street around."

"Believe me, I wish I could. This downturn is killing us," Doug said.

"I know it's tough in the city, and we're looking at a state deficit of at least fifteen billion dollars."

"Ouch." Doug winced.

"Tell me about it." He paused. "Well, I actually didn't call to bellyache about the deficit, although I know you empathize. I wanted to talk to you about the senate appointment."

"Okay."

"You know you're the frontrunner in my mind but officially there are no frontrunners."

"I know. We talked about that." *Here comes the other shoe.*

"The field is opening up in terms of the number of people who want to be considered."

"You're talking about the Attorney General."

"Yes, but let me say again that no decisions have been made."

"I understand."

"I thought you would."

"Thanks for the call, Governor."

"Take care, Doug."

Doug rubbed his eyes. He'd been in politics long enough to know that he had competition, real competition, for the Senate seat. *Things are beginning to get tight.* His thought was interrupted by a knock on the door.

"Yes?" he called.

"It's me, Ki."

"Come in."

Ki entered. He knew something was awry the minute he looked at Doug. "Okay, what's wrong?"

"I just got off the phone with Jim."

"Oh, really," he said with a raised brow. "What did the governor want?"

"In essence he wanted to let me know that I have real competition. I thought you said sixty percent thought I was qualified for the appointment."

"That was a different poll. He's talking about the latest public policy polling. I have the report here." He put it on the desk. "The survey showed that you and Carver polled at 25 percent respectively. "

Doug glanced at it. "Do you think Andy's considering it?"

The Carver family was practically an institution in New York State politics. His father, Anthony Carver, served as governor and was still is active in the Democratic Party. During his father's time as governor he served as an aide and he later was appointed to the Department of Housing and Urban Development for the last Democrat in the White House. He took a brief time out before running for and being elected as the state's Attorney General. Like Doug, Carver had a good pedigree.

"Not after the dog fight he went through to get elected Attorney General."

"It was pretty nasty, wasn't it?" Doug recalled.

"That campaign was a real mudslinging contest. Even though I will admit, Andy had a little less mud on him. Otherwise he would have had a hell of a time climbing the stairs to make his acceptance speech that night."

"Oh, is that why Jane had a hard time making her concession speech? She was weighed down with mud?"

Doug and Ki laughed.

"Listen Doug, I don't think you have anything to worry about. I'm sure you're still the frontrunner by far. The governor has to cover all the bases."

"You're probably right." On the outside he seemed calm, but Doug's competitive nature went from a low simmer to near boiling. He made a phone call.

"Good afternoon, Senator Brennan's office."

"Good afternoon, Julie. It's Doug Brennan. Is my uncle available?"

"Hello, Doug. I think he's in a meeting, but I'm sure he'll want to speak to you. Can you hold a moment?"

"Yes." He tapped the desk during the silence.

"Doug, my boy, how are you?"

"I'm good, Uncle Robert."

"Don't you know it isn't nice to lie to your uncle?"

"I can't call my favorite uncle just to say hello?"

"I might buy that any other day, but I've seen the article in *The Times* about the latest public policy polling data putting you and Andrew Carver in a dead heat."

"I should have figured as much."

"So you called to get the old man's take on it, right?"

"Yes."

"The Carvers are just about as well known in New York as our family is, but there is no real indication that Andrew is even remotely interested in being a senator from what I've heard. What did Jim say?"

"He was the one who told me the field of candidates was getting larger. I was the one who offered up Andrew's name."

"And he confirmed it?"

"Yes."

"That figures." He laughed. "Word is Andrew is considering making a run for governor, and from what I've heard he's got a better than good shot at getting the Democratic nomination."

"So Jim could get rid of his competition." Doug nodded.

"Exactly. I don't think you have anything to worry about."

"Yes, but I'm not crazy about these numbers and with this whole media mess I'm afraid the numbers won't get any better with or without a Carver in the mix."

"I have two words for you. Seth McNeal. He's the best political public relations consultant and pollster I know. If you want to know what you should do next, he's the man to call. He's also convenient since he's in New York. Are you ready for the number?"

"Absolutely." Doug readied his pen.

"His office is 646-555-8965 and his cell is 917-555-7461."

"Got it. Thanks, Uncle Robert."

"Let me know how it turns out. I've got to get back to my staff meeting. Give Elle my love."

"I will." He hung up. *If I want to remain a front-runner, I'm going to have to step up my game. So I have to do what I have to do.*

A short time late Doug gathered his staff for a brief meeting. On his way back to his office his cell phone rang.

"Hi, Doug, it's Rory."

"Hey." He looked around at the people watching him as he went by. "What's up?"

"I know you've seen today's paper."

"Naturally." He smiled and waved to a couple of staffers that passed him in the hallway.

"I talked to Wendy and I've decided to set the record straight."

"What do you mean?" Doug walked back into his office and shut the door.

"I'm going to come clean and admit to the affair with Erica."

"Who's Erica?" Doug sat down.

"She's the woman in the picture. I've been seeing her for a while now."

"And she's okay with that?"

"Yes. We talked about it. I can't do this to you and Elle. The truth has to come out."

"How do you plan to do this?"

"Wendy's going to call a reporter she knows at *The Times* for the interview."

Doug saw his potential senate appointment flash before his eyes. "You can't do that."

"Why? I thought you'd be relieved to have the whole mess go away."

"Then you're more naive than I thought you were."

"What?" Rory was shocked. "You'd rather people think the worst of Elle rather than setting the record straight?"

"Of course not," he huffed. "But now that there's this other thing hanging out there."

"What other thing?"

"You and Elle were seen in the Bronx together. A reporter asked me about it today. It's only a matter of time before that hits the paper."

"We were at the children's clinic. Elle asked me to . . ."

Doug cut him off. "It doesn't make a difference. Someone saw you. So even if *The Times* does a story, the damage has been done. It will be the equivalent of a retraction, and no one reads retractions." He picked up the paper. "I'm sure Wendy told you this already."

"Wendy said she'd stand by whatever decision I make."

"Then you'd better think about it before you open this can of worms." Doug sighed. "Listen, I've got to get back to work. Let me know what you decide. Talk to you later." He hung up abruptly and quickly dialed another number.

"Wendy Kulick."

"Hi, Wendy, it's Doug."

"I wondered how long it would take before you called me. I take it you've spoken to Rory."

"Yes, and I can't believe you'd go along with his plan."

"He's my client, Doug. I work for him."

"You have to talk him out of it."

"I told him it wasn't good in terms of his divorce negotiations, but he's made up his mind."

"He thinks he's helping Elle and me, but he's not. Did you take a good look at his girlfriend? She even looks like Elle."

"That could be written off as a coincidence, Doug."

"The press will have a field day with the comparisons, and you know it." He rubbed his head. "Instead of ending it, this could prolong it. This can't be in his best interests."

"Are you worried about his interests or yours?"

"What?" Doug sounded offended.

"I'm just calling it like I see it, Doug. You're in the running for the Senate, and all this stuff can't be playing well in Albany."

"I'm concerned my brother is making a bad move."

"I apologize for doubting you, but he's still the client and I have to honor his wishes."

"I respect that. I'm just asking that you help him see that this might not be the best course of action."

"Fine." She paused. "I've got to get back to my office. We'll talk later."

"Thanks, Wendy."

I hope Rory comes to his senses sooner rather than later. My political future depends on it. He dialed Seth McNeal and got his voicemail. He waited for the tone.

"Hello, Seth. This is Douglas Brennan. My uncle, Senator Robert Brennan, gave me your number. If you could give me a call at your convenience, it doesn't matter how late, I'd really love to speak with you. My number is 646-555-2354. Thank you." He went into his office.

Elle used her parents visit to slip into the office to get a little Christmas shopping done online. Although they were too old to believe in Santa Claus anymore, Christmas still brought out the little kid in her sons. Every year Elle and Doug had to go to great lengths to hide gifts before their prying eyes and hands got to them.

A puzzled Elle scrolled through a music site. *Who are the kids listening to these days?* She stared and scratched her head as she examined the screen more closely. *I don't know T.I., Lil' Wayne or Young Jeezy from a hole in the wall. Maybe I'll go to the MTV site.* She typed in the web address. *Good grief, what is all this? I thought it was music television. What are The Hills? Maybe I should just get a gift card and let them figure it out.* She sighed.

The phone rang.

"Hello?"

"Hi, Elle."

"Hey, Melissa. It's nice to hear a friendly voice."

"Has it been that bad?"

"I've been trapped in the house all day. What do you think?"

"I'm sorry. I was calling to let you know I'm all set to take you tomorrow."

"Thanks. Oh," she groaned.

"Are you okay?"

"My stomach is bugging me."

"Do you think it's the baby? Do you want to go to the hospital?"

"No, it's not the baby."

"How can you be so sure?"

"I've had this before. It's stomach cramps."

"Like the ones you used to get when we were in Princeton?"

"Right."

"Well, you are stressed out."

"Tell me about it."

"Maybe if you tell Doug about the baby sooner rather than later, you'll feel better."

"I appreciate your concern, Melissa, but I'll tell him once I have all the facts. Besides I'm going to the doctor tomorrow. I'll break the news when I get back."

"Okay. In the meantime you should try to relax and do something to take your mind off of things."

"I'm trying to. I was doing a little online shopping for the kids when you called."

"That sounds easy enough."

"So far it's easier said than done. I think I'm going to get gift cards so they can pick what they want. Looking at all the names has given me a headache."

"I know what you mean."

"I'll tell you, Melissa, between texting and the names of some of these artists, I think the English language is in serious jeopardy."

Melissa laughed.

"I'd better head back into the kitchen and see what the troops are doing. I'll see you tomorrow."

"Okay."

Just as Elle got up she noticed a copy of *The Times* on the secretary desk. "What's this?" she said aloud as she perused the front page. "Carver and Brennan in a dead heat for Senate appointment according to latest poll," she read aloud. *Oh, this isn't good. There is nothing like a challenge to get the Brennan competitive juices flowing at fever pitch.* She sighed. *Maybe I shouldn't have been so gung-ho about this whole thing.* The picture of Rory and his girlfriend flashed in her mind. *Then I wouldn't be a part of this fiasco and I could tell Doug about the baby without the whispers.* She shrugged. "That's water under the bridge now," she said aloud as she left the office and headed down the hall where music was playing. *What in the world?* When she turned to go back to the living room she saw Kevin and Kyle showing their grandparents the latest dances.

"Go Mom and Dad." She chuckled. *I wish I had a camera.*

"I think we've got it." Her mother laughed.

"Yeah Grandma, you're ready for the winter dance," Kevin said.

"Why don't you join us, Mom?" Kyle asked.

"Why not?" As she danced and laughed, Elle forgot all about the troubles of the outside world for a while, and for the time being it was just what the doctor ordered.

CHAPTER 12

With the workday behind him, Doug took advantage of the relative quiet of the car on his way home to check his voice messages.

Doug, it's Rory. I've been doing some thinking and I decided not to go to the press. The way things are going it will only add more fuel to the fire and I know we're all anxious for the flame to be extinguished. I'll talk to you later.

Doug sighed in relief. *Thank goodness.* He picked up the newspaper. *I know I'll probably regret this, but let's see what old Mort has to say about this. I'm sure he couldn't resist.* He opened the paper to Mort's column and began reading. *Well, I'll be a monkey's uncle. He hasn't written a word. He must be the only one.* As the car approached home he noticed reporters were still staked out in front.

"Would you like me to go around back, Mayor Brennan?"

"Yes, Zach."

"No problem."

Walking through the back door, Doug heard Elle and the boys laughing in the kitchen. "What's so funny?" he asked as he entered the kitchen.

"Hey, Dad," Kevin and Kyle said.

"Hey, guys," he said as he set his briefcase down.

"Hi, honey. How was your day?"

"Okay," Doug answered and kissed her.

"You don't look like you had an okay day," Elle said skeptically.

"I'm fine. I promise. What makes you think something's wrong?"

"Twenty years of marriage."

Doug looked over at Kevin and Kyle. Elle recognized his 'let's talk later' look.

"We can talk about it later."

"It's not like we don't know what's going on, Dad," Kevin said matter-of-factly.

"Aunt Angela is just making stuff up because she's mad," Kyle added.

"I suppose we can't hide things from you anymore," Doug said.

"That's right, Dad. We're not babies anymore." Kevin grinned.

The sound of Doug and her sons' conversation faded as Elle's thoughts drifted. *Speaking of babies, maybe I should tell Doug I'm pregnant tonight. Dr. Aranow's test is just a formality anyway . . . .*

"Mom?"

"Elle? Earth to Elle, come in, Elle," Doug said with a smile.

"I'm sorry. What did you say?"

"Where were you?"

"My mind wandered for a minute, that's all. What were you talking about?"

"The boys said your parents were here today."

"Yes."

"They were here together?"

"I know. It's hard to believe." Elle chuckled.

"We were teaching Grandma and Grandpa some of the latest dances," Kevin explained.

"That must have been some sight," Doug said and laughed.

"Hey, don't talk about my parents. They've still got some moves."

"I bet they do."

Just then Frieda entered the kitchen carrying a cardboard box.

Kevin and Kyle nearly bum rushed her. "Food!" they yelled gleefully.

"Wait a minute, you two. This isn't feeding time at the zoo. Give her a chance to put the boxes down," Elle said sternly.

The minute the boxes hit the table, Kevin and Kyle pounced.

"If I were you, Frieda, I'd check to see if I still had all my appendages," Elle said.

Frieda put her hands up. "All ten fingers are accounted for."

Doug laughed.

"I ordered dinner in from the Viand Café, and I got your favorite."

"The Mediterranean Burger Deluxe?" he asked, smiling.

"Yes. It has extra fries and onion rings. To top it off you have the caramel apple pie for dessert."

"Nothing like a little salt, sugar and fat to take the edge off the day," he said.

Frieda handed him a styrofoam carrier. "Here you go, Mr. Brennan. Enjoy."

"It's not exactly a green container, but I'm not going to split hairs." He looked over at Kevin and Kyle. "Are my eyes deceiving me or do they have two double deluxe burgers each?"

"Your eyes aren't deceiving you." Elle chuckled.

Although they were only fourteen, at six feet, five inches apiece, Kevin and Kyle were taller than Doug, who wasn't exactly a pipsqueak at six feet, four inches. Like most growing teenage boys, they could put food away, and tonight was no exception.

"Where do they put it?" Doug shook his head.

"Beats me."

Frieda handed Elle a styrofoam box. "Here's your salad, Mrs. Brennan."

"Thank you." She opened it.

"Is that all you're having?" Doug asked.

"Yes. It's the country Greek salad with chicken. This is more than enough."

"Mom, did you get fries with your salad?"

"No, Kevin. That would sort of defeat the point of getting a salad. You both had double orders of fries. Don't tell me you've finished it."

"Well . . ."

"I knew this would happen. There should be another order of fries there."

Frieda was about to get up.

"No, Frieda." Doug stopped her. "You enjoy your dinner. He can get it."

"Thank you, Mr. Brennan."

Kevin got the fries.

"Don't hog them," Kyle said.

"Put them in the middle of the table and split them evenly."

"Okay, Mom."

Doug shook his head as Kevin and Kyle demolished everything but the container.

Later on that evening, while Doug was in the bathroom, Elle caught up on a little bedtime reading. Although she'd read most a dozen times or more, she enjoyed re-reading the classics. When she looked at the night table she noticed the article from *The Times* and some other poll data. *This is Doug's nighttime reading? This can't be good.*

"So, are you going to tell me what really brought your parents over? I'm pretty sure they didn't stop by for Dance USA," Doug asked as he towel-dried his hair.

"They came by because of all the hullaballoo Angela's drummed up in the newspapers. The dancing was just a bonus."

"What did you tell them?"

"I told them it was just a ploy by Angela to get more money out of this divorce. Naturally they think I should go on the offensive." Elle chuckled. "My mother's ready to take Angela out to the woodshed."

Doug snickered. "I'd pay good money for a ringside seat to that."

"Me, too. In the meantime I told them Rory has a top-notch lawyer and it's only a matter of time before all of this goes away." Elle figured if she sounded confident then maybe she'd believe it, too.

"That's the plan." He paused. "What are you reading?" Doug asked as he sat down on the bed.

"*Anna Karenina.*"

"Oh, that's an interesting choice."

Elle didn't like his tone. "What do you mean it's an interesting choice? You know it's one of my favorite books."

"You're right. I know."

She closed the book and put in on the night table. "I know that tone. What are you getting at, Doug?"

"Nothing," he said and shrugged. "I just think it's an interesting choice considering it's about a married woman who follows her lover."

"And you see a parallel between me and a fictional character who happens to be an adulteress?" Elle's voice got a little louder.

"No, of course not. You're jumping to conclusions."

"Is there another conclusion I should come to, Doug? Are you beginning to buy into this crap Angela's spewing?"

"No. But I wonder why you . . ."

"Why I what? Go ahead and finish the sentence."

"Why didn't you tell me you and Rory were at the children's clinic together the other day?"

"What?" Elle was flabbergasted.

"A reporter from *The Bronx Times* told me that you and Rory were there and asked me if the Brennan foundation was making a donation or gift to the clinic."

"What did you tell him?"

"Even though it was the first I'd heard of it, I told him the foundation was considering ways to help finance many public clinics to help them get through this fiscal crisis."

"Well played, Doug," Elle said curtly.

"Aren't you going to explain?"

"Explain what? It sounds to me like you've already made up your mind."

"I'm just asking, that's all."

"No, you're not just asking."

"Listen, Elle, we don't live in a vacuum. If one reporter saw you, then a dozen saw you."

"So? I wouldn't classify the children's clinic as a clandestine meeting place."

"Maybe not, but it's not the first time you . . ." He stopped himself.

"Go ahead and say it. It's not the first time people have seen me with Rory without you."

Doug didn't answer.

"I don't believe this." She shook her head. "It's not like we were seen at some fleabag motel. And besides, I always tell . . ."

He interrupted her. "Yes. You usually tell me. So why didn't you tell me about the clinic?"

Any other time Elle would have just explained, but her ire was up. "You know, if I didn't know any better I'd think you were accusing me of something."

Doug got quiet again.

"Oh, my God," Elle said as her face fell. "You're starting to believe this crap in the paper. Aren't you?"

"I didn't say that, Elle."

"You didn't have to."

"Come on, Elle, I didn't mean . . ."

She put her hand up. "You know what? I don't want to talk about this anymore. I might say something I'll regret." In a huff she closed the book and turned the light off on her side of the bed.

"You're just gonna go to sleep?"

"Yes. Good night." She pulled the covers up.

It would have been easy enough for me to tell him why Rory and I were at the clinic together if he would have asked me the right way, but he asked like he thinks there's something going on. After being a Brennan all of his life I would have thought Doug would know that he has to take the press with a grain of salt. Elle fluffed her pillow. *It's this Senate thing. It's slowly taking over our lives, and I don't like what it's doing to Doug. What's going to happen when I bring a new baby into the mix? Maybe I should have thought twice before I signed off on this appointment in the first place. Now it seems I've gone from the fishbowl to the shark tank, complete with the theme from Jaws.*

CHAPTER 13

The next morning, while Doug was in the closet mirror adjusting his tie, he heard his cell vibrate. "Hello?"

"Hello, Mayor Brennan, it's Seth McNeal returning your call. I hope it isn't too early."

"No. In fact early is generally better for me. I'm glad to hear from you."

"I have to admit I was surprised to get a call from the mayor of New York City."

"My uncle told me you were the best in the business and I should call you if I wanted to insure my appointment to Senator Clemson's Senate seat."

"I didn't think there was any doubt."

"As you know there's no such thing as a sure thing in politics. And now with the power of the press weighing in on me, I can't rest on my laurels."

"If you don't mind me saying so, your family has been a right-wing target for a long time."

"It's more than that this time."

"What do you mean?"

"Have you read the papers lately?"

"To be honest I've been out of the loop for the past three weeks. I just got back from a European getaway with my wife and daughters."

"Lucky you." Doug grinned.

"It was good to get away." He paused. "So I assume you have some poll data, amongst other things you'd like me to look into.."

"Yes. Are you saying that you'll work with me?"

"Let's just say I'm intrigued enough to review things. Can you email me what you have?"

"Sure, or I can fax it to you."

"On second thought, don't bother. I can do the research from my office. I'll get back to you."

"Thanks. I'll wait to hear from you. Have a good one."

"Thanks. You, too."

Doug walked back into the bedroom where Elle was pretending to be asleep.

"Elle?" Doug tapped her on the shoulder.

"Yes?" She pretended to be groggy.

"Are you going to your office today?"

"No. I'm going with Melissa to an appointment."

"Oh, okay." He leaned down and kissed her cheek. "We'll talk later."

"Okay," she said quietly.

Elle waited a few minutes before she got out of bed and headed to the bathroom. After a quick shower, she went to the closet and pulled out a pair of black slacks and a sweater. Any other day she would have stressed over her fashion choices, but given the state of the media and Doug's attitude, getting a ticket from the fashion police was the least of her problems.

Once she was dressed, Elle sat on the bed and stared at her laptop. *I'm not going to do it. I'm not going to torture myself.* "What the hell? It couldn't be any worse than what is already in the papers." Elle said aloud as she got her laptop and booted up. A few minutes later she was surfing all the newspaper websites and blogs that were devoted to deconstructing the scandal. Elle was hurt and flabbergasted by what she read but couldn't bring herself to sign off.

Melissa knocked and then walked into Elle's bedroom. "I tell you all I needed was the *Mission Impossible* theme and Tom Cruise to get through all those reporters outside. Jeez, I can't believe I had an easier time driving through rush hour traffic." Melissa looked at Elle. "Have you heard a word I said?" She walked over to the bed. "What are you looking at?"

"I'm reading a blog."

"What blog?"

"Someone set up a blog dedicated to the mayor's cheating wife."

"Elle," Melissa groaned.

"No, it's fascinating reading, actually. Here's one that says for women to forget Jenny Craig and to go on the Mrs. Smith's or Sara Lee diet like the mayor's wife. This one says this happened because I married into a white family. And this person says we should go on *Jerry Springer* or audition for *All My Children.*"

"Close the computer," Melissa said sternly.

"I've never really understood why people are so into gossip, but it's been around since the dawn of time. Heck, even the founding fathers used it as political tactic. I think Jefferson and Hamilton set the precedent when the Jeffersonians used James Callender's *History of the United States for 1796* to report Alexander Hamilton's financial dealings as Secretary of the Treasury as well as his 1792 adulterous affair with Maria Reynolds, the wife of James Reynolds, a United States Treasury employee. It was effective."

"Elle, this isn't an empirical study. I know you want it to be."

"Well, I figure if I keep reading, I'll understand why." Melissa closed Elle's laptop.

"Hey, I was reading."

"No. You weren't just reading."

"It's just words. They can't hurt me."

"Do you really believe that?"

"Yes." She shrugged. "I don't know anymore."

"Then why are you torturing yourself reading this junk?"

"My whole life is torture right now, Melissa. I'm practically a prisoner in my own home. This is nothing compared to . . ." Elle's voice caught.

Melissa sat down and put her arm around Elle. "Compared to what?"

"Compared to having your husband look at you like he doesn't trust you?"

"That doesn't sound like Doug at all. Did something else happen?"

"A reporter told Doug that Rory and I were at the Bronx Children's Clinic together after Thanksgiving and he's upset that I didn't tell him."

"What?" Melissa was surprised. "Why did Rory meet you there?"

"Rosario, Dr. Campbell, is a good friend of mine, and when she told me about the high number of cleft palate cases she sees at the clinic I wanted to help. The thing is with so many budget cuts happening across the board, I couldn't get Doug involved. So I asked Rory to come down and meet with her to talk about donating his services as a plastic surgeon and maybe recruiting some of his colleagues."

"Oh, I thought you only worked with clinics in Manhattan."

"I only work with clinics in Manhattan for the hospital. This is something I'm doing on my own outside of the hospital."

"I think that's great." Melissa grinned. "Did you tell Doug that?"

"I was going to, but I didn't like his tone."

"What do you mean?"

"Maybe I've seen too many episodes of *Law and Order,* but he sounded like a man conducting an interrogation and not like a husband asking his wife a question."

"I'm sure he didn't mean it that way. With everything that's happening, he's under a lot of pressure."

"And I'm not? It's bad enough I have to deal with the media and Angela's accusations. Now I'm supposed to deal with Doug's?"

"You're right," Melissa agreed. "Did you tell him how you feel?"

"No. I was too upset and I didn't want to say something I'd regret." She looked down. "Doug is in spin control mode now. Whenever he speaks he sounds more like a press release than my husband."

"I'm so sorry, Elle."

"Thanks." She wistfully looked over at Kevin and Kyle's pictures. "Remember when I found out I was pregnant with the twins?"

"Yes." Melissa smiled. "You were so excited."

"I couldn't wait to tell Doug we were bringing two babies into a world of love and joy." She sighed. "And now here I am fourteen years later, pregnant again, and instead of bursting with excitement I'm filled with dread. This baby deserves to come into a world filled with love, not scandal and doubt." Tears began to stream down her face.

"Elle." Melissa hugged her.

"Thanks." Elle grabbed a couple of tissues and wiped her face. "Well, I've got to pull it together and get to Dr. Aranow's." She stood up. "He usually begins seeing patients at one o'clock, but given the circumstances he's made an exception for me."

"That's good." Melissa looked at her watch. "I guess we'd better get a move on then."

"Right." Elle put on a large coat, sunglasses and a hat. She and Melissa slipped out the back way to her car. Lucky for Elle, Melissa's car windows were tinted so they were able to drive right by a group of reporters unnoticed. Elle breathed a sigh of relief.

"Are you sure you're okay?"

"No. But what choice do I have?" She paused. "I just want to confirm the pregnancy, tell Doug and get on with our lives in relative peace." The frustration in her voice was palpable.

Melissa rubbed her leg. "Calm down, Elle. You don't need to get worked up any more than you already are."

"You're right. I have another person to think about." She patted her stomach.

"Exactly." Melissa reached into the seat compartment and pulled out a CD. "How about a little music for the ride over?"

"Sure."

"I don't have Tori Amos. Is Beyoncé okay?"

"That's fine with me."

Melissa put the CD in and began moving in her seat to "Single Ladies (Put A Ring On It)."

Elle couldn't help but laugh. "What are you doing?"

"I'm doing the 'Single Ladies' dance."

"In the car?"

"Why not? I have booty like Beyoncé. In fact, I have a lot more booty than her." She continued to bounce in her seat.

"Leave it to you to make me laugh."

"What are friends for?"

"You do realize that neither of us are single ladies, right?"

"Neither is Beyoncé, but that didn't stop her. Besides, it's a good song and it will drown out your thoughts, at least for a few minutes."

"That sounds good to me. Calgon isn't quite cutting it for me these days." Elle was grateful for the musical interlude and the chance to put her thoughts on hold, even if it was only for a little while.

Even though it was already yesterday's news, Doug couldn't stop staring at the photo in *The Post*. He rubbed his eyes. *No matter how long I stare at this, it doesn't change.*

"Staring at it won't help," Ki said as he walked in Doug's office.

Doug put the paper down. "I should shred it."

"Then why don't you?"

He tossed it in the garbage. "Who ever thought that I'd welcome a chance to defend the cuts to the new city budget?"

"I think it would be novel for the press to focus on the issues instead of salacious gossip and innuendo."

"It's hard to call it innuendo when there are photos."

"Wait a minute, Doug. You don't believe it's really Elle in that picture, do you?"

"No. Of course not."

"Good. Then what's eating you?"

"It's her relationship with Rory."

"What about it? They're friends and in-laws. They went to lunch at a diner, Doug. I wouldn't call it an illicit meeting."

"I know, and I've never had a problem with them spending time together, but now it's come back to haunt me. I should have put my foot down a long time ago."

Ki folded his arms. "Is that you talking or the latest poll numbers?"

"What?"

"Don't pretend like you don't know today's *Daily News* poll shows Carver with a four percent lead."

"Not too long ago we were in a dead heat."

"The margin of error in a scientific poll is two to three percent. While I'm not denigrating the *Daily News,* it's not *The Times.* Are you saying that not only do you believe the tales Angela and her lawyer have concocted, you think it's hurting you in the polls?"

"No, I don't believe Angela."

"But you are concerned that it's hurting your bid for the Senate."

"No. But . . ."

"What?"

"Then there's the meeting at the Bronx Clinic." He tapped his desk.

"Did you ask Elle about it?"

"Yes, and she wouldn't answer me."

"Did you ask her as a husband or politician?"

"What?"

"You heard me," Ki said pointedly. "Because if you asked her with the same attitude you have now, I can understand why."

Doug was a little taken aback. "You're one of the people who encouraged me to go for the Senate seat. You know the press is already all over me for any little thing since I'm a Brennan."

"Sure, I encouraged you. Do you know why?"

"Why?"

"For the last seven years I've watched you successfully balance being a politician, husband and father. Granted, I might have given you a little grief for making out with your wife in public, but it really made me feel good to know that no matter what went on here, you never really brought it home. So I thought being senator would be a piece of cake for you."

"It will be."

"It won't be if you let your public image come before your family. Elle is a big part of the reason you've been a successful mayor. You need to remember that."

"God, Ki, why don't you tell me how you really feel?" Doug asked somewhat jokingly.

"Listen, Doug, my nose is brown because I'm black, not because it's stuck up your butt." He looked at his watch. "I have some business to attend to outside of the office. I'll see you later."

Ki walked out.

Doug turned and faced the window. *I don't know what Ki is talking about. If it was nothing, why couldn't she tell me?* He sighed aloud. *I know she's pissed. She barely said a word to me this morning. Am I supposed to feel guilty? I wasn't the one with the secret.* His cell phone was vibrating.

"Hello?"

"Mayor Brennan? It's Seth McNeal."

"Seth, I didn't expect to hear from you so soon."

"I figured I'd call you with my preliminary findings. I'll follow up with a detailed hard copy report."

"Great. What's your take? Am I in trouble?"

"Judging from what I've read so far, you're not in any real trouble."

"Yet."

"I didn't say that. It seems that your brother's divorce and the fact that they've brought your wife into it has shaken your numbers up a little, but overall I don't think you have anything to worry about."

"My chief of staff seems to think I should make a public statement showing support for my wife."

"It's not a bad idea. However, I have to ask you something personal."

"Go ahead."

"Are your wife and brother friends? Do they hang out?"

"Of course they're friends. They even occasionally have lunch together. It's been that way for years."

"The problem is even though it's nothing, it has already been made into something. If you come out with a public statement it could make them look guilty. And with Jasper Lyons on the case, you can be sure he'll make a mountain out of a molehill. It's sort of his specialty."

"I thought so."

"If you don't mind me asking, who's representing your brother?"

"Wendy Kulick."

"Your brother is in good hands. She's just as good as Jasper. In my opinion this thing will eventually lose steam, scandals always do. As bad as it sounds you have to wait it out. I'll send you over my analysis and recommendations by messenger this week."

"Wow, my uncle said you were good. Don't forget to include your invoice."

"There's no charge."

"You're kidding me."

"No. The way I see it, this is the equivalent of a loss leader. When you run for your own term, I hope you'll hire me."

"No wonder Uncle Robert likes you."

Seth laughed.

"Well I've got to run to my next meeting. I'll look for your package. Have a good day, Seth."

"Same to you, Mayor Brennan."

Feeling somewhat vindicated, Doug headed out of his office. He looked down at his watch. *I'll give Elle a call a little later.*

Her examination over, Elle waited anxiously in Dr. Aranow's office. She stared at the many photos of all the babies he'd delivered. Dr. Aranow had been an obstetrician for more than twenty-five years. Not much had changed about him in that time. He was average height with slightly stodgy build. He still had a cherub face with just a little more grey hair around the temple.

"Okay, Elle," he said as he walked in with her file.

"What's the verdict, Doc? How pregnant am I?"

He sat down and opened the file. "I'd say you're about eight weeks along. We'll know better after the sonogram, which I would like you to have today."

"All right. Can you do it here?"

"I don't do it in this office. We use the radiologist on the fifth floor. I'll have Terry call down to let them know you're coming."

"Don't I have to drink a gallon of water first or something?"

"No. That was the old way. You don't have to do that anymore."

"That's a relief. I hated that when I was pregnant with the boys."

"There are a few other things that haven't changed for you, Elle. You were a high risk pregnancy with the twins . . ."

"Are you saying that now that I'm over forty, I'm really high risk?"

"We have to follow you more carefully, and you're going to have to slow down and watch your stress levels."

Elle laughed. "I take it you don't read the paper or watch the news. I'm an accused adulteress and home-wrecker. My whole life is one big ball of stress."

"I've seen the news," he said matter-of-factly. "I know you, Elle. I haven't even bothered to look at it."

"You must be the only one."

"Seriously, Elle, you have to be careful."

"I'll do my best. That's all I can promise."

"I'll take it." He took his prescription pad out. "I'm going to write you a scrip for vitamins."

"Please tell me they finally made them smaller. I hated taking those horse pills."

"Sorry."

"You mean to tell me they can make a tiny little pill for erectile dysfunction, but they can't figure out how to make a prenatal pill that doesn't carry the risk of the Heimlich maneuver as a side effect?"

Dr. Aranow laughed. "You haven't lost your sense of humor," he said as he handed her the scrip.

"I have to keep it. If I didn't, I'd never stop crying." She took the paper and put it in her bag. "Thank you."

He stood up. "Radiology is in room 522. It's still early yet, so there shouldn't be many people there."

"Thanks, Doc." Elle got up.

Dr. Aranow walked her to the waiting room.

"Well?" Melissa asked anxiously.

"It's official."

"Great."

"I have to go to radiology on the fifth floor for a sonogram. Do you have time?"

"Sure."

"Do you need me to come back up here, Doc?"

"No. They'll send the report to me. I'll give you a call."

"Okay."

"We're putting you down for another appointment two weeks from today. Same time?"

"Works for me."

"All right, then I'll talk to you soon."

"Okey-dokey."

Elle and Melissa went straight to the radiologist's office, which was empty. Elle had the sonogram and afterwards the technician gave her a copy. As she stared, the pregnancy felt real for the first time. It was no longer conjecture as she looked at a photo of the life she and Doug created inside of her.

Melissa walked over to her. "Are you okay?"

"Yes." She showed her the picture. "It's our baby."

"Aww, Elle. It's precious." She hugged her.

"I'm really having a baby."

They walked out of the office into the hall. "Well, this is a reason to celebrate. I'm going to call Myles and ask him to cover for me for the rest of today."

"Are you sure? It's okay if you need to go back to work."

"No. Don't be silly." She took her cell phone out. "Figures, I don't have a signal here. I'm going to go down the hall."

"Okay. I'll wait for you by the elevator."

"I won't be but a minute."

"Take your time."

Elle walked over to the elevator. She couldn't stop staring at her sonogram. *That little tiny blur is our baby.* She smiled. The elevator doors opened.

"Elle?"

Startled, she looked up. "Rory?" Elle quickly slipped the sonogram into her purse.

He stepped out. "What are you doing here?"

"I had an appointment." She stopped. "I mean, Melissa had an appointment."

"Oh, is she okay?"

"She's fine. She's just down there making a call."

"You know I'm not supposed to be around you with all this brouhaha going on."

"I know. It's not like we planned this. We ran into each other. It is a medical building."

Melissa walked over. "Okay, we're all . . . Oh, hi, Rory."

"Hi, Melissa. How are you feeling? Elle tells me you had an appointment."

"I'm fine, thanks."

"Well, we'd better get going. You never know who may be hanging around with a telephoto lens," Elle said bitterly.

"About that, Elle. I really should explain."

The elevator doors opened. "That's okay, Rory. We have to run." She waved.

"Bye." He waved.

"You told him I had an appointment here," Melissa said, arms folded.

"Yes. I couldn't tell him I was here to see my obstetrician. I haven't even told Doug that I'm pregnant."

"You have a point."

Melissa couldn't help but snicker when Elle put her coat, hat and glasses back on. "Oh, you think this is funny."

"I'm sorry, Elle. You have to admit it is kind of funny."

Elle looked at her reflection and laughed. "I do look like a bugaboo or something."

Melissa put her coat on. "How about we feed the baby? Have you eaten anything today?"

"No."

"Well then I know just the place we can remedy the situation."

"You do?"

"Yes. Are you game?"

"Let's go."

A half hour later, they walked into Amy Ruth's restaurant in Harlem for a little down-home comfort food mixed in with some holiday spirit. The hostess seated them right away.

"The place looks nice and festive," Elle said as she looked around. "With all this garbage going on, I haven't exactly been in the Christmas spirit." She sat down.

"I can't say I don't understand."

Elle looked around the restaurant. "Listen, if I ask you a question, will you tell me the truth?"

"Of course."

"Do you think that I brought this on myself because of all the time I've spent with Rory?"

"No. I can't believe you'd even think that for a minute."

"You've seen the papers and the blog posts. How can I not think that?"

"The media and Angela are like Pavlov and his dogs. She rings the bell and they come running whether or not there is an actual tidbit to devour. Forget about them," Melissa said.

"That is easier said than done."

"Well if you can't forget about them altogether, at least forget long enough to order lunch."

"I'll try," Elle said.

"Good." Melissa grinned as she opened the menu. "Everything is good here."

Elle studied the menu. "Maybe I'll just have the chicken soup."

"You will do no such thing. You're eating for two, remember?"

"All right, I'll have the pan-seared jumbo shrimp with green beans and candied yams. Is that better?"

"That's more like it. Make sure you check out dessert, too." She winked.

"You are too much."

"Listen, if you can't have dessert when you're pregnant, when can you have it?"

"That's so true." She nodded.

The waiter came over and took their lunch order. The restaurant was busy, yet quiet. Elle and Melissa enjoyed their meal in relative peace.

"Mmm," Elle said as she put her fork down. "I don't know that I can eat another bite."

"Oh no, you're not getting out of dessert that easily."

Elle looked pensive.

"You're still thinking about everything, aren't you?"

"I can't help it." Elle sighed. "Back when we were in school things seemed to be clear cut. To me it was black or white, right or wrong."

"Then you stepped into the real world," Melissa added.

"Yes, and I found out that we live in a mixed reality where the lines are blurred, especially when it comes to politics and how people view you."

"Who cares about how people view you?"

"I don't care, but I do worry about how this affects my kids."

"Have they said anything to you?"

"No."

"Then don't go looking for trouble," Melissa said as she sipped her soda.

"Maybe you're right." Elle sighed.

"Of course I'm right. Now how about chocolate cake?" she grinned.

Elle rubbed her stomach. "Let's share a slice."

"I'm game."

After Melissa ordered a slice of cake with two forks, Elle realized her stomach was less than thrilled, but she had a few bites to appease Melissa.

Elle put her fork down. "That chocolate cake was just what I needed," Elle lied.

"I told you."

"Thanks for coming with me today."

"Don't mention it." Melissa sipped her coffee. "So now that your pregnancy is official, are you going to tell Doug?"

"Yes. I'll tell him when he gets home tonight, after I get the boys squared away." Elle shook her head.

"What?"

"Doug and I haven't really talked since last night's conversation. I was so angry with him."

"Well now you have the ultimate icebreaker. 'Honey, I'm pregnant' is a game changer."

"It's a life changer, too. After fourteen years I'm going back to square one with diapers, breastfeeding and sleepless nights. And that's in addition to all the teenage angst we have to look forward to."

"Oh, my God, that reminds me." Melissa looked at her Blackberry.

"What's up?"

"The PTA is handing out the parents' packages for the winter dance today and tomorrow."

"Oh, that's right. I nearly forgot about the winter dance. What did you sign up for?"

"I signed up for the decorations committee and dance chaperone."

"I bet Jason loves that," Elle said facetiously.

"He doesn't think it's chaperoning. He thinks I'm going to be lurking around spying on him."

Elle laughed.

Melissa looked at her watch. "Listen, I can drop you home and then I'll head over to the school."

"Why go out of your way? Besides, I signed up for the winter dance, too. I need to know what I've been assigned to bring by the refreshment committee."

"Are you sure? I can pick up your assignment and bring it over later."

"Thanks, Melissa, but it's okay. I'll go with you to the school. I think I've been entombed long enough."

"If you say so," Melissa said as she glanced over at the dessert cart. "I'm going to order a couple of slices of cake for Myles and Jason first."

"That sounds like a good idea. Do you think they have a whole cake?"

"You want to buy a whole chocolate cake?"

"Please, you've seen my sons eat."

"Oh yeah, you'd better see if they have two, one for each of them."

"I just might do that." Elle chuckled.

"I'll get the waiter." Melissa motioned him over to their table. A few moments later they left the restaurant with dessert.

With a few minutes to spare between meetings, Doug dialed Elle. The phone rang a few times and then went to voicemail. "Damn", he said quietly.

"Did you get her?"

Doug was a little startled. "Ki, I didn't see you there. Where did you come from?"

"I just walked up. So did you get Elle?"

"How did you know I was calling her?"

"Lucky guess."

"Well, I didn't get her. I got her voicemail."

"Maybe she didn't hear it ring or she couldn't get to it fast enough."

"She did say she was going to the doctor with Melissa."

"There's your answer. She probably turned it off at the doctor's office."

"You're probably right." He looked at his watch. "I better run. I have another budget session." Doug quickly scooted down the hall.

CHAPTER 14

The moment Elle and Melissa walked in the gymnasium went from a low roar to near silence.

Melissa quickly turned to Elle. "Listen, you can wait in the hallway. I'll get your stuff, too."

"That's okay, I'll get it. I'm not going to run out of here like I have something to hide. I haven't done anything."

"Okay."

As other parents milled around the gym, Elle and Melissa walked over to the desk where Morgan was seated.

I never thought I'd miss the fashion auxiliary, Elle thought while she waited behind Melissa.

"Here you go, Melissa." Morgan handed her an envelope.

"Thanks."

"Elle, I'm surprised to see you here," Morgan said.

"Really? Why? I did sign up for the refreshment committee."

"I just thought with everything going on you'd . . ."

"You thought I'd forget my obligations?"

"No, of course not," she said hastily, and then handed Elle a paper.

"Thank you." Elle looked it over. "I see I've been given cupcake duty."

"Oh, that's fun." Melissa smiled.

"It's something the whole *family* can do together." Morgan sounded innocent, but Elle knew better.

"Excuse me?" Elle was beginning to get heated.

"I was just saying . . ."

"You were just saying nothing as usual," Melissa quickly interjected. "Let's go. We have what we came for."

Elle and Melissa left Morgan with her mouth agape.

"That Morgan has got some nerve," Melissa huffed as they walked down the hallway. "The woman is in love with her own voice. She should consider going on *America's Got Talent.*"

"What?"

"The woman talks out of her ass. I think that qualifies as more than just a magic trick. Don't you?"

Elle howled with laughter. "I never thought of it that way before. By the way, thanks for getting me out of there before I lost my temper and said something I would regret."

"Don't mention it."

"And thank you for the laugh. I really needed that."

"It's my pleasure."

"I can't let people like Morgan get under my skin." Elle sighed. "Most of them can't believe I got Doug in the first place."

"The fact is you did, and now you're having another Brennan, so the heck with them."

Elle yawned.

"It's been a long day. How about I get you home so you can rest?"

"Yes, please."

"Not to mention you need to get your two chocolate cakes home for the boys. I still can't believe you bought two."

"They have basketball practice today, which means they've gone from eating machines to human piranhas."

As the two women laughed, Elle felt a twinge in her stomach.

"Oh," she said suddenly.

"Are you all right?"

"Sure. My stomach's just a little upset again."

"Why don't you take something?" Melissa popped her forehead. "Duh? You can't."

"Right. Now that I'm officially pregnant, I can't take those medications. But I'm sure it's nothing a ginger ale or a little bicarbonate won't cure."

"Are you sure?"

"Yes." She looked at her watch. "I have enough time to take a nap before I lay the baby news on Doug."

They walked out of the school to Melissa's car.

"I don't know how he's going to take it," Elle said as she got in.

"He's going to be overjoyed," Melissa said as she got in and put her seatbelt on.

"With the senate appointment and this fiasco with Rory going on, I hope you're right."

"Of course I'm right." Melissa smiled as she started the car.

I hope so, Elle thought.

After Melissa dropped her off, Elle went to the kitchen, cakes boxes in hand.

"Good afternoon, Mrs. Brennan. What's all this?" Frieda smiled.

"Hi, Frieda. Hopefully this is dessert for the next couple of nights, but you never know with my sons."

Frieda laughed as she took the boxes from Elle and placed them on the counter. "Mrs. Brennan, the senior Mrs. Brennan is here to see you."

"Oh? How long has she been here?"

"She's hasn't been here long. Twenty minutes at the most. She's in the living room having coffee."

"Thanks." Elle took her coat off. "Frieda, my stomach's a little upset. Would you mind getting me a ginger ale or something?"

"Sure. I'll bring you a glass of ginger ale. Would you like ice?"

"Yes, please."

"Coming right up," she said and smiled.

Elle headed for the living room. Just like she did before she'd seen Mr. Brennan, she made a quick mirror check before she entered the living room. *So much for my nap,* she sighed.

"Hello, Mrs. Brennan," Elle said as she entered the room.

"Hello, my dear." Mrs. Brennan stood up and the two women embraced.

Elle looked over at the tea service Frieda had put on the table. "Would you like another cup?"

"No, dear. I'm good." She sat down. "I'm sorry for just dropping in on you like this."

"That's not a problem, Mrs. Brennan." Elle smiled sweetly as she sat down.

"With everything going on, I was concerned and I wanted to see how you're holding up."

"Thank you. So far I'm none the worse for wear."

"I could kill that Angela." She shook her head. "I didn't like her when Rory first brought her around, there was something about her I didn't like."

Elle was a little taken aback by her candor. "Well, that's water under the bridge now," Elle said.

"It's more like sludge at this point. How has Doug been with you since this happened? I know he's been a bit preoccupied with this Senate business."

"Good. He's been fine."

"Listen, Elle, I've been married to a Brennan far longer than you and I know how they get when it comes to politics."

"He's been busy doing damage control. It's almost like he . . ." She stopped.

"He believes what's in the papers, right?"

"Yes." Elle sank a bit in the chair. "To be honest I haven't helped myself much."

"What do you mean?"

"Rory and I went to Bronx Children's Clinic together after Thanksgiving and I neglected to mention it to Doug. He heard about it from a reporter."

"Well, did you tell him Rory was there to talk about pro bono work with Dr. Campbell?"

"How did you know?"

"Rory mentioned it. Didn't you explain that to Doug?"

"I was going to until he started acting like I'd done something wrong."

"Dear, you should have told him about Rory and how this whole situation is making you feel."

"You're right." Elle nodded. "I tried to tell him, but I clammed up."

"Listen, sweetheart, I understand how you feel, but the Brennan men can be awfully thick skulled. Sometimes you have to use a velvet glove and a big stick to get them to pay attention. Take it from me."

Frieda walked in with the ginger ale. "Excuse me, ladies. Here you go." She handed Elle the glass.

"Thank you."

"Can I get you anything else?"

"No." Elle sipped the soda. "This is great."

"Would you like another cup of coffee, Mrs. Brennan?"

"No. Thank you." She looked at her watch. "I have to be going soon."

"Very good, ma'am." Frieda cleared the coffee service and returned to the kitchen.

"Are you feeling all right, Elle?"

"I'm fine. It' just a little upset stomach, that's all."

"You should get some rest and tell my son how you feel. Trust me, that will help alleviate your upset stomach."

That and getting through the first trimester.

"I will. I promise," Elle said.

Mrs. Brennan stood up. "Well, I'd better be going."

Elle rose, put her glass down and walked her to the door. "Please give Mr. Brennan my love.""I will." Mrs. Brennan hesitated a moment. Then she lightly touched Elle's cheek. "You should get some rest, sweetie. You look a little tired," she said.

"I'm going to lie down for a while before dinner."

"Good." She kissed her on her cheek. "I'll see you soon."

"Okay." Elle watched from behind the door as photographers snapped photos of Mrs. Brennan as she got into a waiting car. She held her stomach as she closed the door.

"Here you go, Mrs. Brennan." Frieda handed her the glass.

"Oh, thank you." She quickly took a long sip.

"I'll get dinner going while you get some rest."

"You're a lifesaver, Frieda."

Frieda disappeared into the kitchen while Elle slowly made her way upstairs to her bedroom. Once she got there she flopped onto the bed. Eventually she managed to pull the covers up. *I'll just rest for a while. I'll talk to Doug when he gets home.* The minute her head touched the pillow she was asleep.

About a half hour later, Elle was awakened by a gentle tap on her shoulder. "Yes?"

"I'm sorry, Mrs. Brennan, but there is a Mr. McNeal on the phone for Mr. Brennan."

"Mr. McNeal? He didn't want to leave a message?"

"No. I can try to get rid of him."

"That's okay, Frieda. I'll talk to him."

"Okay." She left the room.

Elle sat up in bed then composed herself before she picked up. "Hello?"

"Oh, I'm sorry if I woke you, Mrs. Brennan."

"It's fine. What can I do for you, Mr. McNeal?"

"Please call me Seth. Since I'm going to be working with your husband, I thought I'd call to introduce myself."

"I'm sorry. You're working with my husband on what?"

"His senatorial appointment."

Finally a light went on over Elle's head. "You're Seth McNeal. You specialize in political public relations."

"I wouldn't say that's all I do. I really concentrate on taking polls and analyzing data."

"I see."

"Oh, dear, this is the first you're hearing about me, isn't it?"

"Yes, but that's not your fault."

"I'm so sorry. To be honest he hasn't exactly hired me yet, this is all just preliminary stuff."

"Don't worry about it. Doug has been so busy lately he probably hasn't had the chance to tell me." She yawned.

"You sound tired. I should let you go. Again, I am so sorry for the intrusion."

"Thank you. Have a good day."

"You, too." He hung up.

Why didn't Doug tell me he took a meeting with a big gun like him? Poll analyzing, my ass, she fumed. Suddenly her stomach pained her again. *I'd better relax before this gets any worse.* She lay back down, and before long she'd drifted off again.

"Elle?"

She opened her eyes. "What time is it?"

Doug looked at his watch. "It's only eight o'clock. You were out like a light. Are you feeling okay?"

"I was tired."

"Obviously." He sat down, took off his shoes and loosened his tie.

"I did wake up for a phone call, though."

"Yeah?"

"Yes. Seth McNeal called to introduce himself to me."

Doug slumped in the chair. "I meant to tell you about him. Uncle Rob recommended him as the best pollster he knows."

"I know the name Seth McNeal, and that's not all he specializes in. He's the guy who sets up all those infamous mea culpa press conferences when politicians are caught dipping more than just their hands in the cookie jar. Meanwhile their humiliated spouses do their best not to look like deer in headlights."

"You don't think that's the reason I contacted him, do you?"

"Well you didn't bother to tell me about it at all, so I don't know what to think? Maybe you want Rory and me to go in front of the press and confess our friendship."

"That's not fair."

"Well you have been all worked up about that silly clinic thing."

"Silly clinic thing? My poll numbers have been steadily dropping ever since this whole divorce drama broke. A divorce drama that has nothing to do with me."

"It has nothing to do with me, either, Doug."

"I didn't mean for it to sound that way."

"The hell you didn't." Elle jumped out of bed, headed for the bathroom and slammed the door.

"Damn!"

Elle turned the water on in the sink so Doug wouldn't hear her crying.

"Come on, Elle. Open the door. I'm sorry. I didn't mean it." He stood and listened at the door for a few minutes in the hope that she'd open it, but she didn't. Dejected, Doug left the room. *Maybe she needs a little space.*

When he returned an hour later, Elle was curled up in bed fast asleep. Her crying had tired her already spent body out. She and Doug would for the first time in years go to bed upset, and while they both slept it was far from restful.

CHAPTER 15

With Doug and the boys out of the house extra early, Elle went down to the kitchen for a cup of peppermint tea to settle her stomach. Ever since *The Post* ran the photo of Rory and the mystery woman, her stomach, like her life, was in an uproar. She peeked out the window at the reporters still camped out by the front door.

They're like dogs camped around a butcher shop just waiting for any little scrap of meat. I wonder what would happen if I rang a bell. She shook her head in disgust and groaned as she sat down at the kitchen table.

"Mrs. Brennan? Are you all right?"

"I'm okay, Frieda. My stomach is a little upset, that's all."

"Would you like some dry toast or crackers?"

"No, thank you. Tea is fine for now."

"Okay. Let me know if you change your mind."

"I will."

In all the years I've been with Doug, I've never been so angry with him. Maybe it was partly my fault. I should have come clean about the clinic and today we'd be celebrating our impending arrival. She glanced down at her stomach. Suddenly Kyle walked in with the assistant principal, Mr. Gibbs. Kyle looked a little disheveled.

"Kyle? Oh, my God. What happened?" She immediately went over to examine him more closely.

"I'm sorry, Mom."

"What are you sorry about? What's going on?"

Kyle was quiet.

"You're not going to tell your mother, Kyle?"

The boy didn't say anything.

"Kyle and another student got into a scuffle this morning."

"You were in a fight?"

Kyle looked away. "I'm sorry, Mom."

"Why on earth were you fighting at school?"

"I really don't want to talk about it, Mom."

"You might not want to talk about it now, but we are going to talk. Go to your room. I'll be up in a minute."

Kyle turned to Mr. Gibbs. "Thanks for the ride home, Mr. Gibbs."

"That's quite all right, Kyle."

Kyle left the kitchen.

"Mr. Gibbs, Kyle's in the math and chess club. He doesn't have a violent bone in his body. What happened?"

"According to the other students the other kid was giving him a hard time about the . . ."

"You can say it. He was getting teased about me."

"I'm afraid so. Kids can be cruel, even at this age."

"So can adults."

"True. Under the circumstances I thought it best to bring him home."

"Has he been suspended?"

"No. Kyle's a good kid with no discipline problems. He's just going through a bad time, as I'm sure you all are."

"Thank you."

"You're welcome." He looked at his watch. "I'd better get back to the school."

Elle shook his hand. "Thanks again."

"I'll see myself out the back."

Frieda walked in. "That's okay. Frieda, can you walk Mr. Gibbs out the back?"

"Sure. Follow me."

He followed her out of the kitchen.

Elle rubbed her forehead. *Kyle was in a fight over this garbage. I told Doug it wasn't enough to handle the situation for the sake of his political career and to save face for the Senate appointment.* She sighed. *Oh, my poor child had to defend his mother's honor.* She went upstairs.

When she got to Kyle's room the door was open and he was sitting on his bed.

"Kyle?" She sat next to him.

"Yes, Mom. I know you're disappointed in me."

She stroked his hair. "I'm not disappointed. Just tell me what happened."

"I really don't want to talk about it."

"I already know it has something to do with the stuff in the papers. You can tell me."

"I don't want to repeat it."

"Listen, Kyle, I understand that, but you've been teased before and you never let it get you to the point of fighting. So you might as well tell me, because I'm not leaving until you do."

He let out a heavy sigh. "This kid asked me . . ." He hesitated.

"What kid?"

"Shane Whitmore."

Figures it would be Morgan's son. "Go on. Tell me what he said."

"He asked me if Kevin and I will have to call Uncle Rory Uncle Daddy now."

Elle's heart sunk, but she didn't let on. "I know that wasn't a nice thing to say, but they are just words. You can't let them bother you."

"How can you say that, Mom? Aunt Angela and her lawyer are putting these lies in the paper, and you and Dad aren't doing anything about it."

"Your father thinks it's best to work on it through the proper channels."

"Well, it's not working. When is it going to stop, Mom? It's Christmas time and it doesn't feel like it at all." His eyes welled up.

Elle put her arms around him. "You're right. This should be a happy time. I'm going to take care of it. Don't worry."

"How?"

"You leave that to me." She brushed his hair back and kissed his forehead. "Do you feel better?"

"Yes."

"I know it's early, but do you have any homework?"

He nodded.

"Just relax and watch television, go on the computer or play one of your games. You can do your homework later."

Kyle looked shocked. "What did you say?"

"I won't tell if you don't." She winked.

"Thanks, Mom." He hugged her.

"You're welcome, baby." She kissed him again and got up. "I'll see you in a little while."

"Where are you going?"

"I have to run some errands. I'll be back."

"Okay." Kyle flipped his laptop open.

Elle walked out of his room and downstairs to the foyer. "Frieda?"

"Yes, Mrs. Brennan?"

Elle got her coat from the hall closet. "I'm going out for a little while. Kyle's upstairs in his room." She put her coat on.

"Would you like me to have the car brought around?"

"No. I'm going to drive." She grabbed her bag. "I'll have my cell on if anyone needs to reach me."

"Yes, ma'am."

Elle went through the back to the garage and got in her car. *Doug's way isn't working.* She put the car in reverse and pulled away. *It's time for Momma to lay down the law.*

Doug was returning to his office after an announcement and photo op with the Department of Transportation Commissioner for the city's pothole blitz. Though he usually preferred not to dirty his custom shoes, shoveling tar helped to release some of the stress he'd been feeling over the last week.

Alice wasn't at her desk. He looked at his watch. "She must have left for lunch," he mused as he continued to his office. When he opened the door he saw his father sitting there.

"Dad?"

"Hello, son." He got up and the two shook hands.

"Have a seat, Dad. This is a surprise. What brings you here?" Doug took his coat off and sat down behind his desk.

"'I came by to see how things were going."

"It's been a little rough, but I talked to Jim and it seems that he still wants me to be the appointee in spite of the scandal and negative articles."

"I wasn't talking about the senate appointment. I was talking about your family."

"They're hanging tough, Dad."

"You know your mother went by to see Elle. Didn't she tell you?"

"No, but I'm not surprised after the other night."

"I assume it had to do with Rory."

"What else is there these days, Dad? Every time I turn around there's something new."

"What do you mean?"

Doug hesitated for a moment. "Do you know Kent Barlow?"

"Sure. He's a reporter for the *Bronx Times*."

"Well he wanted to know what was going on with the foundation since he'd seen Rory and Elle at the Bronx Children's Clinic a little while back."

"So?"

"So this was the first time I heard of it. Elle never told me."

"Did you ask her about it?"

"Yes, but she got mad."

"I bet she did, and for good reason."

Doug was taken aback. "Dad?"

"Elle arranged for Rory and a few other plastic surgeons to do some pro bono work for cleft palate patients at the clinic. That's why she and Rory were there."

"What? I can't believe she didn't say anything. We've never kept secrets from each other."

"I don't think this really qualifies as a secret, Doug. Elle was trying to do something to help a community center in need without involving you."

"Why wouldn't she want to involve me? I am the mayor."

"That's the reason why she wouldn't involve you. Listen, I don't have to tell you about the city's finances. She figured if she could do this on her own, it wouldn't be stamped as money diverted to a special interest project while you're handing out severance packages."

"Why didn't she just tell me that?"

"I imagine that after twenty years of marriage, she thought she rated more than a little trust."

Doug buried his face in his hands. "Oh. I'm an idiot and a liar."

"What do you mean?"

"For all my pontificating about her not revealing the clinic project, I didn't tell her I'd called Seth McNeal."

"You called Seth?" His father was genuinely surprised.

"I'm surprised Uncle Rob didn't tell you. He's the one who gave me his number."

"Well I'm not surprised that he didn't tell me. I would have talked him out of it."

"You would have?"

"Yes. Seth's a great guy, but calling him in sends the wrong message about the strength of your relationship with Elle. Don't forget Rory's divorce is at the center of this whole storm. You don't want to send a message that your marriage is becoming a victim of collateral damage."

"I never thought of it that way. I just saw my poll numbers dropping and I wanted to fix it." He rubbed his forehead again. "I'm not just an idiot. I'm a colossal idiot. I let my ambition get the best of me."

"It happens to the best of us, son."

"I bet it never happened to you."

"Doug, did you ever wonder why I didn't run for a third term in Congress?"

"Your approval numbers were low and you didn't think you'd have the support of the party."

"That's not the real reason. Approval numbers are like the tides. They go up and down. I could have easily mounted a campaign to court voters."

"Then why didn't you run?"

"At the time your mother and I were getting into a lot of arguments about how much time I spent away from the family. She felt that politics had taken over my life and that I couldn't attend a birthday party without checking to see how I'd fare in the polls first. Naturally I thought she was overreacting. To me she had campaign fatigue."

"What changed your mind?"

"One night I had everyone from my campaign over for a strategy session. We worked into the wee hours of the morning. Once everyone had gone I was in the study when your brother came in and asked me if I was coming to his soccer game. But before I could answer he said he'd wait until I checked with Mr. Max."

"Mr. Max the pollster?"

"Yes. When I asked him why, he said because you always check with Mr. Max for everything and that he'd wait for *his* answer. That's when it hit me. Your mother was right. I did put my political ambitions ahead of family. I decided then that I was done with politics."

"I thought you wanted me to be senator."

"It would be nice to have another senator in the family, but I can live with just one. I really just want you to be happy. The bottom line is your family is more important, you can't let the media, polls or anything else get in the way."

"Are you saying that's what I'm doing?"

"I'm saying that if someone accused my wife of having an affair and I knew she wasn't, I wouldn't wait for some spin doctor to hand me a statement. Political correctness be damned, I'd be in someone's face."

Doug hung his head. "You think I've really made a mess of things."

"Well, you can still do something about it."

"I just hope it doesn't become a matter of too little, too late."

"When it comes to apologizing it's better late than never, son. Make like Nike and just do it."

"I hope it's that easy, Dad. I think I really stepped in it this time."

Still in a huff, Elle rang the doorbell of Rory and Angela's townhouse. Their houseman, Ken, opened the door.

"Hello, Peter. Is Angela in?"

"Mrs. Brennan?" He was surprised to see her.

"Who is it, Peter?" Angela asked.

"It's me, Angela." Elle pushed past Ken.

Angela went white as a sheet. "I'm not supposed to talk to you."

"Well then you're going to listen."

"I'm going to call my lawyer!"

"Go ahead and call him! I have something to say to you, and I'm going to say it!"

Angela made a move to get the phone when Elle grabbed it out of her hand.

"Give me the phone!" Angela was stunned.

"Not until I'm done!" Elle practically roared. "You're the one who started this." She took a deep breath to try to calm down a little. "When this whole thing started I knew it was your way of trying to keep all the extras that came with the Brennan name. You couldn't just get divorced and risk being ostracized by those cows at the country club, you needed to be the wronged woman so people would feel sorry for you."

"I am the wronged one. My husband is in love with you!"

"What!"

"That's right. Not only have I been the second string daughter-in-law, I was second in my husband's affections. In case you didn't notice his little girlfriend looks like you!" She seethed.

"Wait a minute. You knew that wasn't me in that picture. You lied! "

"You don't know what you're . . ." She tried to recover.

"Shut up! I have the floor."

Angela was stunned into submission.

"God knows I should have done this the minute the first story broke, but I took the high road while you crawled with the slugs. That ends today," she huffed. "You were so consumed with your own agenda that you didn't bother to think what would happen to my children with all of this. That's where I draw the line! You call your lawyer and tell him to get ready for the mother of all slander suits. Do you hear me?" A sharp pain hit Elle. "Oh!" she yelled.

"Elle? Are you all right?" Angela started to come near her.

"Stay over there. Don't you help me." Another stabbing pain came on stronger than the first. "Oh, my God!" Elle dropped the phone and grabbed her stomach.

Just then Rory walked in and saw the scene. "Elle? What's wrong?" When she didn't answer he looked at Angela. "What did you do?"

"I didn't do anything. She just doubled over."

"Call 911!"

Angela picked the phone up off the floor and dialed.

"Oh!" Elle's legs buckled.

"Ken, help me get her to the sofa."

The two men helped her onto the sofa.

Elle began to perspire.

"Ken, get a cold compress."

"Yes, sir." He rushed out.

"The ambulance is on its way." Angela looked nervous.

"Good."

"Is there anything I can do?" she added.

"No." He looked at Elle. "The ambulance is coming." He took her pulse. It was racing.

Elle was breathing heavily. "Call Dr. Aranow," she said weakly.

"Dr. Aranow? Elle, are you pregnant?"

A tear rolled down her face. "Yes."

"Oh, my God." Angela covered her mouth.

Ken returned with several cold compresses. "Here you go, sir."

"Thanks." He patted her forehead. "You just hold on. They'll be here any minute."

The ambulance arrived and Rory stepped out of the way as the EMTs rushed to get Elle's vitals. They put an oxygen mask over her face.

"I'm a doctor. I need to tell you that her pulse seems to be way too fast."

"Okay, we're getting her vitals. What's her name?"

"Elle Brennan."

"The mayor's wife?"

"Yes."

The EMTs looked at each other as the first one took her blood pressure. "It's 145/75. That's high. Does she have high blood pressure? Or any other pre-existing conditions?"

"No, she doesn't have hypertension, but she is pregnant."

"How far along?" the second one asked.

"I'm not sure."

Elle lifted the mask. "I'm eight weeks." She continued to writhe in pain.

"Oh, my God." Angela sunk to the floor.

"Okay. Who's her obstetrician?"

"Dr. Aranow. I'll call him to meet you at the ER."

"Good." The EMT turned to Elle. "Now we're going to lift you onto the gurney."

She nodded. They lifted her up. The first EMT went ahead to get the door where a crowd of reporters had gathered.

"I don't believe these people. How did they get here so quickly?" Rory shook his head.

"They listen in on the radio, or sometimes they have friends in the call centers that will give them a heads-up," the second EMT answered. "Are you following us?" he asked Rory.

"Yes," Rory said.

They rushed Elle out past all the flashing lights into the ambulance and sped. The reporters hurled questions at Rory as he tried to get in his car.

"Back off! It's an emergency. Don't you people have any sense of decency?" He climbed into his car and peeled off. He quickly called Dr. Aranow and then dialed Doug.

Doug was still smarting from his father's words when Ki tapped on the door and walked in. "They're waiting for you."

"What?"

"The press conference to announce Henrietta Johnson-Briggs as the new commissioner of aging. Did you forget?"

"Of course not." He got up. "Let's go." He buttoned his suit and walked out and down the hall. Henrietta and Lillian Edwards, the deputy mayor were waiting for him there. "Hi, Henrietta. Are you ready?"

"Yes, sir."

"Lillian?"

"Yes, sir."

"Okay. Here we go." He walked into the conference room and up to the podium. "Good afternoon everyone. New Yorkers are some of the most dynamic people in the world, so it should be no surprise that the 1.3 million seniors who call New York City home would be just as vital. We are committed to making sure that our senior citizens continue to lead independent lives for all that they've done to support their families and communities."

Ki was off on the side listening to the conference when his phone vibrated. He checked it and saw it was Rory. He stepped outside in the hall. "Hello?"

"Ki? Do you know where Doug is? It's an emergency and he didn't answer his phone."

"He's in the middle of a press conference."

"I really need to speak to him, it's an emergency."

"I just can't stop him in the middle . . ."

"Elle's just been rushed to Columbia Presbyterian by ambulance."

"Oh, my God," he gasped. "I'll get him. Just hold on."

"I'm almost at the hospital. Please hurry."

"I will." Ki stepped back into the room and walked over to Doug, who was still speaking.

"As someone with a great deal of experience in the private and nonprofit sector, Henrietta Johnson-Briggs is a wonderful addition to our team . . ."

Doug was taken off balance when Ki tapped him on the shoulder. "Ki?" He turned to the audience. "You all know my chief of staff, Ki."

Ki waved and put his hand over the mike. "I need to speak to you. It's an emergency."

"What?"

"I'm not kidding. Lillian will have to make the announcement."

Doug paused for a moment. "Umm, it seems something has come up. Lillian, if you would please continue."

Lillian was discombobulated, but she took the mike. "Certainly."

"I'm sorry, Henrietta."

Ki quickly escorted him out into the hall.

"What's the emergency?"

"Elle's been rushed to the hospital. I have Rory on the phone." He handed it to him.

"Rory? What hospital?"

"I followed the ambulance to the ER at Columbia Presbyterian."

Doug's face drained. "She was rushed by ambulance? Oh, my God. I'll be right there."

"Doug!"

He'd already hung up and made another call to his driver. "William?"

"Yes, sir."

"Start the car. I need to get to Columbia Presbyterian right away."

"Yes, sir."

"I need to get my coat."

"Forget about it. I'll run and get it." Ki took off down the hall.

Oh, my God. What's happened to my girl? Dear God, don't let anything happen to her before I get the chance to apologize for being such an ass.

Doug quickly went down the stairs, through the security area and to the car. Just as he got in, Ki was on his heels.

"Here." Ki handed him his coat. "Give Elle our love." He shut the door.

CHAPTER 16

Rory paced in the waiting area. They'd taken Elle in right away and he hadn't heard a word. Some reporters were positioned outside, but they were kept at bay by security.

Rory jumped to his feet when Dr. Aranow finally walked out. "Is she okay?"

"She's fine."

"What about the baby?"

"Rory, you're a doctor. You know I can't tell you."

"I know." Rory's heart sank. "Can I see her?"

"Sure. She's resting."

"Okay." Rory walked down to the room. He stopped to get composed before he entered. "Elle?"

She was curled up in the fetal position staring at the wall.

"I'm so sorry." He rubbed her shoulder.

"Thanks," she said weakly.

Things were silent for a moment. "I bet you're wondering why I went to your house."

"It has crossed my mind."

"Kyle got into a fight with Morgan Whitmore's son because he was giving him a hard time about all the crap that's been in the papers this week."

"Oh, no," Rory said.

"It was the straw that broke this camel's back. It was time to give the root cause of all this nonsense a piece of my mind."

"Oh, Elle," he groaned.

"I had to do it, Rory. It's one thing to go after me. I won't allow anyone to get away with hurting my children . . ." Her voice caught.

"I'm so sorry, Elle. I really wish there was something I could say or do."

Elle took a deep breath. "You can do something for me."

"Anything.."

"Help me get out of here and back to my sons."

Rory was hesitant. "I don't think Dr. Aranow wants you to leave just yet. You should get some rest." She turned to face him, eyes bleary from crying. "I want to get home so I can take care of my children. I'll sign whatever."

"Doug's on his way. Don't you want to wait for him?"

"What for?"

"To tell him what happened and the two of you can work through it together."

"I don't want to see Doug right now."

"What?" Before he could say another word Dr. Aranow walked in. "How are you feeling, Elle?"

"I'm fine. I just really want to get out of here. Just give me the release papers. I'll sign them and be on my way."

"Elle, I really don't think you should go home just yet."

"Why? I want to go home. You can't do anything for me. Just have someone take this IV out and I'll be on my way . . ."

It was obvious she wasn't going to budge.

"Fine." He looked over her chart. "I want it to be noted that you're doing this against medical advice."

"Duly noted," Elle answered quickly.

"Then I'll get your release papers."

"Thank you."

Dr. Aranow walked out.

She looked at Rory. "You're a doctor, take this out." She pointed to the IV.

"I really shouldn't."

"If you don't, I'll rip it out."

Rory had never seen Elle like this. It looked like the light she had in her eyes had gone dark. "Fine." He went over to the cabinet and got some alcohol swabs, gauze, tape and gloves. "I'm not supposed to do this," he said as he put the gloves on.

"You have medical privileges here."

He gently took the IV out and bandaged her arm.

"Thank you." She grabbed clothes from the bag underneath the bed and closed the curtain to get dressed.

"I'm here if you want to talk." He stepped away.

"Thanks, but I'm done talking for now." She pulled the curtains closed, tossed the hospital gown on the bed and quickly got dressed.

She just pulled the curtains back when Dr. Aranow came back with her papers. "I see you already have the IV out."

"I didn't want to waste any time. Where do I sign?"

He handed her the clipboard. "Right here," he pointed.

Elle stopped as she was about to sign. "Rory, would you excuse us for a minute? I need to speak to Dr. Aranow."

"Sure." He stepped into the hallway.

Just then Melissa ran up to him. "Rory, what's going on?" she asked breathlessly. "A nurse called and told me Elle wanted me to meet her here."

"Rory, you can come back in," Dr. Aranow said.

"I guess you can ask her yourself now."

Rory and Melissa walked in. Elle was seated on the edge of the bed. "Melissa, I need you to take me home."

"Okay. Oh, God, Elle . . ."

Her eyes welled up. "I can't right now. I really can't. That's why I asked the nurse to call you. I don't want to cry here anymore. Please."

"Sure." Melissa put her arms around her. Elle leaned on her for support as they left the room and went down the hall.

Rory watched until they disappeared from sight.

"Is Doug going to meet her at home?" Dr. Aranow asked.

"He's already on his way here."

"Do you want to let him know what's going on, or do you want me to tell him?"

"I'll talk to him. There are some things he needs to hear from me first."

After getting caught behind a car accident on his way over, Doug finally got to the ER. He rushed down the hall, stopping when he saw Rory.

"Where is she?"

"She's not here."

"What?"

"Come on, we need to talk." He led Doug to an empty room.

"Okay, Rory, you called me because Elle was rushed here and now you tell me that's she's not here. What's going on?"

"Sit down and I'll tell you."

"I don't want to . . ."

"Sit down, Doug," he said sternly.

A little stunned by his brother's forcefulness, he complied.

He took a deep breath. "Elle and Angela got into it this afternoon."

"What?" Doug was completely thrown. "Where did this happen?"

"At my townhouse."

"What? Why would Elle go there? I told her to stay away from Angela."

Rory got a little heated. "For God's sake, can you stop being a politician and be a husband and father? Kyle got into a fight at school over this crap that's been in the papers. Elle decided enough was enough."

"Kyle was in a fight? I would never think of him getting physical," he said in disbelief. "What happened?"

"I wasn't there at the time, but needless to say she let Angela have it with both barrels."

"Were any punches thrown?"

"No. When I got there they were still going at it, and then Elle suddenly doubled over in pain." He swallowed hard before he spoke again. "That's when she told me she was eight weeks pregnant."

Doug's mouth was agape. "She's pregnant?" Doug's joy was quickly tempered by the realization they were in the hospital and he jumped to his feet. "Where is she? Is she okay? What about the baby?"

"Elle's okay."

"And the baby?"

"I don't know."

"What do you mean you don't know? You're a doctor and you're family."

"Yes, but I'm not Elle's doctor, and I'm only the brother-in-law."

Doug flopped back down in the chair and put his hands over his face. "I wasn't here. I should have been here."

Rory patted him on the back. "You can't blame yourself for not being here. You came as quickly as you could."

"No. I mean ever since I got fixated on being senator I haven't been there for Elle or the kids like I should have been. I should have confronted this head on in the media instead of trying the finesse the situation behind the scenes."

Rory nodded.

"I see you're not going to disagree with me."

"No. You have been a jackass."

"Don't sugarcoat it for me," he said facetiously.

"Ever since this whole thing broke you've been a politician on a mission instead of a husband. This was the one time where taking the supposed high road wasn't a good idea. The less you said, the worse it got."

"Don't you think I wanted to say something? But if I did I would have to . . ." He stopped short.

"You would have to what?"

"Admit that my younger brother is in love with my wife."

Rory looked down at the floor. "I wish I could say I didn't know what you're talking about." He took a deep breath. "How long have you known?"

"Since the first time I introduced her to the family."

Rory was a little dumbfounded. "Wow." He took a deep breath. "You know when we were growing up a lot of people used to ask me if I was ever envious of you and all your success."

"Please," Doug scoffed.

"You were the all-round guy, Doug. You were a top athlete, smart, politically astute, and the girls loved you. Hell you were voted the sexiest man alive." He smiled. "But I didn't begrudge you anything. I was happy for you. Then you brought Elle home, and for the first time in my life, I wished I were you."

"Rory, you don't have to say anything else."

"Yes I do. I may have wished I were you, but I'd never think of doing anything."

"I know."

"I tried to find a woman who was like Elle, but there's no one like her so I married Angela." He shrugged. "This whole thing is really my fault. I should have been honest with Angela from the beginning, and then maybe none of this would have happened."

"It's too late for recriminations now."

"I know you're right." He paused. "You do know that wasn't Elle in that newspaper photo, right?"

"Of course I do," Doug said and rubbed his head. "I was an idiot about the clinic, too."

"So Elle told you about the children's clinic."

"No. Dad told me after I practically accused her of hiding something from me."

"Elle wasn't hiding anything from you. She told me she'd tell you once we had everything in place. She figured she'd do it privately since you had to contend with city budget issues. It would be one less thing on your plate."

"After the way I've behaved, God knows I don't deserve her."

"At this moment I'd have to agree with you, but that's not to say you can't change that."

Doug shook his head. "I should have listened to you when you wanted to address this head-on. Then this wouldn't be an issue and Elle wouldn't have wound up here," he said as he looked around the hospital. "I was so concerned with this damn Senate appointment she couldn't tell me she was pregnant, and now I'm too late."

"It's not too late. You love each other . . ." He stopped when he saw Angela arrive with a bouquet of flowers.

"I know I'm probably the last person you want to see, but I wanted to see if Elle was all right."

Doug jumped to his feet. "Now you're concerned with Elle's well-being? You have some nerve coming here." Just as he lurched forward, Rory stopped him.

"Calm down, Doug. You have to concentrate on Elle and the kids now."

"I'm really sorry, Doug. I didn't mean for this to happen," Angela said sheepishly.

"You didn't mean for this to happen? You're the one who caused this whole mess to begin in the first place."

"I brought flowers. I didn't know what else to do."

"You're nuts if you think flowers are going to help." Doug seethed.

"Listen, Doug, you need to go home to Elle. This is my mess and I'll handle it. I have a few things I'd like to say to Angela."

"You're right. I'll talk to you later."

"All right."

As Doug walked by Angela she tried to give him the bouquet. "You're kidding me right?"

"Put the flowers down, Angela, before someone tells you what you can do with them and gives you an assist to do it," Rory said sternly.

"Thanks, Rory. We'll talk later."

"Good luck."

Doug ran down the hallway as quickly as he could. Not even the crush of reporters that had gathered outside the emergency room could keep him from getting to his

SUV. His driver barely had time to open the door before Doug hopped in.

"Where to, Mayor Brennan?" he asked.

"Home."

I only hope it's not too late to apologize to Elle. He sighed heavily. *Pregnant. Elle was pregnant and I wasn't there for her. God, please let her forgive me.*

CHAPTER 17

It was a quiet ride back home. Once they arrived Melissa helped Elle into the house through the back. As they made their way through the hall they could hear Kevin and Kyle in the kitchen with Frieda. Elle stopped to compose herself.

"Are my eyes really red?"

Melissa looked at her. "They're definitely red."

"I don't want to upset the kids. Maybe I should put my sunglasses on."

"That will only make it more noticeable, Elle."

"You're right. I just have to take my chances."

Kyle met them in the hallway. "Mom?"

"Yes, Kyle?" She tried to sound normal.

He rushed over to hug her. "What happened? On the news they said you went to the hospital."

"I didn't feel well, but I saw the doctor and I'm fine now."

"Are you sure?" He didn't seem convinced.

"Yes."

"Mom?" Kevin rushed over to hug her. "Are you okay, Mom?"

Elle squeezed her boys tightly. They were just the medicine she needed. "I'm fine, but I need you to do me a favor."

"Sure, Mom," Kyle answered.

"I need you to go upstairs and pack a few things in your weekend bags. We're going to Martha's Vineyard this weekend."

"We're going to Martha's Vineyard," Kyle echoed.

"Yes. It's just for the weekend. We'll be back on Sunday."

"What about Dad?" Kevin asked.

"He'll be here. Now why don't you two scoot and get your stuff."

They were initially hesitant. "Are you sure, Mom?" Kevin asked.

"Yes."

"Okay, Mom," they answered simultaneously before they slowly went upstairs.

"They know something's going on. They're not . . ." Melissa stopped.

"Were you going to say babies?"

"Listen, Elle, I'm . . ."

She interrupted her. "You don't have to apologize." She went to the kitchen. "Frieda?"

"Yes, Mrs. Brennan?"

"I need you to call Ed to bring the car around for me. Also if you'd please remember to ask him to pick up my car. It's at Rory's townhouse."

"I will. Are you sure you're all right, Mrs. Brennan?"

"Of course I'm sure."

"Very well. Would you like me to tell Mr. Brennan anything?"

"I'm going to leave him a note."

"As you wish." She nodded.

Elle and Melissa then made their way upstairs to her bedroom. Melissa sat on the bed as Elle took out a small suitcase and began tossing things into it.

"Elle, what's the hurry? I really think you should slow down."

She looked over at the clock. "I'd like to make it to the airport sooner rather than later."

"You're flying out this evening?"

"Yes."

"Why Martha's Vineyard? It's warm in California."

"No." Elle shook her head. "I'm partial to seasons. Besides, the time difference makes me feel like I'm in the movie *Groundhog Day*." She opened her dresser drawer, saw the sonogram and broke down.

Melissa rushed to her side to comfort her. "Oh, honey," she said as she hugged her.

"I have to pull it together." She sniffled. "I'm going to splash my face with cold water." She took the phone with her.

"Okay."

Elle went into the bathroom.

Kyle gently knocked on the door. "Mom?"

"Come on in," Melissa answered.

He gingerly entered the bedroom. "Where's Mom?"

"She's in the bathroom, honey."

"Is my mother okay, Aunt Melissa? She doesn't seem like herself."

"She's having a little bit of a rough time, but I'm sure she'll talk to you about it."

"No, she won't. She thinks we're babies."

"Then maybe you should tell her that she can talk to you."

Elle dabbed her face with a towel as she walked out. "Did you pack your sweaters? Technically it's still fall, but you know how the weather is up there."

"We've got them."

"Good." She threw her toiletries in the suitcase. "I guess we're ready to go."

"Aren't you going to wait for Dad?"

"Don't worry. I'm going to let him know where we're going."

Melissa got up. "Why don't you take your mom's bag downstairs?"

Kyle picked up her bag.

"Thank you, sweetie, I'll see you downstairs in a minute." Elle sat on the bed.

Melissa waited for him to leave the room. "I'm going downstairs, too. Why don't you give Doug a call instead of writing him a note? Just a suggestion," she quickly added.

Elle stared at her phone for a minute before she dialed. She was relieved when she heard his voicemail was full. *Thank goodness. I don't think I had the strength to talk to him.* "His mailbox is full. I'll leave him a note." She got a piece of her stationary, wrote the note and put it in an envelope. *God knows I love him so much, but I can't face him, at least not now. I have to get back to where it all started. Hopefully I'll feel that connection again. I need to feel connected.*

"Are you happy now?"

"Not really, but I'll take it."

Melissa followed Elle downstairs where the children were waiting. Her driver Ed had brought the car around back and took the luggage to load the trunk.

"Are you sure you want to do this now? There can't be many flights going to Martha's Vineyard this time of year. Why don't you sleep on it and wait until tomorrow?"

"I already called Fleet Aviation for a private flight. We'll be there in less than an hour."

"Oh, okay."

Elle kissed Melissa on the cheek. "It's sweet that you're worried about me, but I'm fine. This is what I need to do."

"If you say so." She paused. "You know you can call me anytime."

"I know, and I appreciate that." She looked down at the envelope in her hand. "Frieda?"

"Yes?"

She handed her the envelope. "Would you please give this to Mr. Brennan?"

"I will." She tucked it in her apron pocket.

"Thank you."

Ed walked up. "The car is loaded, Mrs. Brennan."

"Thank you, Ed." She turned to Melissa. "Walk us to the car?"

"Sure."

Melissa watched and waved as Elle and the kids got in and drove away. Elle took a deep breath as the house faded in the distance.

"Mom, are you sure you're okay?" Kyle was worried.

Elle rubbed both his and Kevin's hands. "As long as I have you two, I'm more than okay."

Despite her best performance Elle knew her sons didn't quite buy it, but she was grateful they let her keep the charade going.

The car had barely pulled up to the house before Doug leaped out and rushed inside.

"Elle!" he called from the bottom of the stairs. "Baby, are you here?"

Frieda walked into the hallway. "Mr. Brennan, she's not here."

"What? Where is she?"

Frieda took the envelope from her pocket. "She left you this note." She handed it to him.

He stared at it for a moment. "She didn't tell you where she was going?"

"All I know is that she packed a couple of bags and left with the children. She asked me to give you the note. I'm sorry, but that's all I know."

"Okay, Frieda. I understand."

She disappeared back into the kitchen.

Doug lightly ran his fingers over the letter before he opened it. *Please don't let it be a Dear John letter.* He took a deep breath and began reading.

Dear Doug,

The last few weeks I've had a lot to deal with, and now I need some time to think and clear my head. I won't be gone long. The kids have school on Monday. We can talk when I get back. Right now I need some distance. Please respect my wishes. I do love you. Elle.

"Oh, God," he groaned aloud.

Just then the doorbell rang.

"I'll get it," Frieda said.

"Thanks. I'll be in the living room."

Doug went straight to the bar and poured himself a drink.

Ki walked in with flowers. "Hey, how's Elle doing?"

"Your guess is as good as mine." He gulped down his Scotch. "She's not here."

"She's not here?"

"What are you, a mynah bird? That's what I said."

"I know you're upset, but that's no reason to take it out on me." Ki put the flowers down.

"I'm sorry. I'm upset. Elle was pregnant."

"She was pregnant?" Ki was floored. "You didn't know?"

"No. She hadn't told me yet."

"You said she was pregnant. Did she lose the baby?"

"They brought her to the ER because she doubled over in pain at Rory's house."

"At Rory's house? So Angela was there."

"Yes."

"I don't want to know what went on there. What did her doctor say?"

"I didn't see her doctor. By the time I got there she'd already left the hospital." He hung his head. "I hate to think of her going through this alone, but I don't know where she is. All I have is this note." He showed Ki the envelope.

"I'm really sorry, buddy." Ki patted him on the back. "Wait a minute. You can find out where she's gone. I know who you should ask."

Long, lanky and lean with wavy red hair, Myles answered the door. He was still dressed for work, although his tie was a little askew.

"Doug! I mean, Mayor Brennan. How are you?"

"I'm good, Myles. May I come in?"

"Oh, sure." He stepped back to let Doug in and then closed the door. "This is a rare treat. What brings you by?" he asked as they walked towards the den.

"I wondered if Melissa was home."

"Sure. She's in the kitchen with Jason. Do you want me to get her?"

"No that's okay. I'll go to the kitchen."

"Okay. Follow me."

Myles led him to the kitchen, where Jason and Melissa were putting the finishing touches on a science project.

"Look who's here, Melissa."

"Doug."

"Hi, Uncle Doug. Are Kevin and Kyle with you?"

"I'm afraid not."

"Oh."

"Listen, buddy, why don't we leave Uncle Doug to talk to Mom. I'll help you finish your report."

"Okay, Dad. See you later, Uncle Doug."

"You bet."

Melissa began to clean the counter. "I bet I know why you're here."

"And I'm hoping you'll help me. Where's Elle?"

"I don't think she wants to see you right now."

"You know she didn't even call me."

"She tried to call you, but your voicemail was full."

He looked down at his phone. "That explains why she left a note. Melissa, I need to be with her. I love her so much."

"I don't know, Doug . . ." she began.

"She's my life, Melissa. I just want my family. I'll do anything to make it up to her."

Melissa sat down at the kitchen table. "You're not making this easy."

"She was pregnant with my baby, too."

Melissa thought for a moment. "She's going to kill me. She went to Martha's Vineyard."

"Martha's Vineyard. Thank you. Do you know who she flew with?"

"I think it was Fleet Aviation."

Doug jumped to his feet and kissed her on the cheek. "Thanks, Melissa."

He raced past Jason and Myles. "Sorry to run. See you soon." He flew out the door.

Melissa walked into the living room.

"What was that about?" Myles asked.

"He's a man on a mission. I just hope for his sake it's not mission impossible."

In December Martha's Vineyard resembles a ghost town. The year-round residents are buckling down for the long winter ahead and getting recharged for the spring when tourism begins to bloom again. It was dark when Elle and the boys drove through on their way to the compound. Elle stared out the window, lost in thought as Kevin and Kyle chatted away.

Through the darkness she could see Aquila House as they drew closer. The compound was an exquisite eighteenth-century property with modern additions and comforts. It was set in three park-like acres with a very private waterfront. There were eight bedrooms between the main house and carriage house, all with private baths, which served the Brennan clan well as their numbers grew. It had all the old world amenities with its formal living and dining room, several parlors and sitting rooms, as well as a media room and office. It was the best of both worlds as it was near the village yet far away enough to remain secluded.

As they got closer they were met by Henry and Bertha Minton, a hearty New England couple and the compound's longtime caretakers. Despite their somewhat hardened appearance they were the most down-to-earth and caring people Elle had ever met.

Henry opened the car door. "Evening, Mrs. Brennan. Let me help you out of the car," he said with his unmistakable New England accent.

"Thank you, Henry." She stepped out of the car.

"You're welcome. And how are you young fellas?"

"Fine, Mr. Minton." Kyle grinned.

"I'm good. How are you?"

"I can't complain."

"Let's get you inside, it gets a might bit more cold up here than you're used to in New York," Bertha added.

When they stepped inside, there was a fire in the fireplace and the aroma of Bertha's lobster chowder in the air.

"Mmm, is that what I think it is?" Elle asked.

"Indeed. I just finished making a big pot of chowder in case anyone was interested."

Elle looked at Kevin and Kyle. "I know this is a silly question, but are you interested?"

"Oh, yeah," they said in unison.

"We even rustled up some of the oyster crackers you like so much." Henry smiled.

"What about you, Mrs. Brennan? Are you hungry?"

Elle patted her stomach. "I'll take a small bowl a little later. I'd really like to lie down first."

"You go ahead. I'll bring you a bowl."

"Thanks."

"Let me get these things to their bedrooms and then I'll help you in the kitchen."

"Thanks, Henry. Come with me, boys."

Kevin and Kyle happily followed her down the hall while Elle headed for the master bedroom.

Henry opened the door and let Elle go in first. "Here you go, Mrs. Brennan." He put her bag down. "Would you like Bertha to unpack for you?"

"No, that's okay. We're only staying a few days."

"Is Mr. Brennan joining you?"

"No. It's just me and the boys this weekend."

"All right. I leave you to it."

"Thanks, Henry."

Once Henry closed the door Elle took a long look at the master bedroom with its king-sized four-poster bed. *When Doug first brought me here I thought this was the biggest bed I'd ever seen,* she thought as she lay down.

There was a knock. "Mrs. Brennan?"

"Come on in, Bertha." She sat up.

Bertha came in carrying a tray of soup. "Here you go." She put the tray next to her on the bed.

Elle took a whiff. "It smells heavenly."

"Thank you. I'll leave you be to enjoy it." She exited the room.

Elle savored a few spoonfuls of the smooth, creamy broth. *Mmm, I wish I could bottle this feeling.* Her cell phone rang. *I bet that's Doug.* She checked the number. It was her mother.

"Hello?"

"Elle? Are you all right? They're reporting on the news that you were rushed to the hospital earlier."

"I'm fine, Mom."

"Are you sure, honey?"

"Dad?"

"Yes."

"Are you in the same room or is this a conference call?"

"It's a conference call," her mother answered dryly. "Now this is not about us, we want to know what's happening. Did you go to the hospital, or is this another suspect report?"

"I was in the hospital for stomach pain."

"What? Do you have an ulcer? Was it food poisoning? Do you have a stomach virus?"

"Lynette, give her a chance to answer you before you throw the whole kitchen sink."

"Fine. What was it?"

"I had stomach cramps."

"You had stomach cramps so awful you landed in the ER? It must have been food poisoning. Or maybe it was stress."

"What did the doctor say, Elle?"

"He said it was just one of those things, and I'd be okay after I got some rest."

"One of what things?"

"Lynette, maybe she doesn't want to talk about it now. She sounds tired."

"I am tired."

"She needs to get away from all that nonsense with Angela and Rory's divorce."

"I did get away, Mom. I'm at the house in Martha's Vineyard."

"This time of year?"

"Yes, Mom. It's quiet up here. I brought the boys with me."

"How long are you staying?"

"We'll only be here until Sunday, Dad."

"Where's Doug?"

"He's still got a city to run, Mom."

"If you ask me he needs to be tending to you."

"She didn't ask you, Lynette. Didn't she just say the doctor said she should get some rest? So let's not get into that."

"Fine."

"Thank you." Elle yawned.

"You sound sleepy. You should get to bed early."

"Now that sounds like a good idea, Victor. You can give us a call once you feel up to it."

"I will."

"You know I love you, sweetie."

"I love you, too, Dad and Mom."

"You take care," her mother added.

"I promise. Good night." Elle was never one for lying to her parents, but she didn't want to tell them about the pregnancy. It was too soon to deal with all the questions.

Elle stared at her phone for a moment. *I should call and let Doug know that we're safe.* She dialed the house phone. It rang a few times then went to voicemail. "Doug, I just wanted to let you know that the kids and I are all right. I'll see you Sunday." *If I know Doug he's probably wheedled my location out of Melissa by now.* She yawned. *I really am tired.* She turned her cell phone off.

Elle finished her soup and lay back on the bed. She needed time to wrap her mind around the changes that had taken place in her life and to see if she was really ready for the changes she faced ahead. Before long she'd drifted off.

Frustrated with getting Elle's cell phone voicemail, Doug tossed his cell phone on the desk.

"Damn!" He looked at the blinking light on the house phone. "Someone called? I didn't hear the phone." He picked up the phone to see the ringer was turned off. "No wonder," he grunted as he turned the ringer back on. He checked the caller ID until he came to Elle's cell phone number. *She called and I missed it.* In a flash he dialed in and blew past the other messages until he came to Elle's.

"Doug, I just wanted to let you know that the kids and I are all right. I'll see you Sunday."

You can't leave a message like that. I have to talk to you. He quickly dialed.

"Good evening, Brennan residence. Bertha here."

"Hello, Bertha, it's Doug."

"Hello, Mr. Brennan, how are you?"

"I'm fine, thanks. How've you been?"

"Not bad at all. What can I do for you, sir?"

"Has my wife arrived yet?"

"Yes, sir. She and the children got in a few hours ago."

"Good. Where are the boys? I don't hear them."

"Oh, they're in the workshop with Henry."

"That figures. Would you mind putting my wife on the phone?"

"Sure. If you'll hold on for a minute, I'll get her for you."

"Thanks." He waited.

"It seems she's asleep, Mr. Brennan. If it's important I can wake her."

"No, don't wake her. She probably needs the sleep."

"I'll tell her you called."

"Thanks, Bertha. Tell Henry I said hello."

"I will. Bye now."

"Bye." He looked over at the clock. *It's ten o'clock. Ki should be up.* He pressed the receiver down and made another call.

"Hello?" Ki answered.

"Ki?"

"Hey, Doug, I've been waiting to hear from you. Did Melissa tell you where Elle is?"

"Yes. She's at the Martha's Vineyard compound."

"At least you know she and the kids are safe."

"Yeah. Listen, I'm calling for another reason. I need you to set up a press conference around three tomorrow. Can you do that?"

"Sure I can do it, but you have your weekly address tomorrow at ten."

"See if the deputy mayor can handle it. I need you to free up my schedule for the day."

"Consider it done."

"I was expecting you to give me a hard time about my priorities."

"No. Family is a priority, and no one understands that better than me."

"Thanks, and while you're at it, see if you can get some face time with the governor for me before three. I know he's in town."

"Okay." He paused. "Have you spoken with Elle?"

"No. She was asleep when I called. Considering all she's been through she's needs the rest. I'll see her in person Saturday morning."

"So you're flying up?"

"Yes. When I hang up with you I'm calling Fleet Aviation to charter a plane."

"You're going to charter a plane? What about your family's jets?" Ki asked.

"Most of them are in use, and I don't want to waste any more time."

"I hear you. You do know it's after ten. Aren't their offices closed now?"

"Yes. I'm going to call Bud Johnson at home."

"You're going to call the CEO. Talk about going to the head of the line."

"My thoughts exactly. I'm going to let you get back to your family. Give me a call when you have something from Jim's office."

"Will do. You try to get some rest."

"I'll get some rest eventually. Good night, buddy."

"Good night."

It only took Doug a few minutes to make arrangements for the earliest flight possible on Saturday morning. Once he was done he was about to turn on his computer when he stopped and took out a notebook and pen. *Elle's right, some things are better when you put pen to paper.*

CHAPTER 18

When Rory walked into Doug and Elle's home the next morning, he found his brother asleep at his desk.

He turned to Frieda. "Has he been here all night?"

"Yes."

Rory shook his head. "I guess I'd better wake him up."

"I'll get him some coffee. Would you like a cup?"

"Yes, thank you."

"Okay. I'll be back in a flash." Frieda closed the door as she left.

Rory walked up to the desk. "I can't believe he slept in his clothes," he muttered. "Doug?" He tapped his shoulder. "Doug? Wake up."

Jarred, Doug suddenly sat straight up. "Yes. I'm up."

Rory laughed when he saw a sheet of paper was stuck to his cheek. "You must have had some night." He pointed to the paper on his face.

"Oh." Doug pulled it off. "Do I have any ink on my face?"

"No, you're good." He looked around. "Why did you sleep in here?"

He looked down at his notebook. "I had some work to do."

"Where's Elle? Is she upstairs?"

"No. She and the kids are in Martha's Vineyard."

Rory was taken aback. "She went where?"

"You heard me."

"Have you gotten through to Dr. Aranow?"

"I called his service a few times last night. It seems he had four patients in labor."

"Well, that is the life of an obstetrician. Elle's a smart girl. She must have cleared it with him beforehand."

"Her note said she had to clear her mind."

"Then she needed the change of scenery."

Doug stretched. "So how did you get in here? I'm sure reporters are covering both the front and back entrance by now."

"There's no one out there today. I just walked up to the front door."

"Really?"

"See for yourself."

Doug got up and looked outside. Everything was clear. "Well I'll be damned."

Just then Frieda came in with the coffee service. "Here you go Mr. Brennan and Mr. Brennan."

"Thanks, Frieda." Doug smiled.

"Would you like something for breakfast?"

He looked at the clock. "Do we still have muffins?"

"Yes."

"You want one, Rory?"

"Sure."

"We'll grab a couple on the way out."

"Very good." She left the room again.

Doug went over to fix his coffee. "So what else brings you over this early?"

"I thought I would serve up a little good news."

"I could use that." He took a sip.

Rory handed him a paper. "Read this."

Divorce settlement reached between Rory and Angela Brennan.

In a move that shocked onlookers Angela Brennan's divorce attorney, Jasper Lyons, announced that his client and her estranged husband, Rory Brennan, have reached an agreement in their much-publicized divorce battle. The terms of the settlement are private. When asked for comment Angela Brennan would only say that now both parties were free to move on with their lives and that's she sorry for any pain she may have caused the Brennan family, particularly the mayor's wife, Mirielle Brennan. Sources say the move came after the mayor's wife was rushed to the hospital from Angela's Fifth Avenue townhouse.

"Am I reading this right?" Doug was dumbfounded.

"Yes, you are. And not only is it in *The Post,* it's in every daily in New York. Heck, it even made the local television news."

"How in the world did Wendy get her to back off?"

"It wasn't Wendy. After you left yesterday, I let Angela have it, and so did the papers. There was no way to spin it to make her look good. Jasper Lyons might be able to spin thread into gold, but even he couldn't work with manure."

"That explains the lack of media outside. I'm impressed, little brother."

"I thought it was the least I could do for you, the kids and Elle. Enough is enough already."

The two embraced. "I appreciate it."

Just as Rory was about to speak the phone rang.

"Hold that thought." Doug picked up the phone. "Hello?"

"Can you meet the governor after breakfast?" Ki asked.

"Sure." Doug looked at the clock. "What time?"

"Ten o'clock."

"Yes. Is he staying at The Plaza?"

"Yes."

"Okay. Thanks, Ki."

"You're welcome. Oh, by the way, the press conference is set. You know the reporters are itching for a crumb to go on."

"I'm sure they are. They'll have to wait until three. Listen, I've got to jet if I'm going to make it there on time."

"See you later."

Doug hung up.

"What was that about?" Rory asked.

"I have a meeting with the governor this morning. I'll fill you in on the details later. Okay?"

"Okay."

Doug went to the door and stopped. "By the way if I didn't say it before, thanks."

"You're welcome." Rory nodded and then reached into his pocket. "Wait a second. You're going to see Elle, right?"

"First thing Saturday morning."

Rory handed him a CD. "Give this to Elle. I burned the best of Beck for her. Tell her it's got tracks from *Mellow Gold* and *Odelay.* "

"Thanks." Doug smiled and shook his head. "I've yet to figure out her fascination with out-there music."

"Why don't you just ask her?"

"You know, I think I will." He looked at his watch. "I've got to fly." Doug rushed upstairs. He got undressed and grabbed his robe, but as he headed to the bathroom he caught sight of something on Elle's dresser. When his eyes focused, he realized it was her sonogram. He was so overcome with emotion he just sat on the bed for a while thinking of what might have been.

When Elle awoke she was greeted with the sight of seagulls flying over the water in the distance. She smiled and looked over at the clock. *It's almost nine o'clock. I never sleep this late.*

Suddenly Kevin and Kyle burst through the door and onto the bed.

"Good morning, Mom," Kevin lay next to her and kissed her right cheek.

"Good morning, Mom." Kyle lay down and kissed her left cheek.

"My goodness, what's this all about? You two haven't jumped into bed with me in ages."

"Nothing, we just wanted to say good morning and see how you were." Kevin smiled.

Elle saw Doug in his face. "That's sweet of you." She wrapped her arms around them. "You know you're still my babies."

"Yes, Mom, we know," Kyle said.

Elle took a whiff. "Is that blueberry pancakes and bacon I smell?"

"Yes. Mrs. Minton is making breakfast." Kevin grinned. "Do you want us to bring you a tray, Mom?"

"No thanks, sweetie. I'll have breakfast with you in the kitchen."

"Do you want us to wait for you?"

"No, you go ahead, Kevin. I'll be there in a minute."

"Okay, Mom."

They made a beeline for the door. Kevin kept going while Kyle stopped. "Do you want me to close the door?"

"Yes. Thank you."

Elle waited a moment before she picked up her cell phone. *Four missed calls from Doug.* Slowly she got out of bed and then put her robe and slippers on. She looked down at her phone. *I'll call him later. I don't think I have the strength for that conversation, at least not right now,* she thought as she walked out to join her sons at breakfast.

When Doug arrived at the governor's room his aide, Michael, led him to the living room area of the Edwardian suite where Governor Pearson and a few staff members were finishing up breakfast.

"Doug!" Governor Pearson waved him over. "Why don't you pull up a chair? Would like something? Maybe a pastry and some coffee? Or we can order breakfast for you."

Doug sat down. "Coffee sounds good to me, thanks."

"All right." The governor poured him a cup.

"Thanks." Doug added two sugar packets of sugar and stirred.

"Okay everyone, I think that's it for now." He checked his wristwatch. "You can meet me back here in about a half hour or forty-five minutes."

Doug waited until everyone left.

"Before we get into anything else. How's Elle doing?"

"She's as well as can be expected. She's resting at our house on the Vineyard."

"Please give her my best."

"I will."

"So I'm intrigued. Why did you want a meeting with me this morning?"

Doug got right to the point. "I'm withdrawing from consideration for the Senate appointment. I'm planning to make an official announcement later today, but I wanted to tell you in person."

"I see. This doesn't have anything to do with the phone conversation we had a few days back, does it?"

"No. This has to do with getting my priorities straight. I've dedicated my life to serving the citizens of New York City, and, while it would be a privilege to represent the state, it's time I dedicate my life and my time to my family."

"On one hand, I hate to see you drop out because I think you have a lot to offer. However, I understand where you're coming from. Sometimes you have to do what's best for your family."

"And what's best for them is good for me." He stood up. "I know you've got a lot to do today, so I don't want to keep you."

Governor Pearson rose and the two shook hands. "Thanks for coming by, Doug."

"I know it sounds cliché, but it was an honor that you considered me."

"I know you're getting out of politics, but I hope you'll come out to support me for my own bid for governor."

"I'll be there." Doug smiled as he left the room.

Once he was in the hallway, he took a deep breath. *Just one more stop before the press conference.*

Perched in a chair on the beach, Elle watched as Henry, Kevin and Kyle dug for clams.

"I thought it was too cold to look for clams," she called out.

"No. I don't follow the seasons, Mrs. Brennan. I know these beaches like the back of my hand. There's a good shellfish flat here and the tide is low."

"Look, Mom!" Kevin held a clam up.

"Well, I'll be darned."

"Looks like we're having clam chowder tonight boys," Henry proclaimed.

They continued to fill the basket with more clams.

Elle felt her phone vibrate. She checked the number and picked up. "Hi, Melissa."

"Elle, how are you? I've been so worried."

"I'm fine. In fact I'm on the beach watching the boys digging for clams. They're having a great time."

"That's good to hear. What about you? Shouldn't you be in bed?"

"Right now I need to be near my kids. Now please, I don't want to talk about it. Okay?"

"Okay. Have you heard from Doug?"

"He called. I know you probably told him where I was by now."

"He was so pitiful and lost, Elle."

"I know the feeling."

"Have you talked to him?"

"No, not yet. Here I have this whole lexicon of words to use and I still don't know what I'm going to say."

"You know when math equations become complicated, sometimes it's best to get back to basics for the answer. Perhaps it's as simple as saying hi."

"And then take it from there."

"Right."

"That might be a good plan." Elle felt a little chill. "It's getting a little cold out here. I'm going to get the kids and head back up to the house. I'll talk to you later."

"All right. Take care of yourself."

"I will." Elle hung up. "It's getting a little cold out here. How about we head up to the house?"

"Look, Mom, we filled both baskets," Kevin said proudly.

"Great."

"We'll be right behind you, Mrs. Brennan."

"Okay." As she made her way back up to the house she dialed Doug. *It's his voicemail.* She waited for the tone. "Hi . . ." she began and then hung up. *At least it's a start.*

CHAPTER 19

Hugh and Mary Katherine were having a cup of tea when Doug walked in.

"Hello, Mom and Dad," he said as he walked over to kiss his mother's cheek.

"Doug, we were just talking about you. What on earth is going on? We've been trying to reach you since yesterday."

"I'm sorry, Mom."

"What happening with Elle? Why didn't you call us when she went to the hospital?"

"It all happened so fast, Dad. I was in the middle of a press conference when Rory called me. I left straight away."

"Is she all right?"

"I think so, Mom."

"What do you mean you think so? Don't you know?"

"She left the hospital before I got there, Dad. I don't think she wanted to see me."

"What? Why?" Mr. Brennan was floored.

Doug sat down. "Kyle got in a fight at school over some kid teasing him over the stuff that's been in the paper. Elle had enough and went over to confront Angela."

"I wondered why the paper said she was rushed from Rory's townhouse."

"Apparently she doubled over with stomach pains when Rory got there, and that's when she told him she was eight weeks pregnant."

Mr. and Mrs. Brennan were stunned.

"Oh, my goodness. She was nursing a ginger ale when I saw her the other day. And she did say she was tired."

"Please don't tell me she lost the baby."

"She was gone before I could find out, and her doctor has been in the delivery room since yesterday."

"Well then you get him on the phone."

"It's not that easy, Dad. He has four patients in labor. He can't be reached."

"Where's Elle that she hasn't told you anything?"

"She's in Martha's Vineyard with the kids for the weekend. I think she needed to be away from all the reminders."

"Poor thing," Mrs. Brennan sympathized. She had given birth to a stillborn child, Ruth, when Doug was five years old, and a part of her had never gotten over it.

"That brings me to the reason I'm here." He paused. "I met with Governor Pearson this morning and I told him that I'm withdrawing my name from consideration for the Senate appointment. I'm having a press conference this afternoon to make it official. This means this is my last year in politics, Dad."

"I know."

"Uncle Robert will be disappointed."

"He'll get over it," Mr. Brennan said reassuringly.

"After the press conference is over, I'm going to clean up some odds and ends at the office and then I'm off to

Martha's Vineyard first thing Saturday morning to be with my wife and children."

"Good. Now that this fiasco with Angela is over with you can have some peace in your life," Mr. Brennan interjected.

Mrs. Brennan got up and kissed Doug on the forehead. "I'm proud of you, son."

"You are? Even though I've been a jackass?"

"A real jackass doesn't know he or she really is a jackass."

Doug laughed. "Thanks, Mom, you always know what to say." He looked at his watch. "I'd better get going. I've got to change before I head over to City Hall." He stood up and gave his mother a hug. "I'll talk to you later."

His father rose and went over to hug him. "Remember we support you in whatever you choose to do."

"Thanks, Dad."

"Be sure to give Elle our love," Mrs. Brennan added.

"I will." Doug kissed his mother's forehead before he left the room. He only had a couple of hours to change and go over his notes before the press conference.

After a quick change at the house, Doug was in his office at City Hall. As he looked over his notes, Ki walked in.

"Everything's set up in the Blue Room."

"Thanks." Doug looked up from his notes. "Listen, before we get started I wanted to talk to you first."

"If you're going to tell me that you withdrew your name from the running for the Senate seat, I figured as much."

"I'm sorry, Ki."

"Don't be sorry. You're doing what you need to do, and I completely understand that."

"I know you were looking forward to the challenges of Washington."

"If you ask me Washington politics are overrated." He smiled. "I'll just dust off my résumé and see what's out there."

"Well I was hoping you'd put your name on a shingle next to mine."

"What?"

"I'm going back to my civil rights practice. I'll likely take on a lot of pro bono cases, but you'd have a good salary."

"Does that include dental?" He grinned.

"Of course."

"Then you've got yourself a deal."

They shook hands.

"Oh, by the way, this came for you." He handed him an envelope.

Doug saw that it was from Seth McNeal.

"Aren't you going to open it?"

"I don't need it anymore." He tore it in half and tossed it in the wastebasket. "Can you do me one more favor?"

"Sure."

"Find out what Seth charges so I can pay him for his services. This loss leader isn't going to pay off like he thought."

"You got it." Ki looked at the clock. "It's about that time. Are you ready?"

Doug took a long deep breath. "I'm as ready as I'll ever be."

When Doug walked into the Blue Room there seemed to be more press than usual. As he approached the podium he took a sheet of paper out.

"Earlier today, I informed Governor Pearson that I am withdrawing my name from consideration for the United States Senate. I was honored to be in the running for Senator Clemson's seat and to have the opportunity to represent the people of this great state. I will continue in my efforts to guide our great city through this economic crisis until the end of my term, after which I am looking forward to spending more time with my family. Thank you." Doug turned and walked away.

"Mayor Brennan, does this decision have anything to do with what happened to your wife?" A reporter shouted.

Ki went to the microphone. "The mayor isn't taking any questions. Thanks for coming."

Doug went back to his office and sat down at his desk. He picked up the photo of Elle and the kids. *I'm coming, guys.*

"Mayor Brennan?" Ki said as he knocked.

"Come in."

"You certainly know how to leave them wanting more. There's a feeding frenzy out there."

"I can imagine."

"Mort Barnes is out here. He says you called him. Is he trying to pull a fast one?"

"Nope. I did call him."

Ki looked at Doug like he'd taken leave of his senses. "You called *him?*"

"Yes, and I'm fine. Show him in."

"If you say so." He opened the door. "Mayor Brennan will see you now."

At sixty-eight, Mort Barnes was from the old school of journalism. He wore a conservative blue suit with a white shirt. Unlike his younger counterparts, he still used a pen and pad to take notes for his interviews and he never went anywhere without them.

When he came in he looked as confused as Ki did, since he was always vocal in his criticism of the liberal Brennans.

Doug stood up. "How are you, Mort?" He shook his hand.

"I'm good. Although I have to admit I'm a little perplexed at the moment."

Doug chuckled. "I bet you are. Please have a seat."

"Thank you." He sat down.

Doug pulled up a chair next to him. "I bet you're wondering what you're doing here."

"The thought has crossed my mind."

'I'm going to give you an exclusive and tell you why I decided to withdraw from the Senate race."

Mort's ears perked up. "You are? Why me? I would have thought I'd be the last person in the world you'd give an exclusive like this to. We aren't exactly on the same side."

"True. But you were the only journalist who didn't run a story about my brother's divorce and my wife's supposed role in it."

"I'm a journalist, not a tabloid reporter. To me you don't go after a man's family. I may not subscribe to your politics but I won't go after your family just to make a point. Family is off limits."

"I have to say it didn't go unnoticed. Thank you."

"You're welcome. But if you tell your father I'll deny it. This is off the record." He grinned.

Doug laughed. "I'm ready when you are."

Mort took out his pen and pad. "Now we're on the record."

"Fire away."

Elle was resting in the master bedroom when Kyle burst in.

"Quick, turn on the TV, Mom. They're talking about Dad on the news."

"What?" She grabbed the remote and turned the TV on. "What channel?"

"It's Channel 5."

Elle turned the volume up.

In other news New York City Mayor Douglas Brennan announced that he is withdrawing from that state's hotly contended Senate race to fill the seat of junior Senator Rita Clemson, who has been tapped by the president-elect to be the next secretary of state. Mayor Brennan was widely reported to be the odds-on favorite. His decision leaves the door open for a line of Democrats competing quietly for the coveted high-profile seat. In other news . . .

"Did you know about this, Mom?"

"No." Elle was in a daze.

"I guess that means Dad will be around for us more." Kyle grinned as he left the room.

"I'll be damned," she said aloud. Her cell phone rang. She picked up.

"Hello, Elle?"

"Rory?"

"Yes. How are you?"

"A little stunned at the moment."

"I take it you heard the news."

"Yes. I just saw it on Channel 5. Did you know about this?"

"I had a feeling, but Doug never said anything specific."

"Well, I didn't see this coming."

"So how do you feel about it?"

"If the scrutiny we've been under for the last few weeks was any indication of life in Washington, I'm relieved."

"Well you don't have to worry about the media anymore, at least as far as Angela is concerned."

"I don't?"

"We reached an agreement in the divorce. All the papers have been signed and filed. It's over."

"I'm speechless. I thought she and her lawyer were digging trenches for another Hundred Year War. What happened?"

"Let's just say that after what happened at the town-house, I made her an offer she couldn't refuse."

"I see."

"The less you know the better."

"I'll take your word for it."

"Are we okay? I know Angela said some things that day . . ."

"You don't have to say anything."

"No. I feel like I should. It's not everyday you find out that your brother-in-law has been in love with you for years."

"I should hope not." Elle tried to add a little levity.

Rory laughed. "Now that's what makes you so special, Elle. You always know just how to make people feel comfortable."

"You know for someone who is supposed to be so smart, I had no idea. I didn't unknowingly lead you on, did I?"

Rory laughed. "No. I've always known that this could never be more than a crush, and that's okay with me. I just don't want things to be weird between us now that the cat's out of the bag, so to speak."

"It won't be as long as you know that . . ."

He interrupted her. "You're totally in love with Doug. I know."

"Good. Besides, who else could I enjoy my weird music with?"

"Speaking of weird music, I got the definitive Depeche Mode."

"Get out of here. Is the original 'Personal Jesus' on it? You know I hate remixes."

"Of course. I'll burn you a copy for your CD player."

"Cool."

"I'm going to get you into the iPod if it kills me."

"Don't say that. It might. You know when it comes to science, math and linguistics I have a brain for the new millennium, but when it comes to all the innovative electronic gadgets, I need training wheels. "

Rory laughed. "So are you okay?" he asked somewhat hesitantly.

"Yes, and that's all I want to say about it. Okay?"

"I can respect that."

"Thank you." She yawned. "Oh, excuse me."

"I should let you go. You sound tired."

"I am."

"I'll talk to you later."

"Sure. I'll see you when I get back on Sunday. Bye."

"Bye."

"Mrs. Brennan?" Bertha called as she knocked.

"Come in, Bertha."

She poked her head in. "I'm about to start dinner. I wanted to know if you need anything."

"I'm good, Bertha. In fact I think I'm going to soak in the tub for a little while. I'm a little achy."

"There's some Advil in the medicine cabinet if you need it."

"Okay."

After Bertha closed the door Elle got up and went into the bathroom. She filled the old fashioned tub with warm water and bath oils and then she climbed in. Elle sighed as she let her cares drift away. *I'll call Doug once I'm out of the tub. I can't believe he dropped out of the Senate race and now we can have a normal life. At least something that resembles normal for the Brennans. Either way, I'll take it.*

Though she had every intention of calling Doug, Elle drifted off to sleep. When she woke up it was too late to call Doug, so she decided to do it first thing Saturday morning.

Just as Doug got into the car on the way to the airport on Saturday morning, his driver handed him a copy of *The Post.* Once he was settled in the back seat he read the cover headline: *Exclusive: Mayor Brennan talks to Mort Barnes After His Bombshell Announcement.* He turned the paper over and placed it on the seat.

"You're not going to read it, sir?"

"No." Doug smiled. "I know what it says."

Elle sat at the kitchen table with a cup of tea at her side. She'd been trying Doug on his cell since five a.m. to no avail. She looked up at the clock. "It's after seven. Where could he be?" She sighed.

Bertha seemed startled when she entered the kitchen. "Mrs. Brennan, I didn't think you'd be up so early."

"It seems I went to bed with the chickens, so I got up with the worms."

She laughed. "Would you like some coffee? I'm getting ready to brew a fresh pot."

"Maybe later. I have my tea for now."

The beautiful view outside the window called to Elle. "You know I think I'm going to take a little morning stroll on the beach."

"Okay. You make sure to bundle up now. It looks warmer than it is."

Elle got up from the table. "I will." She went into the hallway and grabbed her coat and scarf. When she stepped outside the morning air was chilly but invigorating. With a little pep in her step she went down the stairs and onto the sandy beach. Elle walked for a while and then stopped to admire the beauty and expanse of the ocean. "Smell that salt air." She closed her eyes and sighed.

"Elle!"

The sound of her name broke her trance and she turned around. "Doug?"

Doug ran up to her as fast as he could. "There you are." He was out of breath.

"What are you doing here?"

"You're here. Where else would I be?" He wrapped his arms around her tightly.

Elle felt a well of emotion come up. "Doug, I'm . . ."

"No. You don't need to say anything. Baby, I'm so sorry about everything. I shouldn't have let my ambition get in the way of our life and our love. Can you forgive me?"

"Can you forgive me? I should have told you about the baby, but then I got angry."

"You don't have to apologize to me."

"I was going to tell you the morning of . . ."

"You don't have to say a word. All I'm going to say is that from now on nothing is going to get in the way of our family."

"I know. I saw the report on the news yesterday."

He pulled her closer to him. "That's a promise, my love. Once the year is over we'll be private citizens again. And there's no Seth McNeal."

"Sounds like heaven to me." She looked down at the sand. "I'm sorry I ran away without talking to you. I should have been more honest about my reservations from the beginning."

"If I'm honest with myself I didn't give you a lot of room to say no. I had D.C. ambitions in my eyes and I couldn't see everything you've been through . . ."

She interrupted him. "Everything we've been through. It wasn't just me."

"But you've been getting the brunt of it, and I'm sorry." A tear ran down his cheek.

Elle wiped it away.

"I love you so much, Elle."

"I love you, too."

Their lips came together with a mix of passion and healing they both needed.

Doug ran his hands through her hair. "This is kind of like your dream, isn't it? The two of us on the beach just like when we first met."

"It's not quite like my dream. There are three people here." She touched her stomach.

Doug's breath caught. "But I thought . . ."

"You thought I lost the baby." She looked down at her stomach. "The Brennan and Abbott children are from tough stock. My stomach pains were due to stress, and combined with the fact that I hadn't been eating much, I got the mother of all cramps."

"I remember you telling me about it once. I think you said it happened when you were in college."

"Right. The last time I had pain like this I was working on my doctoral thesis, but I could take medication for it. Now I've got to rely on ginger ale, peppermint tea and crackers, at least for the next seven months."

"So that's why Dr. Aranow released you so quickly."

"Yes. If there was anything wrong with the baby, I'd still be there."

A wave of relief hit Doug. "Thank God." He dropped to his knees and kissed her middle.

Elle giggled.

He got up. "We're having a baby." He kissed her passionately again.

Just like that nineteen-year-old on the beach all those years ago, Doug still made Elle weak in the knees. "Yes, we are. Do you think you're ready for diaper duty again?"

"Oh yeah."

"I don't have my calendar, but you can be sure I'm going to mark this down."

"Please do." He paused. "I guess we're going to have to call Sheri and change your wardrobe order for the next seven months."

"Oh, my God, I hadn't even thought about that. I was more concerned with how soon we'd have to get on a list for preschool."

"You're thinking about preschool already?"

"In New York City? These days most people think about preschools before they get pregnant."

"I think she'll be okay."

"She? You think we're having a girl?"

"Yes. Don't you?"

"I hate to break it to you, Doug, but I'm pretty sure we're having another boy."

"Did the doctor tell you that?"

"No. It's just a feeling I have."

"Wow. I just thought of something."

"What?"

"What if this baby looks more like you?"

Elle laughed heartily. "Wouldn't that be a switch?"

"That would be cool with me. I'll just have to hit the tanning salon, that's all."

Elle smiled.

Doug reached into his pocket. "Wait a second, I have something for you." He handed her a CD. "It's the best of Beck. There are tracks from *Mellow Gold* and *Odelay* on it."

Her eyes lit up. "Thanks. I can't wait to play it."

"Elle, we've been together for over twenty years and I still don't know why you love this . . ."

"Why I love weird and out-there music?"

"Yes."

"It's really not all that original. It was rebellion." She looked down at the case. "I love Tchaikovsky, Mozart, Bach and Beethoven but they didn't bother my parents and The Clash did."

"So that's it? That's the reason?"

"That and I love it. I did say it wasn't original." She glanced at the CD again. "Are you afraid the new baby will share his mother's taste in music?"

"No, and if he does, that's okay with me." He felt a chill. "It's a little cold out here. I think we should head back to the house." He took her hand in his.

"Really? I hadn't noticed."

He kissed her hand. "So how much time do you think we have before the boys get up?"

"It's Saturday morning and they're teenagers. They don't get up until noon. Why?"

"I'd like to indulge in a little extended make-up time on that lovely king-size four-poster bed." He winked.

Before she could stop it, Elle blushed. "Oh, this is ridiculous. We've been married twenty years. I'm two months pregnant and still I blush."

"That's what I love about you."

"Funny, I was going to say the same thing."

Hand in hand Elle and Doug made their way back up the beach to the house. They were brought together again by the very same place where it all started. They were older and wiser. Their love had stood the test of time, and they were ready for whatever the future had in store for them as long as they were together.

ABOUT THE AUTHOR

A native of Amityville, New York, Chamein Canton is a freelance wedding/fashion and romance writer, author and literary agent with a small agency that bears her name. She holds a Bachelor's Degree in Business Management from Empire State College and still lives on Long Island. Chamein is the proud parent of twin sons Scott, who holds a B.A. in Black Studies from SUNY Geneseo, and Sean, who is attending CUNY Lehman to pursue a degree in English.

MIXED REALITY

2010 Mass Market Titles

January

Show Me The Sun
Miriam Shumba
ISBN: 978-158571-405-6
$6.99

Promises of Forever
Celya Bowers
ISBN: 978-1-58571-380-6
$6.99

February

Love Out Of Order
Nicole Green
ISBN: 978-1-58571-381-3
$6.99

Unclear and Present Danger
Michele Cameron
ISBN: 978-158571-408-7
$6.99

March

Stolen Jewels
Michele Sudler
ISBN: 978-158571-409-4
$6.99

Not Quite Right
Tammy Williams
ISBN: 978-158571-410-0
$6.99

April

Oak Bluffs
Joan Early
ISBN: 978-1-58571-379-0
$6.99

Crossing The Line
Bernice Layton
ISBN: 978-158571-412-4
$6.99

How To Kill Your Husband
Keith Walker
ISBN: 978-158571-421-6
$6.99

May

The Business of Love
Cheris F. Hodges
ISBN: 978-158571-373-8
$6.99

Wayward Dreams
Gail McFarland
ISBN: 978-158571-422-3
$6.99

June

The Doctor's Wife
Mildred Riley
ISBN: 978-158571-424-7
$6.99

Mixed Reality
Chamein Canton
ISBN: 978-158571-423-0
$6.99

2010 Mass Market Titles (continued)

July

Blue Interlude
Keisha Mennefee
ISBN: 978-158571-378-3
$6.99

Always You
Crystal Hubbard
ISBN: 978-158571-371-4
$6.99

Unbeweavable
Katrina Spencer
ISBN: 978-158571-426-1
$6.99

August

Small Sensations
Crystal V. Rhodes
ISBN: 978-158571-376-9
$6.99

Let's Get It On
Dyanne Davis
ISBN: 978-158571-416-2
$6.99

September

Unconditional
A.C. Arthur
ISBN: 978-158571-413-1
$6.99

Swan
Africa Fine
ISBN: 978-158571-377-6
$6.99$6.99

October

Friends in Need
Joan Early
ISBN:978-1-58571-428-5
$6.99

Against the Wind
Gwynne Forster
ISBN:978-158571-429-2
$6.99

That Which Has Horns
Miriam Shumba
ISBN:978-1-58571-430-8
$6.99

November

A Good Dude
Keith Walker
ISBN:978-1-58571-431-5
$6.99

Reye's Gold
Ruthie Robinson
ISBN:978-1-58571-432-2
$6.99

December

Still Waters...
Crystal V. Rhodes
ISBN:978-1-58571-433-9
$6.99

Burn
Crystal Hubbard
ISBN: 978-1-58571-406-3
$6.99

Other Genesis Press, Inc. Titles

Other Genesis Press, Inc. Titles (continued)

Blood Seduction	J.M. Jeffries	$9.95
Bodyguard	Andrea Jackson	$9.95
Boss of Me	Diana Nyad	$8.95
Bound by Love	Beverly Clark	$8.95
Breeze	Robin Hampton Allen	$10.95
Broken	Dar Tomlinson	$24.95
By Design	Barbara Keaton	$8.95
Cajun Heat	Charlene Berry	$8.95
Careless Whispers	Rochelle Alers	$8.95
Cats & Other Tales	Marilyn Wagner	$8.95
Caught in a Trap	Andre Michelle	$8.95
Caught Up in the Rapture	Lisa G. Riley	$9.95
Cautious Heart	Cheris F. Hodges	$8.95
Chances	Pamela Leigh Starr	$8.95
Checks and Balances	Elaine Sims	$6.99
Cherish the Flame	Beverly Clark	$8.95
Choices	Tammy Williams	$6.99
Class Reunion	Irma Jenkins/	$12.95
	John Brown	
Code Name: Diva	J.M. Jeffries	$9.95
Conquering Dr. Wexler's	Kimberley White	$9.95
Heart		
Corporate Seduction	A.C. Arthur	$9.95
Crossing Paths,	Dorothy Elizabeth Love	$9.95
Tempting Memories		
Crush	Crystal Hubbard	$9.95
Cypress Whisperings	Phyllis Hamilton	$8.95
Dark Embrace	Crystal Wilson Harris	$8.95
Dark Storm Rising	Chinelu Moore	$10.95
Daughter of the Wind	Joan Xian	$8.95
Dawn's Harbor	Kymberly Hunt	$6.99
Deadly Sacrifice	Jack Kean	$22.95
Designer Passion	Dar Tomlinson	$8.95
	Diana Richeaux	
Do Over	Celya Bowers	$9.95
Dream Keeper	Gail McFarland	$6.99
Dream Runner	Gail McFarland	$6.99
Dreamtective	Liz Swados	$5.95
Ebony Angel	Deatri King-Bey	$9.95
Ebony Butterfly II	Delilah Dawson	$14.95
Echoes of Yesterday	Beverly Clark	$9.95
Eden's Garden	Elizabeth Rose	$8.95

Other Genesis Press, Inc. Titles (continued)

Other Genesis Press, Inc. Titles (continued)

Indigo After Dark Vol. IV	Cassandra Colt/	$14.95
Indigo After Dark Vol. V	Delilah Dawson	$14.95
Indiscretions	Donna Hill	$8.95
Intentional Mistakes	Michele Sudler	$9.95
Interlude	Donna Hill	$8.95
Intimate Intentions	Angie Daniels	$8.95
It's in the Rhythm	Sammie Ward	$6.99
It's Not Over Yet	J.J. Michael	$9.95
Jolie's Surrender	Edwina Martin-Arnold	$8.95
Kiss or Keep	Debra Phillips	$8.95
Lace	Giselle Carmichael	$9.95
Lady Preacher	K.T. Richey	$6.99
Last Train to Memphis	Elsa Cook	$12.95
Lasting Valor	Ken Olsen	$24.95
Let Us Prey	Hunter Lundy	$25.95
Lies Too Long	Pamela Ridley	$13.95
Life Is Never As It Seems	J.J. Michael	$12.95
Lighter Shade of Brown	Vicki Andrews	$8.95
Look Both Ways	Joan Early	$6.99
Looking for Lily	Africa Fine	$6.99
Love Always	Mildred E. Riley	$10.95
Love Doesn't Come Easy	Charlyne Dickerson	$8.95
Love Unveiled	Gloria Greene	$10.95
Love's Deception	Charlene Berry	$10.95
Love's Destiny	M. Loui Quezada	$8.95
Love's Secrets	Yolanda McVey	$6.99
Mae's Promise	Melody Walcott	$8.95
Magnolia Sunset	Giselle Carmichael	$8.95
Many Shades of Gray	Dyanne Davis	$6.99
Matters of Life and Death	Lesego Malepe, Ph.D.	$15.95
Meant to Be	Jeanne Sumerix	$8.95
Midnight Clear	Leslie Esdaile	$10.95
(Anthology)	Gwynne Forster	
	Carmen Green	
	Monica Jackson	
Midnight Magic	Gwynne Forster	$8.95
Midnight Peril	Vicki Andrews	$10.95
Misconceptions	Pamela Leigh Starr	$9.95
Moments of Clarity	Michele Cameron	$6.99
Montgomery's Children	Richard Perry	$14.95
Mr. Fix-It	Crystal Hubbard	$6.99
My Buffalo Soldier	Barbara B.K. Reeves	$8.95

Other Genesis Press, Inc. Titles (continued)

Naked Soul	Gwynne Forster	$8.95
Never Say Never	Michele Cameron	$6.99
Next to Last Chance	Louisa Dixon	$24.95
No Apologies	Seressia Glass	$8.95
No Commitment Required	Seressia Glass	$8.95
No Regrets	Mildred E. Riley	$8.95
Not His Type	Chamein Canton	$6.99
Nowhere to Run	Gay G. Gunn	$10.95
O Bed! O Breakfast!	Rob Kuehnle	$14.95
Object of His Desire	A.C. Arthur	$8.95
Office Policy	A.C. Arthur	$9.95
Once in a Blue Moon	Dorianne Cole	$9.95
One Day at a Time	Bella McFarland	$8.95
One of These Days	Michele Sudler	$9.95
Outside Chance	Louisa Dixon	$24.95
Passion	T.T. Henderson	$10.95
Passion's Blood	Cherif Fortin	$22.95
Passion's Furies	AlTonya Washington	$6.99
Passion's Journey	Wanda Y. Thomas	$8.95
Past Promises	Jahmel West	$8.95
Path of Fire	T.T. Henderson	$8.95
Path of Thorns	Annetta P. Lee	$9.95
Peace Be Still	Colette Haywood	$12.95
Picture Perfect	Reon Carter	$8.95
Playing for Keeps	Stephanie Salinas	$8.95
Pride & Joi	Gay G. Gunn	$8.95
Promises Made	Bernice Layton	$6.99
Promises to Keep	Alicia Wiggins	$8.95
Quiet Storm	Donna Hill	$10.95
Reckless Surrender	Rochelle Alers	$6.95
Red Polka Dot in a World Full of Plaid	Varian Johnson	$12.95
Red Sky	Renee Alexis	$6.99
Reluctant Captive	Joyce Jackson	$8.95
Rendezvous With Fate	Jeanne Sumerix	$8.95
Revelations	Cheris F. Hodges	$8.95
Rivers of the Soul	Leslie Esdaile	$8.95
Rocky Mountain Romance	Kathleen Suzanne	$8.95
Rooms of the Heart	Donna Hill	$8.95
Rough on Rats and Tough on Cats	Chris Parker	$12.95
Save Me	Africa Fine	$6.99

Other Genesis Press, Inc. Titles (continued)

Secret Library Vol. 1	Nina Sheridan	$18.95
Secret Library Vol. 2	Cassandra Colt	$8.95
Secret Thunder	Annetta P. Lee	$9.95
Shades of Brown	Denise Becker	$8.95
Shades of Desire	Monica White	$8.95
Shadows in the Moonlight	Jeanne Sumerix	$8.95
Sin	Crystal Rhodes	$8.95
Singing A Song...	Crystal Rhodes	$6.99
Six O'Clock	Katrina Spencer	$6.99
Small Whispers	Annetta P. Lee	$6.99
So Amazing	Sinclair LeBeau	$8.95
Somebody's Someone	Sinclair LeBeau	$8.95
Someone to Love	Alicia Wiggins	$8.95
Song in the Park	Martin Brant	$15.95
Soul Eyes	Wayne L. Wilson	$12.95
Soul to Soul	Donna Hill	$8.95
Southern Comfort	J.M. Jeffries	$8.95
Southern Fried Standards	S.R. Maddox	$6.99
Still the Storm	Sharon Robinson	$8.95
Still Waters Run Deep	Leslie Esdaile	$8.95
Stolen Memories	Michele Sudler	$6.99
Stories to Excite You	Anna Forrest/Divine	$14.95
Storm	Pamela Leigh Starr	$6.99
Subtle Secrets	Wanda Y. Thomas	$8.95
Suddenly You	Crystal Hubbard	$9.95
Sweet Repercussions	Kimberley White	$9.95
Sweet Sensations	Gwyneth Bolton	$9.95
Sweet Tomorrows	Kimberly White	$8.95
Taken by You	Dorothy Elizabeth Love	$9.95
Tattooed Tears	T. T. Henderson	$8.95
Tempting Faith	Crystal Hubbard	$6.99
The Color Line	Lizzette Grayson Carter	$9.95
The Color of Trouble	Dyanne Davis	$8.95
The Disappearance of Allison Jones	Kayla Perrin	$5.95
The Fires Within	Beverly Clark	$9.95
The Foursome	Celya Bowers	$6.99
The Honey Dipper's Legacy	Myra Pannell-Allen	$14.95
The Joker's Love Tune	Sidney Rickman	$15.95
The Little Pretender	Barbara Cartland	$10.95
The Love We Had	Natalie Dunbar	$8.95
The Man Who Could Fly	Bob & Milana Beamon	$18.95

Other Genesis Press, Inc. Titles (continued)

The Missing Link	Charlyne Dickerson	$8.95
The Mission	Pamela Leigh Starr	$6.99
The More Things Change	Chamein Canton	$6.99
The Perfect Frame	Beverly Clark	$9.95
The Price of Love	Sinclair LeBeau	$8.95
The Smoking Life	Ilene Barth	$29.95
The Words of the Pitcher	Kei Swanson	$8.95
Things Forbidden	Maryam Diaab	$6.99
This Life Isn't Perfect Holla	Sandra Foy	$6.99
Three Doors Down	Michele Sudler	$6.99
Three Wishes	Seressia Glass	$8.95
Ties That Bind	Kathleen Suzanne	$8.95
Tiger Woods	Libby Hughes	$5.95
Time Is of the Essence	Angie Daniels	$9.95
Timeless Devotion	Bella McFarland	$9.95
Tomorrow's Promise	Leslie Esdaile	$8.95
Truly Inseparable	Wanda Y. Thomas	$8.95
Two Sides to Every Story	Dyanne Davis	$9.95
Unbreak My Heart	Dar Tomlinson	$8.95
Uncommon Prayer	Kenneth Swanson	$9.95
Unconditional Love	Alicia Wiggins	$8.95
Unconditional	A.C. Arthur	$9.95
Undying Love	Renee Alexis	$6.99
Until Death Do Us Part	Susan Paul	$8.95
Vows of Passion	Bella McFarland	$9.95
Waiting for Mr. Darcy	Chamein Canton	$6.99
Waiting in the Shadows	Michele Sudler	$6.99
Wedding Gown	Dyanne Davis	$8.95
What's Under Benjamin's Bed	Sandra Schaffer	$8.95
When a Man Loves a Woman	LaConnie Taylor-Jones	$6.99
When Dreams Float	Dorothy Elizabeth Love	$8.95
When I'm With You	LaConnie Taylor-Jones	$6.99
When Lightning Strikes	Michele Cameron	$6.99
Where I Want To Be	Maryam Diaab	$6.99
Whispers in the Night	Dorothy Elizabeth Love	$8.95
Whispers in the Sand	LaFlorya Gauthier	$10.95
Who's That Lady?	Andrea Jackson	$9.95
Wild Ravens	AlTonya Washington	$9.95
Yesterday Is Gone	Beverly Clark	$10.95
Yesterday's Dreams, Tomorrow's Promises	Reon Laudat	$8.95
Your Precious Love	Sinclair LeBeau	$8.95

Order Form

Mail to: Genesis Press, Inc.
P.O. Box 101
Columbus, MS 39703

Name _____

Address _____

City/State _____ Zip _____

Telephone _____

Ship to (if different from above)

Name _____

Address _____

City/State _____ Zip _____

Telephone _____

Credit Card Information

Credit Card # _____ ☐ Visa   ☐ Mastercard

Expiration Date (mm/yy) _____ ☐ AmEx   ☐ Discover

Qty.	Author	Title	Price	Total

Use this order

form, or call

1-888-INDIGO-1

Total for books _____

Shipping and handling:
  $5 first two books,
  $1 each additional book _____

Total S & H _____

Total amount enclosed _____

Mississippi residents add 7% sales tax